OUT OF TIME

AN ATTICUS WOLFE NOVEL

DAVE SINCLAIR

ALSO BY DAVE SINCLAIR

For Kristi.
Monkey + Heart + Unicorn

PROLOGUE

Mutt was pretty sure everyone was going to die. He was an expert on these things.

It was just after dawn and he was in his bedroom, most of the way through a Nicolas Cage all-night movie marathon. He was about to press play on the cinematic masterpiece *Con Air* when movement in the lane behind his parents' house caught his eye.

From his window on the second floor he watched the team of heavily armed soldiers slink down the cobblestone laneway. It looked like something out of one of Mutt's movies, surely a tactical assault team of some kind. It certainly wasn't something he saw in the flesh every day. Sometimes called London's poshest suburb, Knightsbridge was exclusive and elitist. And, as far as Mutt was concerned, the most boring place on the planet. Except today.

The black helmets and military gear made it difficult to determine genders in the team of eight. They were heavily armed and moved silently, with intent. Using short, sharp hand signals to communicate, each had a short machine gun tucked into their shoulder, aimed forward. From the way they moved, it was clear they were deadly serious.

An action-film afficionado, Mutt was unrivalled at school in his knowledge of the collected works of Arnold Schwarzenegger, Steven Seagal, Sylvester Stallone, Jackie Chan and Jason Statham. The posters adorning his bedroom were a shrine to movies made decades before he was even born. Kids from his school rarely came to visit.

The soldiers or whatever they were seemed to be homing in on the rear of the townhouse diagonally across from Mutt's house. He'd only met the mysterious resident of number 12 a handful of times. He lived alone and always seemed nice. He'd even helped Mutt with his algebra homework once at the local coffee shop.

The soldiers in the lane remained faceless and inhuman. It was a well-known fact that if the main character of the film wasn't part of an assault team they were destined to meet a sticky end. To Mutt, these clowns looked like the FBI guys who stormed Nakatomi Plaza in *Die Hard*. That hadn't worked out so well for them. That's how Mutt knew these guys were all going to die.

Two of the soldiers broke off from the group and approached the gate in the middle of the tall red brick fence. One aimed a shotgun at the top hinge and nodded to the group.

Something was about to go down. Mutt unwrapped his last Snickers bar. With his other hand he hit record on his mobile phone, framing the action in the lane below. *This shit will get me so many upvotes on Reddit.*

Down below, the faceless group tensed. The soldier nearest the gate fired two shots in quick succession, blowing the hinges. Every member of the team stormed through the smoking opening, guns raised, all screaming incoherent orders.

For a second nothing happened, and Mutt thought maybe that was all he'd get to see. Nose pressed against the frosted window, he continued to record, hoping something more would happen.

It did.

A huge explosion rocked the backyard of number 12. There was a blinding orange flash followed by a massive dirty grey mushroom cloud that billowed into the sky. Several members of the group lay on the ground, unmoving, their shouting suddenly silenced.

Mutt stopped recording and took a bite of his Snickers. *Called it.*

ONE

It's not every day you spot a terrorist walking the posh streets of London.

MI6 agent Atticus Wolfe would have called it his lucky day, but people had already died. Pulling out his phone, he called Paul Cavendish, Head Spec Ops. His superior answered on the second ring.

"Where the hell are you?" His voice was strained, like he wanted to yell but was conscious of the multitude of people in the Tactical Operations Centre. Part of a joint operation between SO15, MI5, MI6, CIA, NSA, GCHQ and any other acronym you could think of, the multi-departmental taskforce had spent the best part of a year tracking the mysterious Omar Ganim: the very man Atticus was 50 metres behind.

Walking briskly down the leafy street in the early morning sunshine, Atticus made sure he stayed far enough back to avoid arousing suspicion, while keeping the target in sight. Hurriedly moving towards the Thames, Ganim wasn't checking for a tail – but he wasn't taking in the sights, either.

Cavendish went on. "I'm sitting here with a pleasant smile on my face and my thumb up my arse while my star tactical officer has gone walkabout."

It was true. Atticus was part of the taskforce, as an observer, and his work had finally pinpointed Ganim. Today was the day they were meant to bring him in. They'd failed.

Atticus had left the Tactical Operations Centre in a hurry after the assault on Ganim's townhouse had gone fatally wrong. Entering via the rear laneway the tactical assault team were wiped out by a booby trap device. The cramped trailer had rapidly descended from collegial bipartisanship into denunciation and backstabbing as soon as the assault team had triggered the explosion. Atticus had exited the tumultuous operations centre to gather his thoughts and wander the streets.

"I have something to report."

Cavendish huffed down the phone. "It better be good. Every agency is tearing this city apart searching for Ganim."

"They're looking in the wrong place."

"The wrong...? Is this the famous Atticus Wolfe arrogance again?"

"Not this time."

"Fine, I'll bite. Why are they looking in the wrong place?"

"Because I have eyes on the Tango. Male, black hoodie, green camouflage backpack, heading south from TOC, along..." Atticus checked the sign, "Sloane Street. It was blind luck I found him, Paul. I was wandering the street composing what I was going to write up in the report and boom, there he was. He must have snuck out minutes before we got there. But I've got him now."

There was the briefest of pauses. "Location?" All

sarcasm had been scrubbed away, leaving only the raw business layer.

Atticus gave his precise position. Up ahead, Ganim showed no sign that he knew he'd been discovered. It was only a matter of time. Contrary to what movies suggested, surveillance wasn't meant to be carried out by one man. Usually a team of at least a dozen would pursue a target, or Tango, backed by multiple vehicles with concealed cameras and access to CCTV systems. They would triangulate the target's phone and utilise high-altitude drones to track the Tango's position at all times, even when the human pursuers had lost visual. None of those tools were available to Atticus as he walked briskly down the Knightsbridge street.

As a member of MI6, Atticus had no authority to operate within the United Kingdom. His role in the task-force was purely advisory. As an experienced spy, the passive position did not sit well with him professionally or personally. He should have been careful what he wished for. Now the entire mission was on his head.

"I'm going to need some help, Paul. And soon."

As he spoke, Ganim sprinted ahead, glancing over his shoulder. That brief turn gave it all away – the fiery eyes looked directly at Atticus.

There was mumbling in the background as Paul went on. "Team en route, ETA five minutes."

Atticus broke into a run. "That won't be quick enough. I've been made."

Hanging up, the spy put his years of recreational running to good use, and there was an additional spring in his step. The terrorist had broken the cardinal rule when under surveillance: never run.

Without the disadvantage of a backpack weighing him

down, Atticus quickly closed the gap between them. Now a new set of concerns had to be assessed. While he may have worked for the same organisation as James Bond, Atticus certainly didn't have a licence to kill. He didn't have a gun, either. Not even a reasonably sharp pencil. Regardless, he ran on.

With a sense of trepidation, Atticus watched the backpack bounce as Omar sprinted wildly. Having noticed his pursuer, the criminal seemed to be running blind. He turned down streets seemingly at random, stumbling often. Atticus sucked in air between his teeth every time he did. Anything could have been in that backpack. Having just detonated a bomb, and given his history, Atticus highly doubted Ganim had eluded an assault team and fled the scene with his dirty laundry.

Losing visual as Ganim rounded the corner of a narrow residential street, Atticus doubled down. Tearing past quaint little terrace houses with their even quainter window boxes, Atticus ignored his lungs screaming for respite. He couldn't slow down, not now. Not with so much at stake.

Turning the corner, Atticus finally slowed. He could afford to. Ganim really had been running blindly. He'd stumbled into a dead-end lane and was trapped. The trouble was, he knew it. By the time Atticus entered the lane, Ganim had already removed his backpack and was fiddling with the large grey metal device within. He barely flinched as Atticus approached.

"Omar!"

The newly crowned terrorist frowned in frustration and reluctantly glanced up. "Go away. You don't know what you're doing."

"I have a reasonable idea." Atticus slowed his approach. He knew the drill. No sudden movements. Calming voice.

Every fibre of his being screamed at him to run. The man before him was preparing a bomb. Atticus should be putting as much distance between himself and the device as humanly possible. But he just couldn't do it. Not if there was a chance of stopping this madman. Perhaps it was his stubborn nature, perhaps it was his passionate sense of duty, but Atticus had to stop Ganim from detonating that bomb.

Or die trying.

Palms raised, Atticus attempted to appear non-threatening. "Look, I just want to talk, okay? Is it alright if we talk for a bit?"

Seemingly buoyed that he hadn't been shot, Ganim went back to fiddling with his device. Atticus could have really used that sharp pencil right about now.

"Nobody else has to die."

"I don't kill people." Ganim's jaw was set.

"The six dead members of this morning's SO15 counterterrorism assault team beg to differ."

"*Assault* team. The very title provokes consequence."

No one knew if it was a tripwire, an early detection device or remote operated; all they knew was that, of the eight men and women in the assault team, only two continued to draw breath.

Ganim turned to Atticus. "I'm not a murderer. Before you people attacked today, I hadn't killed anyone."

"You've broken into scientific laboratories across the globe, often violently. You're hardly a saint."

"But I'm not a killer." He paused. "Until today."

"The security guard in Zurich?"

Ganim waved his hand dismissively. "He had a heart attack while we were tying him up. Hardly—"

"The police officer in Seoul?"

"He was killed by so-called friendly fire—a bullet from his own team. I've taken great pains not to harm..." He paused. "Stop...you're stalling. I won't have it." He went back to his tinkering.

Atticus had to admit, the man was right. Before today, Ganim hardly deserved the label "terrorist". But the instant that bomb exploded at his townhouse, Omar Ganim had graduated from mysterious globetrotting criminal to fully certified terrorist.

The morning's operation was meant to be a peaceful takedown of the mysterious Ganim and his cell of fanatics. What was it Robert Burns said about the best laid plans?

Realising he was running out of time before Ganim finished whatever it was he was messing about with, Atticus went on, keeping his voice neutral. "I know that, before today, they were accidental deaths, not at your hand. I can't promise you leniency, it's not my place, but I will testify that you refused to take any more lives. That has to count for something, right?"

It was a lie, of course. The man was a terrorist and would be tried under the stark, unforgiving eye of public scrutiny. If he somehow escaped, there wouldn't be a rock on the planet the man could hide under now. Atticus was sure Ganim had no intention of being caught, or of running. All his attention was focused on the bomb. Atticus swallowed hard.

Flailing an arm in the air, Ganim let loose an annoyed grunt. "Like any of that matters. The whole system is corrupt, all of it. I'm going to fix it. I'm going to fix it all!" His eyes were wild; he seemed more unhinged by the second. "Everything needs to be reset. All of it. No one who's not white has ever received any sort of justice. Never." He stabbed the air with a finger. "You're a man of colour, you understand."

Atticus refused to take the bait. His heritage wasn't on the list of discussion topics right now. "What I understand is whatever plan you had in mind has failed." Atticus slowly moved a step closer. Faces appeared in the tiny windows of the terrace houses. Most were curious, some concerned. None of them knew they were about to die. "Listen, Omar, I know everything seems overwhelming right now, but if you step away from the device we can talk, alright? Just to talk, that's all I'm asking."

Ganim was too far away for Atticus to rush him. By the time he'd closed the gap, Ganim would have flicked the switch. Instead, Atticus had to incrementally make his way closer. It would take time; time he suspected he didn't have.

"Talk?" Ganim let loose a humourless laugh. "My people have had a century of talk. And where did it get them?" He pulled out a small palm-sized device which was attached to the metal box via a series of wires. At the bottom of the keypad was a wide red key. Atticus thought big red buttons only existed in the movies, but there it was.

Ganim grunted. "I'm going to fix the mess the French and the English made of the Middle East. You carved my homeland up like a cake and set us on a path of self-destruction and dependence on the West. This," he waved the button, "will end it all."

"That must be one hell of a bomb."

"You have no idea."

He was right. Atticus didn't know what the bomb was. No one did. The multi-nation taskforce that had been tracking Ganim as he slashed his way across the globe accumulating parts, tech and scientific knowledge had no idea what he was building. The type of bomb, its explosive yield and destructive potential were all unknown. It seemed Atticus was about to find out firsthand. Pity he wouldn't live long enough to tell anyone.

"Omar, listen..."

The newly crowned terrorist flipped the clear plastic cover over the big red button. The manic, unhinged persona gave way to a calmer exterior. It was far more menacing. The glee on his face had been replaced with a veneer of determination. That was when Atticus knew for sure that he was going to die.

They stood alone in the deserted laneway waiting for the inevitable.

"Wait." Atticus had to think. There had to be a way. "Wait!"

Ganim didn't wait.

He pressed the button.

The bomb exploded.

CHAPTER

TWO

E yes fluttering open, Atticus inhaled deeply. That was his first mistake. The sudden stabbing pain was excruciating. His ribs felt like he'd been impaled on a pitchfork. Instinctively, his hand darted to his side and gently touched a bulge under stiff fabric. Bandages.

It took several moments, but eventually his eyes adjusted to take in the starkness of the room. Every surface was a blindingly white. It was a hospital room like no other he'd seen. The fit-out was simple in the extreme; there wasn't even a TV. Bare white walls, a single hard wooden visitor's chair, and a white wrought iron bed, where he lay. It was like something out of the fifties. His sheets and pyjamas were starchy and stiff. The whole room reeked of disinfectant.

Was he dead? The whiteness of the room would have been enough to convince some people, but not Atticus. Never one to believe in an afterlife, his brain scrambled to make sense of his surroundings. He came up short.

The blast should have surely killed him, Ganim and

anyone else in the vicinity. It seemed impossible that he could have survived. And yet, here he was.

Taking in a few more painful inhalations to make sure he was still breathing, another memory surfaced. Well, more a colour. Atticus remembered seeing a flash of vivid green when the bomb detonated. *Why green?*

Before Atticus could stumble down that particular rabbit hole, a grey-haired man entered the room. His age, the arrogance in his strut and his white coat all screamed doctor, but Atticus wasn't convinced. Perhaps it was the cigarette dangling from his lips.

"Now then," the possible-doctor/possible-escaped-inmate said, "cracked rib, probable concussion, a few scratches, singed here and there but you'll be right as rain in a few days, lad."

He picked up the wooden clipboard at the end of bed and scribbled a note, then strode across the weathered linoleum floor, worn down from years of use. Extracting a torch, he waved the light in Atticus's eyes.

So, doctor then.

Atticus did his best to not cough. "Are you... are you trying to get fired?"

"What's that, young man?" The doctor scribbled another note.

"The cigarette..." Atticus couldn't believe he was having this conversation with a medical professional.

The doctor let out a frustrated sigh. "You mean the confounded RCP report from last year? Pure poppycock."

"Well, now I'm more concerned about your use of the word 'poppycock', if I'm completely honest."

"Responses normal, you'll be right for discharge tomorrow." The doctor checked his antique Omega watch. "I have rounds to attend to."

"How did I get here, uh, sir?" Atticus was still reluctant to use the word "doctor".

The man took a drag of the cigarette, his features curious. "Found you in the middle of the lane, they said. No one else around. Right in the middle of Knightsbridge, of all places. Not somewhere someone such as yourself should be."

Someone such as yourself. He could have been referring to Atticus's age, or his expensive suit, but instinct and years of practice told Atticus of the man was referring to his skin colour. Knightsbridge was considered one of the poshest neighbourhoods in the world. It seemed the doctor believed it was somewhere Atticus didn't belong.

Refusing to rise to the bait, Atticus changed the subject. "I need to call my boss. His name is Paul Cavendish, he's at SIS. You'd know it as MI6."

The doctor let out an amused snort. "Right. Does he have a direct number, or do I have to call Miss Moneypenny first?"

Before Atticus could issue a snide remark of his own, a nurse slunk into the room. Not just any nurse. Instead of the usual scrubs, she was dressed in what appeared to be cosplay. Bouffant hair, crisp white uniform, equally pallid shoes and a nurse's cap, like something out of *The Flying Nun*. Atticus didn't know whether to laugh or applaud.

She leaned over to the doctor conspiratorially. "Did you hear about Kennedy?"

"Of course I bloody did." The doctor handed her the clipboard. "It's all anyone can bang on about. I have rounds then I'm off home where I can close the doors and not have anyone ask me about bleedin' JFK."

The doctor left in a puff of cigarette smoke and arrogance. Atticus's head swum, and not from the smoke.

Nothing made sense. Maybe he really did have a concussion.

"Would you like some water, sir? You're looking a bit pallid there."

"Perhaps that's a good idea, thank you."

As he sipped, Atticus tried to gather his fragmented and chaotic thoughts.

Bobbing his head in thanks, he handed back the heavy glass. "Can I at least have my phone? I need to call SIS immediately, see who else was hurt."

In retrospect, he found it odd that no one from his organisation was present. No security detail, no operation heads. Hell, he would have settled for someone from the Press Office at this stage.

The young nurse's head crumpled in confusion. "*Your* phone? You can use the one down the hallway, like everyone else, sir. But why don't you just relax and read the paper instead? It's *The Daily Herald*."

She placed the heavy newspaper on the bed beside him, then left in a waft of pungent perfume. Atticus had heard of the paper, but he was reasonably sure it had ceased circulation in the seventies. All this was not aiding his chaotic thoughts. *What the fuck is going on?*

With a shaky hand, he reluctantly picked up the paper. It was crisp, no sign of age on its freshly printed pages. Steeling himself, he inspected at the date in the top right corner. *Saturday November 23, 1963*. Splashed across the front page was the headline "Assassinated! Kennedy shot dead in car".

Atticus sat up with a jolt and then screamed from the pain. Flopping down on the bed caused similar agony.

Thumping the bed with an angry fist, he yelled, "What the actual fuck is happening?"

His head swam. None of this made sense. None of it. Perhaps he was in a coma and this was his body's way of dealing with it. If so, why would his subconscious pick this era, one he knew so little about? Atticus would have preferred a more interesting era; maybe his early twenties, when he was in Ibiza and spent the better part of a week in his hotel room with an Italian girl. That would have been far preferable to flying nuns and smoking doctors.

"Hope I'm not intruding?"

Atticus turned to see a slightly plump, slightly balding bookish man in his thirties. He poked back his thick oval glasses and smiled pleasantly.

"My name is Oliver Preston. I was wondering if you had a moment?"

Atticus rubbed his temples and slowly sat up. It was less painful now.

"Why are you here, Oliver Preston?"

"The doctor called me." Oliver held a small cardboard box. From it, he extracted Atticus's black Tom Ford wallet and flipped it open without asking. "Said one of mine had been found in the middle of the street unconscious, all banged up."

"One of yours?"

Oliver took a card from the wallet. Atticus knew it well. It was his Secret Intelligence Service ID, with the subheading MI6, complete with his picture. The anti-counterfeit hologram flashed in the sunlight.

Holding it between his thumb and forefinger, Oliver considered it with disdain. "You see, officially, there's no such organisation as MI6, at least as far as the public is concerned. You just said 'MI6' to the doctor." He grinned sheepishly. "My apologies, I've been lurking in the corridor. Habit of the trade, I'm afraid." He frowned. "I'm wondering,

Mr Wolfe, what you think you're going to achieve with this... thing?"

Oliver's appearance was so unremarkable, so unmemorable, Atticus knew he'd make a good spy. Anyone's gaze would just naturally slide off the man, like Teflon, as if he wasn't there.

Atticus rubbed his temple. "I... I'm a bit out of sorts, to be honest, Mr Preston."

"No doubt."

Oliver's expression was expectant, as if he was still waiting for an answer. But all Atticus had were questions of his own.

"I don't even know where I am."

Oliver's eyes crinkled at the corners. "St Thomas' Hospital."

Atticus nodded, but wasn't sure he believed it. He wasn't sure he believed any of it.

Thinking out loud, he said, "This has to be some elaborate trick, surely? I've been kidnapped and I'm really in some underground bunker in Tehran, or I'll walk out that door and find an army of MI6 psychologists and overpaid behavioural consultants."

Pulling a *let's see, shall we?* face, Oliver jutted his head towards the window at the end of the hospital room. Helping Atticus stand, he assisted him into a starchy robe and gingerly escorted him across the cold linoleum floor. Carefully they made their way across the room. It was surreal. Atticus really did feel he was in another world. Why was he filled with such dread? He gazed out the window breathlessly.

It was London.

Except it wasn't. Not at all.

Gone were the skyscrapers he was so familiar with. No

Shard, no Gherkin, no Strata. No London Eye. But the rest of the buildings—well, it was London alright.

Atticus still couldn't accept it. It couldn't be real. *It couldn't.* It was a projection, surely, albeit a very convincing one.

The wooden window had a latch. With a shaking hand, Atticus unhooked the heavy metal mechanism and flung the window open. The sounds and smells of London flooded the room. Outside, dozens of red double-decker buses motored along; old-school buses, with bonnets and rear exits. The heavy scent of diesel mixed with smoke and smog. Brown vans honked at Minis and Austin-Healeys as men in bowler hats and thick-rimmed glasses strolled past girls in bright vintage knee-length dresses. It was London alright, but not one Atticus had ever seen in his lifetime.

He gripped the window frame. "I think..." Atticus's legs buckled, but Oliver held his arm firm, "I think I need to sit down for a spell."

THREE

The room spun.

Lying on the bed, Atticus smothered his face with his hands. Bombarded with a million thoughts, he was unable to process a single one.

"You look terribly pale." Oliver's voice was comforting. "I'll fetch you some tea."

How very British of you, Atticus thought as he fought the compulsion to say it out loud. His amusement was fleeting. His mind soon returned to the present. Well, the past, it seemed.

Oliver left the room, and Atticus was alone with his tumultuous thoughts. It was like a dream, except in a dream one flitted from one moment to the next without remembering how one got there. Atticus had steadfastly remained rooted in this moment. He didn't flit from one scene to the next. He was conscious and aware. It just didn't make sense.

How could a man travel sixty years back in time? That was impossible, wasn't it? Atticus took in the room. The extremely sixties room. What was it that Arthur Conan

Doyle said? Once you eliminate the impossible, whatever remains, no matter how improbable, must be the truth.

He *must* have travelled in time. But *how*? Was time travel even possible? Atticus vaguely remembered a little about Einstein's equations of General Relativity and a train moving near the speed of light. He even recalled reading that Stephen Hawking had said time travel was possible, but there was something about wormholes and infinite mass and other ideas that completely went over his head. At that moment, Atticus really wished he had more than a generalist's knowledge of scientific theory.

Disregarding that hypothesis, Atticus instead tried to wrestle with the how of it all. How did he get there? There was only one likely scenario.

The bomb.

It had to be the bomb.

All along they had assumed Omar Ganim had been building an explosive weapon, but there were things that didn't add up. The only explosives ever found were those used to kill the breaching team at the townhouse. He'd broken into scientific facilities, think tanks and bleeding-edge tech start-ups across the globe. Why scientists? Most agencies chalked it up to a bad man doing bad things, but what if there was more to it?

Atticus recalled Ganim's crack about "fixing the mess the French and English had made of the Middle East". Was that what this was all about? Was he planning to go back and "fix" it? That was what he'd said, that he'd fix it all. Whatever *it* may have been.

Then, of course, there was the explosion itself. Atticus had seen his fair share of explosions. None of them had ever been green. Even the most rudimentary bomb would have killed him at that range, yet he'd survived with minimal damage. But *how*?

Atticus's brain felt like an egg slowly being boiled inside its shell. He was trying to make sense of a senseless situation; attempting to solve an impossible puzzle without any of the requisite pieces. Down that dark path madness lurked.

With impeccable timing, Oliver returned with two white paper cups. He handed one to Atticus.

"The tea's appalling, but at least it's strong." Oliver chuckled politely.

Taking a sip, Atticus agreed. The tart bitterness revived him.

The spy quietly placed the cup on the floor beside him and once again examined Atticus's ID.

"It seems to me," Oliver turned the MI6 card over in his hand, "a spy agency that makes their people carry identification cards is not a very good spy agency."

Atticus chuckled. "Operatives never visit Vauxhall Cross, I mean, MI6 headquarters. My headquarters. They'd be dead if they ever did. We know any rival foreign government has surveillance on anyone who enters. If we meet, it's in one of the safehouses scattered around the city."

"I see."

"To the rest of us, headquarters is just an office building. I'm a Tactical Officer now, I don't go around lurking in shadows in far-off lands anymore. I'm strictly nine to five. It's a job, like everywhere else."

Oliver dipped his head to indicate he understood, yet it was clear he didn't. "Earlier, when you were speaking to the nurse, you asked for your phone. A strange word to use, I would have thought. *Your* phone." He picked up the cardboard box. From it he extracted a small black device. "Is that what this is?"

In his hand, Oliver held Atticus's mobile phone. It was still locked, but the latest Samsung glowed bright, the colourful screen completely out of place in the dull 1960s setting.

"Yes, that's my phone."

Confusion creased Oliver's features, as if the answer was nonsensical. "And this?" He held up the device. "There's a picture here, of you in front of, I'm guessing a car? It looks like a spaceship."

Oliver's tone was friendly, but Atticus was in no doubt he was being interrogated. It was then that Atticus realised Oliver might be a good spy.

"It's a Lambo." Atticus kept his manner as even as he knew how. "Lamborghini. The photo was taken at the Frankfurt Motor Show last year." Suddenly, the words "last year" seemed fraught and bewildering.

"And this." Oliver brought the screen closer to Atticus, but still out of reach. His finger pointed to the date on the screen. March 28, 2024. "How is this being projected? We have nothing like this." He judged the weight of the phone, giving it a few tiny hefts. "It's so clear. So thin. Is it...Soviet?"

"What?" There was no way Atticus could hide his surprise at the question.

"Is it Soviet? It's quite a simple question, one would have thought."

With a shake of his head, Atticus said, "No, it's South Korean."

Oliver laughed, awaiting the punchline. When none came, his face dripped with confusion. "No, really." Seeing Atticus's unchanged expression, he turned the device over several times. "Well, I'll be." Oliver harrumphed. Atticus hadn't thought people actually harrumphed, but there it was. "*South* Korea. There's still a South Korea in 2024. Fascinating."

In 1963, the Korean war had only been over for ten years. The scars were still fresh. The world, Oliver included, seemed to think the peace of the two halves of the country wouldn't hold. A new set of thoughts tumbled into Atticus's already tumultuous mind.

With his knowledge of future events, could Atticus somehow derail the future? Wasn't there a Prime Directive in *Star Trek*? Did it apply to time travel? Could his mere presence here alter the time he came from? His addled brain was rather quickly becoming hard-boiled.

"So, this phone," Oliver's pronunciation of the word retained a hint of scepticism, "what does it do?"

"It makes phone calls, though most people don't use them for that anymore. Here, let me show you."

With some reluctance, Oliver relinquished the phone. It was as if he were letting a stranger take away his newborn child. It didn't feel right for Atticus to be demonstrating a device from the future to someone he didn't know, but if he was stuck in the past—and Atticus was quite a way off accepting that reality—he was going to need allies. Oliver seemed to be the best—and if he were honest, the only—ally available.

Unlocking the phone with his fingerprint, Atticus scrolled through photos for a gobsmacked Oliver. Recalling the sense of wonder he'd felt when iPhones first came out, Atticus could only imagine what that would seem like fifty years earlier. He was reasonably sure Oliver wasn't ready for Angry Birds just yet.

He locked the device and handed it back to a dumbfounded Oliver. Handling it with the reverence one might show a Gutenberg Bible, he placed the phone back in the box. It was plain the man was enamoured with the phone but needed to move on.

Oliver extracted one more item from the box, his face etched with intrigue. It was a keypad, with a large red button at the bottom of its front panel. A wire spiralled from the base for a few centimetres before stopping suddenly in a tangle of exposed wires.

"And this?"

"Where did you find *that*?"

"Next to your unconscious body, apparently. Given your attire, and the *phone*," the word still seemed new to him, "I assumed it belonged to you as well. What is this? Don't tell me it's your car?"

Honestly, Atticus didn't know what the device was. The keypad was what Ganim had pressed to send him here, but being neither an engineer nor scientist, he understood nothing about its true purpose. All he knew was that it should stay out of the hands of anyone in this time period, or who knew what sorts of butterfly effects could ensue.

Thankfully, Preston placed it back in the box without further questions and considered the man opposite him. There was a new, casual air about his manner. To Atticus, he appeared just a little too casual. He wanted something.

"So, tell me, Future-Man, who wins the Cold War?"

Atticus didn't need to be a spy to detect the eagerness in Oliver's tone. It was the same question he would have asked if their roles were reversed.

"We do. The West. It's touch and go a few times, that's for sure." Oliver would have just lived through the Cuban Missile Crisis, so would know that only too well. "But in my time, there's no such thing as the USSR. Russians buy Coca-Cola just like everyone else."

"Good Lord." Oliver shook his head, genuine surprise on his face.

It suddenly dawned on Atticus how uncertain life would have been in this time. To him, history was just a linear list of events that led to his own time. Not so for Oliver. The ever-present threat of nuclear war hung over everyone on the tiny island nation like a spectre. They went to bed wondering if the next day would be their last, if some madman really would push a button and wipe them off the face of the Earth. To Oliver and the rest of his organisation, the Cold War was very real and very dangerous. In Atticus's time they faced a completely different set of threats, but no less deadly.

"So the Soviets are friends in your time?" It was plain Oliver was wrestling with the concept.

"Russians", Atticus gently corrected him. "And, well, let's go with a tentative no."

That confused Oliver. "But if the Soviet Union collapsed as you said, doesn't that mean an end to conflict?"

"I think Georgia, Chechnya and Ukraine would have something to say about that."

Atticus let the idea sit for a moment. As he did a completely new thought hit: what if Atticus was stuck here? He had no money, no friends, no way to earn an income. How was he going to live? His deliberations had quickly escalated from worldwide implications to the awfully immediate and personal. It's funny how the human brain can switch to self-preservation in an instant.

Once again, it seemed that Oliver was reading his mind. "It seems to me, Mr Wolfe, that a tactical officer from the future would be rather a valuable strategic asset, would you not agree?"

"What if I screw everything up? Make things worse? Fuck, I don't know, start a nuclear war?"

"Or...", Oliver scratched his chin, "what if you were always meant to be here and your presence guides humanity down the path you recall so vividly? Your existence could guarantee our very survival."

Closing his eyes, Atticus's boiled-egg skull cracked. He rubbed the back of his head. "Do you believe that, or are you trying to manipulate me into doing what could give you a strategic advantage?"

With a splayed hand across his chest, Oliver said, "I take umbrage at the suggestion that a member of the espionage community would ever manipulate a conversation to his own end." Amusement danced in the corners of his green eyes. "If you really are from the future, I think Her Majesty's government should keep you rather close, don't you, Mr Wolfe? What if the USSR got hold of you, hmmm? Imagine what those wretches would do, knowing how events unfold? They would do their utmost to foil that particular outcome, would you not agree?"

"I thought you just said my presence here guaranteed the future I remembered?"

Oliver shrugged. "I don't know anything for certain. I'm merely a public servant who must make strategic decisions based on the partial intelligence he is supplied. I make calculated determinations in the best interests of the United Kingdom. And right now I'm thinking, what better way to do so than by giving you a job at MI6?"

He tilted his head, appearing thoughtful, but Atticus detected an urgency in his delivery. Oliver was intensely interested in Atticus's answer, but didn't want to show it.

Atticus scoffed. "Me work at MI6?"

"Surely it wouldn't be much of a stretch for you?" He dangled Atticus's ID to emphasise the point.

"No, of course not." Atticus gave it a moment's thought. "Actually, yes, it would be. I don't know anything about spying in this time period. It's all invisible ink, dead drops and umbrella guns, isn't it?"

"I do believe you've been reading too many trashy spy novels." Leaning back in the rickety wooden chair, Oliver interlaced his fingers. "You're here now, Mr Wolfe, so the question is what to do with you. You need to eat, afford a flat, live a life. That requires an income, does it not? We also need to keep you away from Soviet agents, yes? Are you aware of any organisation better suited to this task than MI6? It seems our interests have converged."

"Your phrasing suggests I don't have much of a choice."

"Now you're getting it."

Atticus rubbed his temple. "Where do we start?"

FOUR

T he car trip from the hospital was brief. Through the thick windows of the bumpy Triumph Mayflower town car, Atticus saw a city bustling with life. Horse-drawn carts jostled with vans and pedestrians. Girls in bright dresses clashed with women wearing oversized coats and sour demeanours. Men in stiff camel-hair coats scowled at young men with quaffed hair in colourful suits and cravats. Mod fashion poked out amongst the staid brown sameness of the older generation. The streets were filled with contrasts, conflicting realities. It was the personification of clashing cultures and Atticus was there to see it firsthand. This was no elaborate MI6 fidelity assessment. This was the real deal.

The shock was still too fresh for him to fully process. The previous night had been sleepless. He drifted off occasionally, but every time he stirred he expected to find himself in his king-sized bed in his stylishly appointed flat. Instead, he opened his eyes and was confronted with the staid white walls of an archaic hospital. Atticus was doing his best to keep his head, but it seemed everything was encased in a shell of incongruity, an unreality which made it difficult to accept. But accept it he must; if he was to live in this time, he had to acknowledge his plight and do the best he could. The first step was finding a place to live.

That's why they were here. The slender worn stairs creaked with every step. Atticus followed the bony legs encased in coarse, worn lavender tights, layered with a tattered tweed skirt. They belonged to a woman with the most bird-like face Atticus had ever seen. Mrs Astor seemed officious and cold. She also appeared to be his new landlady.

When he and Oliver had first discussed renting him a flat, Atticus had asked about Notting Hill, recalling that it was *the* place to be in the sixties. Oliver had scowled and explained that it was full of grubby tattoo parlours, bikers' cafes and prostitutes in small ugly bedsits. Not a place for a member of Her Majesty's Government to live. Instead, he'd suggested Covent Garden, the epicentre of the emerging cultural revolution. As he put it, what better place for a man who didn't fit in to be than amongst a whole generation who felt the same way?

Reaching the third-floor landing, Mrs Astor extracted a huge set of keys from the front pocket of her apron and unlocked the dilapidated white wooden door. With a cigarette dangling from her bottom lip, she gave a half-hearted flourish, ushering Atticus and Oliver in. Although she was inviting them to enter, she didn't seem too pleased about it. Unsure if he'd done something wrong or this was Mrs Astor's everyday demeanour, Atticus stepped into the sunlit flat.

The top-floor loft was spacious. Bare wooden floor-boards, and huge floor-to-ceiling windows on each side which flooded the space with light. White paint peeled off the metal windows, which contrasted against the bare brick wall at the south end. The furniture was straight out of the fifties. A Norwegian wood sideboard sat next to a matching kitchen set, and a single bed sat in the corner under a faded handmade quilt. A freestanding brass ashtray sat in the centre of the room, between a couple of mid-century green cocktail armchairs. In front of them was a large TV cabinet, next to which stood a huge RCA Victor Victrola record player and radio. All of it in immaculate condition. If this was the twenty-first century, it would be a hipster's paradise.

"The old girl's a bit dated," Mrs Astor said, unimpressed, from the doorway, "but she's cheap."

From the huge windows, Atticus could see the Covent Garden Flower Market, a few blocks from Leicester Square, Piccadilly Circus and Trafalgar Square. In his era, there was no way anyone could afford to live here unless they had a few lazy million in the bank.

Mrs Astor remained at the threshold, allowing them to explore the space. Atticus did his best not to grin from ear to ear. The place was perfect. If he was to be marooned here, there were worse fates, surely.

Reading Atticus's expression, Oliver beamed. He turned to their host. "He'll take it."

With a curt bow, Mrs Astor hobbled across the floor. Now on an even surface, it was clear that the woman had a pronounced limp. She made her way to the sideboard and back to hand Oliver a set of paperwork and a pen. Atticus quickly glanced away, but not before she noted his gaze at her uneven gait.

She sighed. "8 October 1940, t'was." Her voice held no emotion, as if she'd repeated the words so many times they'd lost all meaning. "We were visiting my parents, 39

Bow Street. 7.30 at night. We was just a bit slow heading down the Underground, unfortunately. The Luftwaffe must have got up early that day. Got the limp the same time I lost me 'usband, if that's what you were wonderin'." She shrugged. "Rent's due on the first of the month, no exception."

In response, Atticus gave half a sympathetic tilt of his head. What more could one say to such a story? In the stillness that followed, he realised he was not without loss himself. Everyone he knew, everyone he loved was gone. Probably forever. What remained of his family, his loyal and dependable friends, the young blonde advertising executive he'd had one date with and intended to message again; they had all vanished, or rather, he had. All the people he depended on when he was down or lonely, or propped up when they were; all gone. The realisation made his stomach churn with anxiety he hadn't felt in an age. Atticus was alone.

A retro flat hardly made up for the loss. At first, it seemed like a lark, a quaint throwback he could take sabbatical in for a time. But this was no holiday. With no Ganim, no tether to his own time, he was stuck, a refugee in a time not his own. The quaint flat suddenly felt like a prison.

Oliver, ignorant of Atticus's inner strife, merrily filled in the pages of paperwork. Mrs Astor absentmindedly fluffed a pillow that required no fluffing.

As his darkening mood descended upon him, Atticus looked down at the small box he'd brought from the hospital. The pitiful contents were his sole possessions in the world. The dusty box contained his phone, smart watch, Ganim's keypad and wallet. Unpacking wouldn't take long. Atticus gazed out at the market, trying to distract himself. A shopping and tourist site in his time, the edifice was at once both familiar and foreign.

Mrs Astor poked her chin in the direction that Atticus was looking. "There's talk of 'em tearing it all down. Bloody absurd, if you'll excuse the language." Atticus wasn't aware there'd been any language, but let her continue. "Because of the traffic, they say. Pure twaddle. They're talking about demolishin' the lot and buildin' a bleedin' motorway, of all things. London'll riot before that happens, mark my words."

Atticus nodded, realising he was in a conversation. "Do you live locally, Mrs Astor?"

"Oh, lord no. This place stopped being for the likes o' me years ago. Can't seem to let go of the old girl though. Mr Astor'd turn in his grave, I think. No, live out in Islington now. The old neighbourhood's turned into an enclave of freaks, immigrants and bohemians." She shot Atticus an awkward expression. "Other immigrants, obviously." She quickly moved on. "Now it's a hive of the literary and artistic avant-garde," she spat the words with disdain. "Most of 'em come from Oxford and Cambridge and not a steady pay cheque amongst the lot of 'em." Her gaze swivelled to Oliver. "Rent's thirty-two guineas a month. First month in advance."

Atticus didn't know how much thirty-two guineas actually was. She may as well have asked for thirty-two dragon eggs.

"Certainly, certainly." Oliver pulled out a billfold and proceeded to count fresh notes onto the table. "Let's say, the first two months, as well as the last month to keep everything simple, shall we?"

"That'll be fine." She pursed her lips into an almost-smile, which was the first semblance of humour Atticus had seen on her birdlike features. As soon as Oliver had finished counting his notes, Mrs Astor shoved them into her bra before he changed his mind. "Just fine, Mr Oliver."

For a moment, she seemed pleased, but it was fleeting. Her expression soon returned to its sour default.

"There won't be no," she squinted, shifting her gaze between them, "funny business up here, will there? I can't condone it, mind. Me and Mr Astor's always been devout C of E, but my nephew, bless his soul was... one of them, you know. In the Navy for ten years, but ended up locked up in Shepton Mallet up in Somerset. Should o' seen him when he got out. Ghastly t'was. No, I don't like the idea of men, you know... but neither do I like locking folks up for it neither. I'll just say as long as no police knock down my door, and leave it at that, shall I?"

For Atticus, it was another reminder he wasn't in Kansas anymore. This was an era when homosexuality was considered a crime. Although, from memory, the term wasn't even used in these times. It was 'gross indecency'. The likes of Alan Turing and generations of men and women were outcasts, or worse, simply because of who they happened to love.

For the first time, Atticus noted a slight shift in Oliver's normally inert demeanour; a minute hardening of his jaw, a slight straightening in his back. Tiny, almost insignificant, but it was there. It didn't necessarily mean Oliver was gay, just that he seemed to have a strong opinion on the subject. Interesting. It seemed the invisible spy had tells after all. A topic for another time.

For now, Atticus concentrated on the conversation at hand, forced to play along. "I assure you there's nothing to fear in regard to... funny business, Mrs Astor. I have a fiancée, Debora, she's in Australia, studying biochemistry.

We're to be married in August next year when she returns."

The statement seemed to sate Mrs Astor. With a jutted beak, she responded, "Well, alright then. I'll be 'ere Friday at three to do the weekly clean, but you keep the place nice, understand?"

"Thank you, but I'm quite adept at cleaning."

Mrs Astor shook her head. "I've yet to meet a man whose cleaning wasn't complete tosh." She dipped her head curtly as if that was the end of it. "Every Friday at three."

Atticus realised there was no arguing with Mrs Astor. "Of course."

They made polite small talk as they ushered Mrs Astor out. She handed Atticus two keys and then disappeared down the stairs. It seemed Atticus had a place to live.

Oliver smirked as he slumped into one of the armchairs. From his coat pocket he pulled out a small bottle of brandy and gave it a gleeful shake. "A housewarming present. Grab a couple of glasses from the kitchen, will you?"

Atticus rummaged around the grimy kitchenette with its butane burner, which was the only cooker there. It amused him how quickly Oliver had assumed the manager persona by ordering him to retrieve the glasses. For the first time, he wondered what position Oliver held.

In the third cupboard he found two brightly coloured anodised cups. The archaic surroundings only reminded Atticus he would never see his own studio apartment again, with the drinking glasses he'd imported from Barcelona. Why had the thought of some glasses made him suddenly homesick? In that instant he'd give anything to call his best friends, Bester and Kate, and tell them he was coming over with a bottle of wine. Atticus placed his hand on the bench, overcome with the sickening realisation he'd never see them again.

"I say, you wouldn't happen to know who killed Kennedy, would you?" Oliver appeared hopeful. "I mean, they have the Oswald chap, but there's scuttlebutt there's more to it. I was hoping to save a lot of fellows a few rather late nights."

And hand you the biggest intelligence scoop of the century, Atticus thought to himself. Not that he could blame Oliver. If the roles were reversed, he'd ask the same question. Besides, he was glad of the chat; it diverted him from his own maudlin thoughts.

Atticus made his way across the room with the cups. "I'm afraid that one's still debated in my time." When he saw the disappointment in Oliver's features, he added, "But if it makes you feel any better, I and most folks think Oswald acted alone."

"I see." Oliver stared nowhere in particular, disappointed. "I'm thinking, with your knowledge, you could influence history, world events—you could make world-spanning changes to the future. Have you thought about that?"

"A little. Mainly, I really want to find the lead singer of Smashmouth and tell him the world's going to roll him."

"I... I... I'm not sure I know how to respond to that."

"Believe me, in my time the gag would be... mildly amusing at best."

Seemingly eager to move on, Oliver shifted his weight. "That business with the fiancée in Australia." He poured and gave an impressed tilt of his head. "It seems you are a spy after all. I was almost convinced myself, if I'm completely honest."

Atticus sat in his newly acquired chair. "And I know you're not."

"Touché." Oliver simpered. "And what happens if you're still here next August and dearest beloved Debora doesn't show?"

Atticus's mood soured once more. Everything had happened so fast; his head had been spinning since the moment he'd awoken in this time. When Oliver had first spoken of a flat, back in the hospital room, he'd assumed the arrangement would be temporary, that somehow he'd make his way back. But every extra moment spent in this time made it clear that was a laughable pipedream.

The explosion had come out of nowhere. If the device had indeed been some sort of time machine, he had only one broken component of Ganim's technology with him. And even if he'd had the rest, he wouldn't know the first thing about how to operate it. All logic dictated Atticus was stuck here, forever to be a man out of time.

He wasn't quite ready to accept this new reality. Perhaps that acceptance would come, but when or if it did, it would be on his terms, and may or may not involve a very large bottle of Scotch.

Doing his best to shake off his spiralling thoughts, Atticus re-joined the conversation. "I'll have to inform the dear Mrs Astor that poor unfortunate Debora met with a freak wombat incident. There was nothing left of her but her glasses and a picture of us by the seaside in Blackpool."

Oliver wrinkled his nose. "I'd lose the picture—a touch too much detail—but otherwise, a solid plan."

"And the wombat incident?"

Oliver chuckled. "Maybe we could work on that one."

Despite the banter, Atticus was still confronting the

reality of his plight. It had all seemed otherworldly, surreal. Atticus exhaled deeply.

Oliver caught the expression. "You alright?"

Atticus rubbed his eyes. "Sure, sure. Just trying to keep up. It's been a crazy twenty-four hours."

It was an understatement. A ridiculous, beyond all comprehension, understatement. Atticus wasn't alright. He didn't know if he'd *ever* be alright. He couldn't even see alright if he had the Hubble telescope. Not that there would be such a thing for thirty years.

He was in the sixties. *The sixties*. The concept made no sense whatsoever. Atticus felt himself at the outer edges of a panic attack. He did his best to try a breathing technique he'd picked up in meditation class, but it was difficult as he was simultaneously trying his best to hide it from Oliver. In a few seconds the dread eased, but he knew it was there, an existential crisis in waiting.

If he were alone Atticus would very much like to curl up in a foetal position until the whole thing blew over. But it wasn't going to blow over, as much as he wanted it to. As bizarre, incomprehensible and utterly unbelievable it was, he was here and somehow had to get his head around it. *Somehow*.

Oliver gave him a knowing, slanted grin, unaware of Atticus's internal break down. "It will get better, you know. Trust me on that."

Trust. *Right*. Whether Atticus trusted the man before him was still up in the air, even as he topped up his cup. The question that plagued him the most was why Oliver was helping Atticus at all. Yes, sure, it made sense to keep the future-man away from the Soviets, but there had to be more to it. Oliver had believed him so quickly—perhaps too quickly.

When he thought about it, all Oliver had was Atticus's word, a shiny phone and a MI6 ID. To anyone of this time his story should be gossamer thin at best. Perhaps the reasoning for Oliver's acceptance was equally flimsy.

If one was cynical—an advisable trait in a spy—one would question if Oliver had an ulterior motive. Atticus was indeed cynical, and absolutely questioned Oliver's motives. Sitting opposite him, Atticus tapped the wooden armrest. Everything had happened too quickly; it was all he could do to keep up. He was alone in a strange world, with no support, no resources, no income and, for the time being, no escape route. He would cautiously trust Oliver for the moment, but there was something in his nature that told Atticus he wasn't being told the whole story. Then again, it may boil down to the fact that the man before him was a professional spy.

Atticus liked Oliver, even if he wasn't sure he trusted him. For now, Atticus needed an ally. Time would tell how far their alliance went. In his experience, some allies were more dangerous than enemies. It remained to be seen which category Oliver would fall into.

"You start at MI6 tomorrow." Oliver's chipper words jolted Atticus back into the present. Well, *a* present. "Please do try to keep a low profile, will you?"

"Great in theory, but," Atticus moved his hands around his head, "I don't exactly look low-profile."

"Just do the best you can." Oliver simpered. "Be the chap who buttons his lip in meetings, blends into the wall-paper, that type of thing."

Rubbing the stubble that was emerging on his chin after a couple of days without his razor, Atticus hefted an eyebrow. "Keeping quiet's not entirely my style, I'm afraid." He tilted his head. "Oh, I'll do my best, but anyone I've ever reported through to will tell you a great many things—mainly that being a wallflower is not my strong suit. Ever since I was a snotty little kid with glasses, I've never been one to keep quiet. I tend to speak my mind, often to my own detriment. I, ah, can be a little abrasive at times, I'm afraid."

There was a mild veneer of horror on Oliver's face, as if he was beginning to regret his life choices. "You don't have glasses now."

Atticus gestured to his eyes, smirking. "Lasered."

Oliver's mouth dropped open. "You have laser eyes? Is it like X-ray vision or can you—"

"Lasic surgery, I mean. It corrected my near-sightedness. I don't have lasers flying out of my eyes, Oliver."

"Oh." He pushed his glasses up the bridge of his nose, looking disappointed. "Well, I'll pick you up in the morning and introduce you around." It was his turn to have an amused expression. "I'm sorry I don't have any plastic ID passes for you."

"I'm keen to understand just how you managed my appointment so quickly. Surely even in this time period there's security clearances, background checks..." Atticus stopped, detecting a hardening of Oliver's features.

"Well, even in these backward stone-age times, I've managed to forge documents to make you a new appointment to MI6." With a hint of self-satisfaction, he managed to overcome the slight. "And I have orders from the Home Office to prove it."

With clear pride, Oliver explained how Atticus had supposedly been transferred from the Naval Intelligence Division, the intelligence arm of the British Admiralty. It dealt with matters concerning British naval plans, with the collection of naval intelligence. The Admiralty were winding up the department and members were being dispersed to numerous organisations.

Oliver went on to describe how the NID had conveniently erased Atticus's past. The secretive organisation also known as "Room 39" was as enigmatic as MI6. There would be no one to ask about Atticus's transfer, as neither organisation was meant to exist.

Even the existence of MI6 was not confirmed publicly until the 1990s. Atticus apparently now worked for an organisation the public wasn't certain existed outside the pages of Ian Fleming novels.

"But I don't know the first thing about the Navy." Atticus scratched the back of his neck. "I don't even know what a yardarm is."

Oliver considered the statement for a moment, then his eyes twinkled. "If anyone asks you what you did, I'd suggest you tell them it's classified."

"If they ask about yardarms?"

Oliver topped up his cup and shrugged. "Fake a heart attack?"

"So helpful." Atticus smirked.

Once more, Atticus's thoughts turned to the man pouring the brandy. He realised he didn't know the first thing about Oliver.

"What is it you do at MI6?"

Oliver pushed his bookish glasses back onto the bridge of his nose. "Oh, my dear boy, a great many things."

"See, that's the sort of answer you've repeatedly given me. Pleasant but evasive." Atticus put down his cup. "Just who are you, Oliver?"

"Is this the abrasive part of your personality, is it then?" Oliver sipped his brandy. "I probably deserved that question." He shifted in his chair. "You don't know me, nor if I have an ulterior motive." Atticus nodded, but said nothing. Oliver went on. "I'm a Business Support Officer at the Circus."

It took effort for Atticus to control his expression. In his time, that was a relatively junior position. Like any other business, MI6 required admin teams. Business Support Officers were sold as essential "behind-the-scenes" branches of MI6, but what the role actually boiled down to was accounting and passing around paperwork nobody else wanted to do. Not exactly the sexy side of the organisation.

The role seemed out of step with what Oliver had achieved for Atticus. He had to be senior to have the level of clearance needed to forge documentation and push through a new hire without question, especially on a weekend. It was yet another aspect to the man that didn't quite add up.

Then again, it wasn't like Atticus had a great deal of choice. Beggars and choosers and all that. He'd have to accept Oliver at his word and take it from there. There were more pressing concerns.

"What about—" Atticus used his hand to make a circular motion around his face. "Can't imagine there are many who work at MI6 who have my... complexion."

Oliver seemed to concede the point with a raise of his eyebrow. "In light of the spate of Cambridge defections, there's been chit-chat about drawing fewer of our numbers, shall we say, from the same stagnant pool. The Chief has asked for more variety in our ranks. We almost hired a chap who had Chinese parents. We promoted a lass from the typing pool. We even have a young lad with long hair who wears those skinny suits like those god-awful Beatles."

"You're positively the United Nations." Atticus leaned

backwards. "And by the way, those god-awful Beatles change the face of music forever."

"Those idiots?" Oliver's face turned sour. "Really? I can't stand them, with all that head shaking and screeching."

"Then you're going to love the Sex Pistols."

The blood drained from Oliver's face. "The what?"

THE TWO TALKED LATE into the night. Atticus did his best not to give too much away about the future, but the occasional thing slipped out. He'd had to explain what googling meant, which necessitated explaining at a high level what the internet was.

At one stage he thought he'd given away too much by mentioning the Berlin Wall, but was relieved to learn it had been erected two years previously. Atticus realised he'd need to modify his manner of speech and everyday topics, which would either be completely foreign or give him away as a man displaced in time.

He was already finding it difficult to not continually reach for his phone. Other than some photos, saved memes he intended to send to his friends for a laugh, and as a handful of downloaded songs, shows, books and movies, it was now a futuristic paperweight. When he thought about trying to explain how one could become so addicted to a small black rectangle, he decided to leave it. He'd let some future version of Oliver discover that for himself. Speaking of learning for himself, he knew there was at least one book on his phone that Oliver would have loved to get his hands on—Westad's *The Cold War: A World History*. It was something Atticus had to make sure stayed out of circulation for the next fifty years.

Atticus had mixed feelings about seeing the new, that is, old MI6. It would be like stepping into history, although it was now his present. There was a reason he looked forward to working at MI6, but not one he was willing to share with Oliver yet. That would be for him alone.

Oliver, in his own words, pulled up stumps at around 11 pm, only to arrive the next morning at 8 am sharp. He brought what he referred to as a suit befitting a man of Atticus's stature. To Atticus it resembled something a grandfather would have worn to a funeral. With that came a sudden realisation: he could see the members of his family who were alive in this time period. It wasn't a welcome thought. Atticus's relatives in the sixties were well known. Notorious was probably a more apt description. That was something he could explore at a later date—or he could just do what he'd done for the better part of his life: try his best to deny he was even related to the infamous lineage.

The Tube was familiar yet unfamiliar at the same time. The Circle line was still the Circle line; even the sound wasn't dissimilar. Out of habit, when they approached the gates Atticus redundantly reached for his wallet. The most surprising thing was that there were no ticket barriers. That, and that everyone seemed to move at a much slower pace. In the twenty-first century, if people moved this slow there'd be a riot. Another notable difference was the sheer volume of newspapers. Almost everyone was reading a paper, each one with headlines about the Kennedy assassination, and Jack Ruby's slaying of Lee Harvey Oswald.

The two exited St. James's Park tube station and made their way up Broadway. Once again, Atticus was mesmerised by how alive the city seemed. It was bursting at the seams. The traffic was chaotic, and crowds of people jostled one another in an endless dance. The most common segment of the crowd were men in coats, most of whom had accompanying bowler hats. Occasionally a hatless man's long hair poked out, but the featureless businessman was by far the most prevalent.

Idly, Atticus wondered how long before it all changed. When would the freakish younger generation exert themselves on the mainstream and shock the English establishment to its core? It suddenly dawned on Atticus that Jimi Hendrix or Keith Richards could wander around the corner at any moment. Just as quickly, he realised he could go see Clapton, Hendrix, The Stones, Pink Floyd, The Who, all in their prime. He'd need to make a list.

"Here we are," Oliver announced in a cheerful tone.

They had halted before 54 Broadway, an unremarkable building with a prominent mansard roof, seemingly built decades before. Next to the entrance was a brass plaque identifying it as the offices of the "Minimax Fire Extinguisher Company".

Atticus regarded Oliver questioningly.

In return, Oliver checked to ensure no one was within earshot, then opened the front door. "Atticus Wolfe, welcome to MI6."

CHAPTER
FIVE

T he ground floor office appeared to be what it said on the plaque outside, a humdrum office of an equally uninteresting fire extinguisher company. The pleasant middle-aged receptionist greeted them as they walked in. Oliver made introductions and Atticus met his second contemporaneous MI6 staff member, Mrs Abernathy. She greeted Atticus warmly, but he sensed he was being sized up by this wool-suited maiden. While maintaining a pleasant air, her sharp blue eyes pierced into him. She pressed something under the hardwood desk and a low mahogany gate opened. The two men strode to the elevator.

Not for the first time, Atticus wondered what the hell he was doing. Yes, he knew spy craft, but could he fool this antiquated organisation into believing he knew *their* spy craft? Espionage in the twenty-first century was about data mining, satellite tracking, digital encryption cracking, facial recognition software and so much more, all of which relied on vast fields of servers. Atticus doubted there was even one computer in this whole building. He wiped his sweaty palms on his pants as they waited for the elevator.

Oblivious to Atticus's inner turmoil, Oliver glanced over his shoulder. "Don't let the congeniality fool you. Mrs Abernathy once strangled three SS officers in one night. Apparently, not one of them made a sound." He made a slashing gesture across his neck for effect.

"Uh, good to know, I guess."

The elevator arrived with a loud *thunk*. The door opened to reveal an ancient lift. When the two stepped in the whole thing bounced. Inside, a man, barely in his twenties, stood rigidly tall next to the floor lever and greeted them with a cheerful smile. He wore a suit identical to those Atticus had seen in black and white footage. The Chesterfield suit was pale grey with winged lapels of black velvet. It was complemented by a long black tie. With his mop top hairdo, the young man even bore a passing resemblance to a young George Harrison. Which, of course, is exactly what George Harrison would be at this time.

"Floor, gentlemen?" the young want-to-be-Beatle asked, hand hovering over the lever.

"Six, thank you, Henry."

The young kid leaned forward and slid the heavy scissor gates closed with a thud. Atticus felt a growing sense of claustrophobia. Henry clanked a heavy handle and the ancient mechanism issued a series of hefty groans, but nothing happened.

Henry thumped the wall with his fist. "This thing is pants." He hefted the lever several more times, apparently hoping for a different response.

Taking advantage of the lull, Oliver said, "New suit, Henry?"

The kid beamed and thumbed the black velvet lapels.

"Do you like it? Bought it Saturday from Dougie Millings up in Soho. Cost a bomb. The boss hated it, naturally."

"Of course he did." Oliver turned to Atticus. "What did you say? The Beatles were going to save the world?"

Atticus rocked on his heels. "Change music forever, I believe it was."

The lift finally began its slow, juddering upward trajectory. Atticus felt sure this archaic mechanism would tumble down the darkened shaft. The whole thing groaned like an asthmatic dragon.

"You like them too?" Henry beamed. "Outstanding! They're brilliant. Have you heard the new album that came out Friday? I'm going to need another one because I've been playing it nonstop!"

His enthusiasm was infectious. Atticus liked him.

Oliver grunted. "It's just a lot of twang and screaming. Hardly music at all."

That stifled the conversation for a few moments. The ancient lift wheezed its way skyward.

Atticus smirked as he addressed Henry but looked at Oliver. "I think *With the Beatles* is a real step forward in the band's song-crafting genius."

The mask of horror on Oliver's face amused Atticus no end.

"That's what I said!" Henry almost squealed.

"And the yearning of McCartney's 'All My Lovin' is a major step up, and Harrison's first songwriting effort 'Don't Bother Me' is a stellar contribution to the Lennon-McCartney powerhouse."

Henry's mouth dropped open, glee wrapped around his young face. Oliver tutted.

"Wait until you hear *Rubber Soul*, it's going to blow your mind." Oliver elbowed him in the ribs, his eyes flared in warning. Atticus went on quickly, "Always a pleasure to meet a fellow Beatles fan."

Rolling his eyes, Oliver groaned. "Oh god, don't encourage him, that's all we need." In an obvious attempt to change the subject, he addressed Atticus. "Remind me, I have a briefing at one, I believe. Something on the Soviet sphere of influence in Asia or some such palaver. I have to find out what room. I'll invite you along."

"Woolley's chairing the Soviets in Southeast Asia quarterly analysis, but it may as well be conducted by a trained monkey. That human colostomy bag thinks he's knowledgeable about statecraft because he was in the same room as Churchill once. I could agree with his analysis of the Vietnam situation, but then we'd both be idiots. It's impossible to underestimate the man." Straightening his back, Henry seemed to realise he'd spoken aloud. "Room four twelve, at one o'clock." Seeing the flabbergasted expressions on Atticus and Oliver's faces, he added, chagrined, "People talk in elevators." He shrugged. "I pick up the odd snippet."

"The odd snippet, huh?" Atticus chuckled to let him know it was fine. "How long have you been here, Henry?"

"Nearly two years." His demeanour soured. He turned to Oliver. "Any word from His Highness on getting out of...?" Henry motioned to the four walls.

"Nothing yet, I'm afraid." Oliver grimaced apologetically.

"Rathdowne hates me, I swear the old man hates me. He's never going to give me anything more than pressing buttons."

"Patience." Oliver's tone was soothing. "He'll come around. It's only a matter of time."

"They'll have flying cars before I get a desk. He doesn't think I'm cut out for this line of work, does he?"

"Oh, I don't know. It seems this job has a lot of responsibility."

The two gawped at Atticus, confused. The elevator jolted to a halt.

He went on. "You see all comings and goings of this place. You're trusted enough to handle the sensitive conversations between floors. You are the sentinel, the guardian of MI6, Henry."

Henry tugged the scissor gates open. "The sentinel?" He puffed out his chest. "I like that. Yeah, I like that a lot. Thanks Mr..."

"Atticus. Atticus Wolfe." Only too keen to step out of the ancient lift, he replied, "You're welcome, Henry."

"Ta, Mr Wolfe."

Oliver and Atticus made their way into MI6 proper. The offices were nothing like those of Atticus's time. Vauxhall Cross was a bright, modern office building, bustling with activity. This was the polar opposite. Polar was an apt word. 54 Broadway was a rabbit warren of interconnected offices which were uniformly freezing cold, despite the prehistoric bar heaters lining the walls. Atticus wasn't quite sure what he'd expected, but it certainly wasn't a dingy building overstuffed with wooden partitions and frosted glass windows. Nor had he expected the constant clickety-clack of typewriters or the ever-present haze of cigarette smoke hovering at head height. A teletype machine clattered noisily in the corner. This was most definitely not his MI6.

Heads turned in his direction. Atticus hoped it was due to him being a new face, and nothing more.

One aspect that struck Atticus was the mismatched

desks. The whole set-up seemed cobbled together, borrowed from wherever they could source it. It was hardly the jetsetting first-class-all-the-way MI6 of fiction. Atticus knew that in reality spies didn't travel first class. They carried themselves in such a way as to ensure they created the least impression possible. Martinis at thirty thousand feet were purely for the movies.

The once-white paintwork was patchy and dirty. The memories of past cigarettes clung to the yellowing ceiling like guilt. The expressions of the staff urgently moving about was a reminder this wasn't some quaint guided tour of a once-important building. It was etched on their earnest faces; this place, right here, right now, was of great significance. The decisions made in these offices saved lives; or, just as easily, condemned them. Nations could thrive or fall according to whether a piece of intelligence was passed to the right party. The men and women who walked these halls did so in the knowledge that if they didn't perform their duties to the best of their abilities, there would be dire consequences. A nuclear bomb makes a much worse stain than cigarettes ever could.

It was all too claustrophobic and insalubrious. After the day was done, Atticus would definitely need to go for a run. His skin was already crawling and he'd only been there ten minutes.

Oliver wove through the labyrinthian office, clearly on a mission. Atticus had to jog to keep up. The man only slowed when he reached a closed cherry red door at the far end of the floor.

"Stay here. I'll let him know you've arrived." Oliver pursed his lips and blew air out his nose, as if gathering courage. "Leave the talking to me."

"Really? Because I was about to blurt everything I know about Tamagotchis and the Spice Girls' back catalogue."

Opening his mouth to respond, Oliver seemed to think better of it. Instead, he knocked and went in.

Through the crack in the door, he heard Oliver speak. "Mr Rathdowne, I have Atticus Wolfe outside, just transferred over from Room 39. You received the communique last month from the Home Office, remember?"

Mr Rathdowne? The formality indicated a subordinate role for Oliver and then some. If Atticus's saviour was kowtowing to this man, how low on the totem was he?

"Of course I bloody recall, Preston. Bring him in, this isn't some King's College graduation ceremony, you don't need all this pomp and ceremony, alright?"

"I thought it would be advisable if I first—"

"Just bloody bring him in."

Oliver leaned out the door and jerked his head for Atticus to follow him in. Inside, the tiny office was overfilled with filing cabinets. A battered desk at its centre in the classic power play move. Piles of papers teetered, threatening to cascade to the floor at any moment.

Behind the desk sat a small man in a big suit. His combover would have been laughable if it hadn't been so earnest. He had the unwavering beady eyes of a man perfectly suited to be either a dictator or a parking officer. The sneer beneath the thick moustache gave Oscar Rathdowne the disposition of someone who was angry at the world, but not entirely sure why.

A messy office could sometimes suggest a creative mind. Atticus studied Rathdowne's face and wondered if he'd ever had a creative thought in his life. Perhaps in his new boss's case, the messy room simply indicated that he was busy, and didn't have time to clean it.

Rathdowne stamped out a cigarette and looked up. On seeing Atticus, he recoiled. "Good lord, he's a darky."

Clenching his fists, Atticus stepped forward. Oliver's hand darted to Atticus's forearm.

Clearing his throat, Oliver addressed his superior. "Like I said, sir, from the Admiralty. He comes highly recommended." He opened his briefcase, balancing it against his chest. "I have his certificates of commendation, references and letter of introduction right here."

As Oliver pulled the papers out of the case, Rathdowne waved his hand. "Fine. Fine."

Oliver's face fell. "Don't you want to see them, sir? There's some very fine—"

Atticus was still fuming, but not livid enough to miss the realisation that Oliver must have spent the better part of the night forging the contents of the briefcase. His shoulders slumped and he closed the case, disheartened.

"Stop banging on, Preston." Rathdowne waved an annoyed hand. "The Admiralty says it's fine, it's fine. There's nothing I can do about it." He huffed. "Seriously, with the blowback from the JFK mess, the Minister's having an absolute fit. He wanted to shunt the PM off to Chequers, which did not go down terribly well. The new PM doesn't want to show his back to his enemies; the bugger hasn't even been in the job a month. Paranoia's rife right about now, let me tell you. Everyone above the position of tea lady in this organisation thinks the Soviets will take advantage." He ran his palms down his face in frustration. Rathdowne assessed Atticus, from his clompy second-hand brown shoes all the way up to his shiny bald head. "We'll put him in the African bureau. Take him down to Bridgeman on two—"

"No."

Both men turned to Atticus. Oliver's bookish face was panicked; Rathdowne's stunned.

"Eastern Europe." Atticus stood rigid.

Rathdowne's jaw hardened as his eyes bore into Atticus. "Look, I don't know how they do things at the Admiralty, but here, my boy—"

"And don't call me boy." It took all of Atticus's willpower not to throttle the man.

The two men glared at one another. Both knew his assignment was based purely on the colour of his skin and nothing to do with abilities. Atticus had faced racism all his life, for as long as he could remember. One of his earliest memories was as child—he couldn't have been more than five—having urine poured over him by an older white kid at school. It hadn't ended there. To say his life had been a constant battle would be untrue, but to say his life was as easy as his white contemporaries would be an outright lie.

Deep down, he knew the sixties were going to be tough, and that he'd face bigotry, both explicit and covert, but he didn't expect it quite so fast, and not from his own beloved organisation. Having grown up in proud black family in a proud black neighbourhood, Atticus had never been afraid to call out discrimination. He'd made it his life's work to not back down in the face of prejudice. Every backward step meant the journey would be that much longer.

At the same time, he realised this period was not his own, nor was this his organisation, even though it shared the same name. As much as it pained him to admit it, he couldn't change this world with defiance alone. It would take many brave souls decades of struggle, and even then, they still had far to go. The Brixton race riots were years away. As tough as it was to concede, he was a stranger to this time and he'd have to learn to compromise. A little, at least.

"Steady on, old... chap." Oliver's tone was an attempt to sound amused, though his eyes were pure panic. He'd stuck his neck out for Atticus and now it appeared it had been placed in a guillotine.

Atticus ground his teeth. "You don't know me." His eyes drilled into Rathdowne. "And you don't know how I work. Fine, I understand that." His tone held a modicum of conciliation. "Let me show you. Let me earn my stripes, that's all I ask. I'm not demanding any more than anyone else here, all I'm asking is for the same chance they have. Let me earn Eastern Europe. How does that sound?"

The rigidness of Rathdowne's posture eased slightly. "We'll see." He smoothed out his moustache. "You won't half stand out walking through the middle of Berlin, mate."

"All the more reason for them not to suspect me." Atticus raised one eyebrow. "Who'd be fool enough to assign a black spy to Berlin?"

Rathdowne rubbed the back of his neck. "I'm asking myself the same thing." The faintest outline of a smile creased the corners of his mouth. "Let's play it by ear, shall we?"

It wasn't a win, but Atticus would take it for now. He tilted his head in agreement, and Oliver sighed in relief.

Clearing his throat, Rathdowne shifted his weight, keen to move on. He jutted his chin at Oliver. "I say, how did you go with that loon the other day, the one in hospital?"

The right part of Oliver's mouth twitched into a smirk, but the rest of his mouth refused to follow suit. "Oh, it ended up being a wild goose chase, sir. Just a vagrant making up stories, I suspect, nothing more. The fool even had an ID card with MI6 written on it."

Atticus could tell Oliver was doing his damnedest not to look in his direction.

Rathdowne let out a boisterous laugh. "Ha, plonker. Probably written in crayon, no doubt." He picked up a pack of Embassy Filter and lit one. "I tell you, they better not make any more of those damned preposterous Bond pictures or we'll be up to our armpits in delusional want-to-be spies. I appreciate you taking time out of your weekend." Rathdowne's face paled slightly and he regarded Oliver in alarm. "Saturday, Jesus. I sent you on Saturday. I didn't even think."

"That's quite alright, sir. It wasn't a bother, really."

Rathdowne waved his cigarette about. "Good, good. I don't know what you lot get up to on the... you know..."

"The Sabbath?"

"Hmmm, yes, that. Well, as long as it wasn't a problem, then fine." He paused, then stared contemplatively in Atticus's direction, ruminating. "Where do we put you then, I wonder?"

Thankfully, Atticus had been mulling over that very subject and already had an answer. "I'm a tactical officer, a highly trained and experienced strategic analyst. I don't wish to be blunt, but you'd be putting this organisation at a disadvantage by placing me in the mailroom. Put me to work somewhere in that capacity and let me earn my place, but please don't make the mistake of underestimating me."

Beside him, Oliver let out a surprised burst of air from his lips. He seemed shocked at Atticus's sheer audacity, but remained silent.

"You're not shy, are you?" Rathdowne's eyes narrowed.

"Last time I checked, MI6 wasn't one for hiring shrinking violets." Atticus hefted his chin. "Test me out, and if I'm not up to the task we'll shake hands and be done with it. How does that sound?"

The proposal earned him a smile from Rathdowne. "I don't take my meetings at lunch over brandy and canapés, and I certainly didn't get this job because my uncle's in the House of bloody Lords. I didn't have a privileged public-school upbringing, I got here because I work damn hard. I expect the same from everyone else here."

Atticus tilted his head. "Then we'll get on just fine."

Rathdowne blinked as if the thought hadn't occurred to him. "Yes, I imagine we might." He picked a piece of tobacco off his tongue. "So, Mr I-Want-Eastern-Europe, what did you do at the Admiralty?"

"Quite a variety of activities, really." Atticus's mind raced. "My last assignment was primarily focused on the intelligence gathering on Soviet shipyards and under-standing their nuclear capabilities." Atticus was quite pleased with this piece of on-the-spot bullshit. The expression on Rathdowne's face suggested his new boss was just as impressed. "My role was focused on cultivating and developing assets who could supply intelligence. Nothing to do with yardarms, as such."

Atticus made sure he didn't glance in Oliver's direction in case he burst into an ill-timed smile. The line about his past work wasn't entirely untrue. His recent assignment at MI6—*his* MI6—had been cultivating assets, only those particular assets had terrorist ties. In fact, one of those assets had led him directly to Omar Ganim.

That was one reason Atticus was so eager to take up the offer to work at MI6; something he hadn't and wouldn't share with Oliver. Yes, he was an expert in spy craft who needed a job, but that wasn't his main motivation. MI6's role was primarily intelligence gathering. What better place to determine if Omar Ganim had travelled back in time with him? Atticus had been found alone on the street; who's to say Ganim hadn't arrived with him, and fled before anyone arrived on the scene? If that was the case, Atticus had to find him.

In time, Atticus would have all the resources of this organisation at his disposal, far beyond the capabilities of a mere civilian. If Ganim was here, he was the only man who could tell Atticus what had happened to them. There was even the more remote possibility he could return Atticus home. It was an unlikely proposition, one he did his best not to cling too readily to, for he knew that way madness lay.

"I see, I see." Rathdowne smoothed out his moustache again. It seemed he did this whenever he was contemplative. "What did you find about the Soviets? We've heard rumblings about a new class of submarines out of the Nikolayev Shipyard. Anything of interest?"

Atticus clasped his hands behind his back. "That would be a question for the Minister, sir. I'm not at liberty to divulge anything at an inter-departmental level. I'm loath to say it's classified, but I don't believe it is my place to determine what is and isn't an appropriate intelligence exchange. I'm sure you understand." Atticus was sure he did. He was just as sure Rathdowne wouldn't like it. He added, "I know that's not the answer you were looking for."

Rathdowne blew out a frustrated exhale of smoke from his nostrils. "I might not like the response, but I respect your professionalism, Wolfe."

Did he detect a slight tone of admiration? That was a bonus.

His new superior steepled his fingers. "Well, if you're

not bound for the African bureau, we're going to have to find you something to do."

He squinted at his new member of staff, as if contemplating something, but it seemed to Atticus he'd already decided, and was just going through the theatrics of mulling it over. It seemed Oliver was right. All Atticus had to say was classified and that put an end to the questioning. For the first time, he believed he could actually pull this off.

Rathdowne scratched the back of his head. "Listen here, there's a... we have a gathering at eleven. An outsider..." he coughed, "someone new to the organisation might be just what the doctor ordered. Room 503." His head swivelled to Oliver. "You too, Preston. About time we put you to work for a change."

"Yes sir, very good." Atticus could almost hear Oliver roll his eyes.

After some minor pleasantries the two were dismissed. Once clear of the office door, Oliver sighed deeply and leant against an unoccupied desk.

"That went... I'm not entirely sure what happened there."

Atticus grinned, and jerked his head towards the office they'd just left. "As soon as I walked through the door, I knew the type. A brown coat, clipboard and correct paperwork. He's been fighting against privilege ever since he got here. It's a subject I'm somewhat familiar with. Same war, different battles."

Oliver gave his head a slight shake. "I thought you were a strategist, not a psychologist."

"A good strategic officer is absolutely a psychologist. We have to anticipate moves, tactics, millions of decisions before they're even made. If you can't read people, you're in the wrong job." He turned to Oliver and showed his teeth. "Some things haven't changed in sixty years."

OVER THE NEXT HOUR, Oliver took Atticus on a tour of MI6. Each floor had its speciality, its own unique feel. The third floor was pure intelligence gathering and was suitably quiet; dark and enigmatic as a church rectory. The fifth was operations, and felt like they'd stumbled into an after-polo match party.

No one gave Oliver the slightest hint of respect. At most, there was a grudging acknowledgement of his existence. In each of the departments they visited, everyone seemed to know Oliver, but no one seemed too pleased to see him.

Almost no one.

"Oliver!"

The woman leapt from her desk and wove through the clattering typing pool. Amidst the *clickety clack* of dozens of women typing away, the brunette in her twenties bounded towards Oliver and embraced him in a fierce bear hug.

Struggling for oxygen, Oliver squeezed out, "This. Is. Maggie. Dunbar."

The woman's figure-hugging A-line pinafore started a couple of inches above the knee. The fact that every other woman in the office had theirs well below the knee seemed telling.

As she relinquished her hold, Atticus greeted the newcomer. "Ms Dunbar."

"Ms?" Maggie gave Oliver an amused expression, as if to say *la di da*. She jutted her chin at her friend. "Who's this?"

"This is Atticus Wolfe." He gave a theatrical flutter of his hand. "He's new."

"No way?" Her voice drowned in sarcasm. "Pretty sure I would have noticed Mr Atticus Wolfe walking the halls." Atticus didn't know the intent of the statement. Turning her attention back to Oliver, Maggie gave him a playful slap on the arm. "Word of the day test. Ready?"

"I'm not sure if now is quite the best—" Oliver gave Atticus a sideways glance, slightly embarrassed.

"If I said you're the ticket, you'd be?"

Oliver's eyebrows curved in concentration. "Just the ticket," he winced, unsure, "good?"

Maggie adorably screwed up her face and shook her head. "Opposite. As in, third-class ticket, basically a bad Mod. Like, I don't know, someone still wearing last week's fashion, their hair's out of place or not enough mirrors on their scooter. If someone calls you a ticket, Oliver, punch them."

"Good to know." He twisted around to Atticus. "One must keep up with emerging trends and so forth. Maggie has been giving me Mod language lessons."

It seemed a familiar ritual the two shared. Their camaraderie was infectious. Perhaps the two were more than friends?

"So, you're bilingual, then?" Atticus attempted to sound witty, but felt gangly and self-conscious. "Mod and English."

"Quadrilingual, actually," Maggie replied, showing off her dimples. "English, Russian, German and Mod. Quinquelingual if you count Cockney."

The young woman had an air of defiance he hadn't expected in this time period. Atticus chastised himself for being so naive. Feminism didn't start in the seventies. Women had been fighting male privilege for centuries. It only made him like her even more.

"And what is it you do here, *Ms* Dunbar?" Atticus asked, good-naturedly emphasising the word. He liked the interaction between Oliver and Maggie, and felt comfortable enough to join in.

She seemed to catch the humour and appreciate it. "I'm in Signals."

"Maggie was recently promoted into the role after showing a natural aptitude in the typing pool." Oliver seemed to take pride in the statement. "I may have put in a good word."

"But you're still located down here?" Atticus had already been to Signals; it was three floors above.

Maggie seemed impressed he'd noticed. "Upstairs want me to stay put among this picturesque sea of typewriters."

Atticus appeared to have no issue reading Maggie's expressions, and there were many. It was an admirable trait in a colleague, deadly in the field.

"But why?"

She grunted and held up a fist. "Take your pick." She flicked out her thumb. "I'll be too much of a disruptive influence for the blokes upstairs." She kept going, counting off progressive fingers as she spoke. "Not being able to keep up, because, you know," she pointed to her face and crossed her eyes, "woman." She uncrossed them and continued to unfurl fingers. "There will be material unsuitable for a lady. I'll ruin the boys' club atmosphere. I'd have to share the bathroom." She stared at her hand. "I've run out of fingers. "Oh, and I need to be protected from the foul language." She rolled her eyes. "Like that's a fucking issue."

A woman with thick cat-eye glasses typing nearby gasped and covered her mouth. Her eyes darted over to the group, then she immediately returned to winding back the roller of her typewriter. Using liquid paper to make a correction, she tutted and shook her head.

Maggie ignored the woman and went on. "I'm as capable as that daft lot up there. I was the one who spotted that the Minsk letters were fake. They were written by two separate typewriters, not the one by the ex-agent like they wanted us to believe." She turned to Atticus. "Every typewriter slug has a unique characteristic if you look close enough. In this case, the e and s were totally different. Saved a whole operation months of work on a false lead. Do I get any thanks?" She shook her head in case there was any doubt. "They dismissed my hard work, said 'clever secretary', and quickly moved on. They steadfastly refused to acknowledge that it was damn good intelligence work. Isn't that what good spies do? Use *all* their knowledge to solve problems? Never in the history of this place has a working knowledge of polo ever resulted in a breakthrough, but the one time *I* use past experience they give me a pat on the head and send me back to the typing pool. It's so bloody..."

"Condescending?" Atticus tilted his head.

"Yes, that." Amusement crossed her lips, as if impressed by Atticus's enlightened understanding. "So here I am shuffling papers with a shiny new title but the exact same desk." She huffed. "I thought my promotion might shake things up, but apparently it was a just a frivolous girl's featherbrained daydream."

"Upstairs could use a disruption." Atticus noted her enquiring gaze. "From what I've seen, it's about as diverse as sliced bread."

Maggie looked Atticus up and down. "It seems slightly more diverse than it did last week."

In spite of her animated facial expressions, Atticus found it difficult to get a read on Maggie Dunbar. He couldn't tell if the crack was complimentary or the exact opposite. It seemed she could play her cards close to her chest. Maybe she could make a good field agent after all.

Atticus felt compelled to keep the conversation going. "What made you join MI6, Ms Dunbar?"

Her expression turned frosty and she folded her arms. "I have my reasons."

That was a dead end. Atticus felt compelled to fill the swirling silence that ensued with something, anything to change the subject.

Stretching his arms above his head, Atticus asked, "Anyone know where I can get a decent pair of runners? I might pop out at lunch if there's a store nearby."

Only after he'd said the words did Atticus realise he didn't have any money. That posed all sorts of issues in itself.

"Runners?" Oliver's face was deeply confused. "Do you need people to run something?"

"No, like sneakers. Running shoes."

Maggie was equally perplexed. "Why would you run?"

"For fitness. You know, fun?" Their matching blank expressions told him it was a foreign concept. It seemed recreational running wasn't yet a thing. To himself, he mumbled, "I won't ask about a good yoga studio then."

The incessant noise of typing grew louder. Atticus stood self-consciously in the centre of the floor, feeling exposed. Again, he was inherently aware that he was an interloper—in more ways than one.

"Atticus? That's an odd name." It appeared Maggie was doing what he had attempted moments before, filling the uncomfortable silence with small talk. "Is it a family name?"

Atticus shrugged nonchalantly. "My mother was a big fan of *To Kill a Mockingbird*."

Maggie tilted her head. "Your...? The book only came out a couple of years ago."

"It's been lovely," Oliver piped in, threading his arm through Atticus's and guiding him away, "but we have to dash. Lunch tomorrow?"

"That would be lovely, especially since it's your turn to pay."

Oliver practically dragged Atticus towards the elevator, his face half amused, half annoyed. The sentiment was clear. *You have to be more careful.*

He was right. Atticus had been far too casual, too careless. This wasn't an amusing dream he would soon wake from. Like it or not, this was his life now; he had to treat it as such. It was too easy to slip into his casual persona and risk blurting out something that would let everyone know he was an outsider, an intruder in this time. If he wasn't careful, he could be exposed at any moment. At best, he'd be fired; at worst, killed. This wasn't a game. He had to start acting accordingly.

CHAPTER
SIX

Room 503 appeared to be designed to seat six comfortably. Unfortunately, well over twenty people were squeezed into the dark wood-panelled room—and they were all men. Dense with smoke and testosterone, the room felt more like a seedy nightclub than a meeting of key members of the intelligence community.

When Atticus walked through the threshold, every head twisted in his direction. He was examined from head to toe. It wasn't an unfamiliar sensation, although Atticus was at a loss to recall a time it had been so intense.

Rather than warmly greeting familiar co-workers, Oliver slunk into the room. He hunched his shoulders and aimed for the periphery, trying to make the smallest impact possible. Once again, Atticus was conscious of the lack of interaction between his benefactor and the rest of the organisation. Aside from the occasional reluctant sidestep to let them through, every person in the room seemed to ignore Oliver completely. The short bespectacled spy was an invisible man amongst invisible men.

Perhaps that was the reason Oliver had taken Atticus in so readily. With Future Man under his wing, Oliver would have a potential inside line to success. He could leverage Atticus's knowledge of upcoming events to demonstrate unsurpassed intuition and insight. He could manoeuvre himself into a position of power within the organisation, finally clawing out some semblance of the respect he so clearly lacked. Atticus had to admit, as plans went, it wasn't terrible.

Nearing the back of the room, a weak-chinned man sneered in their direction. He blew out smoke as Oliver approached. "Here he comes, boys. Backs to the walls."

There was general sniggering, and Atticus took particular note of the fact that no one came to Oliver's defence. It seemed there could be another reason Oliver had befriended him. Atticus treated him as an equal, while his compatriots mocked and treated him as a joke at best, at worst, an affront. In their eyes, his sexuality was his defining feature. Was that the reason he was looked down upon, or was it the foundation from which their derision was built?

Reaching the smoking man, Oliver sighed heavily. "Move, Henderson."

The other man tutted and failed to move a muscle. He turned his head slowly and blew smoke from his nose. "You need to learn respect for your betters, Preston."

"As soon as I find any, I'll let you know. Now, move."

As if it were the greatest effort ever experienced by man, Henderson moved three inches to let the two of them pass. Once they'd taken their places, Atticus had time to read the room. There was a clear undercurrent; everyone was tightly wound. Atticus heard words like "Kennedy", "Oswald", "Soviet" and "ramifications", but there was far more in what they didn't say. It was the clenched jaws, the sleep-lessness of their darkened features. These men were on edge. All of them were coated in a slick veneer of fear. The room positively reeked of it. What made it worse was none of them, not one, knew exactly what they were afraid of.

Barging in with folders stuffed under his arm, Rath-downe positioned himself behind the podium at the front of the room. He slapped down the files and loudly cleared his throat.

"I'll keep this short and to the point." Rathdowne's forehead crinkled as the room remained obstreperous, disinclined to quieten at Rathdowne's command. It seemed he didn't have the respect of the room either. In retrospect, that shouldn't have been a surprise. He was blue collar; the rest of the room, bar Atticus and Oliver, seemed entitled. The audience smacked of pomposity and contemptuous-ness; Atticus could almost taste its vile stench.

"Gentlemen." Rathdowne's frustration was palpable. If anything, the volume in the meeting room increased. "Pillar!"

The target of Rathdowne's wrath appeared to have walked off a polo field. The man with premature grey on his temples, which added to his handsomeness rather than detracting from it, continued his conversation. He had an air about him that suggested he was the kind of person who might say "forsooth" without irony.

Again, Atticus was reminded of the class war currently raging in English society. The likes of Rathdowne on one side; Pillar, Henderson and their ilk on the other. Rath-downe's fight for class equality seemed to be playing out right before his eyes. It was telling that none of these upper-class men knew their time was ending. The working-class success of the Beatles meant that anyone could make it. Society no longer cared where you came from. The working class were becoming successful in art, music and fashion, and they were leaving the aristocrats behind. In a few short years their heritage would be forgotten, their titles meaningless. Society would move on, leaving their kind resigned to history. They just didn't know it yet.

And it was plain from Rathdowne's frustration that they weren't quite there yet.

He puffed out his chest and slammed his fist into the podium. "Our new man in East Berlin has been kidnapped."

That shut the room up. Every head turned in his direction.

"Alistair Jayne was discovered missing at 3 pm yesterday afternoon, German Standard time. We suspect foreign intervention."

A young man with a ridiculously large chin at the front of the room waved a cigarette in Rathdowne's direction. "We all know you think the communists are behind everything. Christ, it was only last week you suspected the Soviets of being behind the missing biscuits in the tearoom. How do we know—"

"His room was ransacked," Rathdowne interrupted, "his blood type strewn across the room. Upturned furniture and broken pictures and mirrors suggest a significant struggle. The walls were hacked into; his mattress slashed. All his books were sliced open. Whoever took him was searching for something. Our man was targeted. *We* were targeted, gentlemen." He cast a contemptuous expression. "Does that answer your query, Hildebrand-Burke?"

To his credit, Hildebrand-Burke remained silent and issued a reluctant tilt of his head, yielding the point. It didn't garner Rathdowne more respect, but it did quell further questioning on the matter.

A grey-bearded man, the oldest in the room, poked a pipe at Rathdowne. "What if it was a defection made to appear like a kidnapping?"

Rathdowne inhaled deeply. "We're eliminating nothing at this point. All stations in Europe have been placed on high alert. Given what's going on in the US, you can imagine that's put a few knickers in a twist. As far as we know he wasn't in possession of classified materials, but we can't afford to make assumptions. If our man has been kidnapped, the clock is ticking. Recovering him is our top priority. Are we clear?"

Despite the lack of initial respect, the room was now all business. The already tense atmosphere ratcheted up another notch. Backs straightened; cheer melted from arrogant expressions. Pockets of whispering broke out, but now with one intent.

"I say," Hildebrand-Burke waved his cigarette about. "He must have given himself away, surely, said something to a bird who gave him up." He shook his head. "They must have been watching him for months, he'll have created a pattern they picked up on."

"He'd been in the city for a sum total of thirteen hours." Rathdowne's voice was even.

"Christ."

"Exactly. Are we on the same page now?"

There were nods all around. Rathdowne had won the room over. Atticus was impressed, but his thoughts soon spiralled. Alistair Jayne wasn't a name he was familiar with, but that was no surprise. Spies rarely made headlines, and it wasn't like MI6 had ever been eager to educate anyone on its past failures.

The grey-bearded man spoke up again. "If this wasn't a defection and he has actually been kidnapped..."

Rathdowne lowered his chin. "Then we have a mole in MI6." He waited for the alarmed mumblings to subside. "If we do have a leak, I'm here to make damn sure it doesn't bloody well sink us. Make no mistake, this could potentially be the most grave breach in our short history, gentlemen. We have no idea what this could mean. Given the chaotic state of the world right now, who knows? Worst-case scenario, this could be a prelude to a new Soviet push."

Oliver turned to Atticus, alarm in his eyes. Making sure no one else could see, Atticus gave a slight shake of his head. He knew the future, but for everyone else in room, their fear was palpable.

Rathdowne once again called for their attention. "This meeting wasn't organised to find Jayne; every station in Europe is on that. No, we're here to find any evidence that Jayne's assignment was leaked to the other side. If, and let me blatantly clear on this, *if* his mission was compromised, it came from this office." He slammed his palm on the podium to quell the chatter. "Settle down! I said *if*. I know it's a big if. But we must consider it a possibility until proven otherwise. Let's do what we do well, gentlemen. MI6 isn't about finding truth. It's about uncovering lies."

Taking moment to steady himself, Rathdowne went on. "If Jayne was nicked because he was reckless and blew his cover, that is unfortunate. If he was betrayed by his own countrymen who knowingly sent him to his death, well, that is not only a disaster, it puts every person in this room, this building and this country in peril. Make no mistake, until we know what occurred, nobody is above reproach, nobody is can be trusted and above all, nobody rests. Do I make myself clear?"

Atticus's mind reeled. An MI6 mole? Atticus knew moles were a part of the history of this time. In fact, he'd written his Political Science doctoral study on the subject. The term "Five" was first heard by MI6 in the early sixties, when KGB defector Anatoliy Golitsyn named two spies directly. The first, Donald Maclean, was a British diplomat who spied for the Soviet Union during World War II and early on in the Cold War. He'd studied at Cambridge in the early 1930s, where he met the second of the five, Guy Burgess, another diplomat who spied for the Soviets at the same time as Maclean. They both disagreed with the idea of capitalist democracy. A decade prior to this time, both had disappeared in what was known rather uncreatively as the "affair of the missing diplomats", reappearing years later at a press conference in Moscow. Since that odious event, MI6 had been battling its own demons, none more satanic than the spectre of Kim Philby, who had been known as the "probable" third man.

Atticus realised it had only been months since Philby, fearing abduction by MI6, had defected to the Soviet Union under cover of night. The organisation would still be reeling. The scars were still visible in Atticus's time, but they would be red raw to everyone in this room.

The involvement of the remaining two of the infamous "Ring of Five", Blunt and Cairncross, would only be discovered years later, but in this time, both men were already long gone from the halls of MI6. Neither would have the access needed to expose a new agent in the field. If MI6 had a mole, it wasn't one Atticus knew of. That was potentially the most concerning aspect. If there was a mole, had MI6 buried it so deep that Jayne had remained an unknown casualty of the Cold War, or was something else at play?

"Where do we start?" It was the first time Oliver had spoken in the meeting.

"The exact opposite of what you suggest, I'd say,

Preston," Pillar chuckled, to the accompanying mirth of those seated around him.

Someone Atticus couldn't see said, "That's not helping, old chap."

"It's quite alright." Oliver waved a hand. "Pillar knows he's Hildebrand-Burke without the talent. But then again, so is Hildebrand-Burke."

"Alright, you lot." Before the room erupted further, Rathdowne slammed his folder down. "We *do* need to start. That's why you're all here. I want to hear from you. So, let's have it."

"We start with affiliations, obviously." Hildebrand-Burke turned and pointed to a younger man two rows behind. "Bridgeman, start digging into the history of everyone in the Berlin station—university associations, anything to tie them to connections to anyone with a socialist leaning. We go through their... Have I said something wrong?"

The room was quiet. Atticus looked up. The entire meeting room gawped in his direction. Without realising it, he'd been shaking his head, and now Hildebrand-Burke was staring directly at him.

"Do you have something to offer, Mister—?"

"Wolfe, Atticus Wolfe."

Rathdowne called from the front of the room, "Mr Wolfe comes to us highly recommended by Naval Intelligence."

"That's all fine, but we're not here to pick barnacles off our peckers. This is an MI6 issue, not some outsider's—"

"He started here this morning." Oliver tried to come off as authoritarian, which might have worked if his voice hadn't broken.

"I don't care if he's been here for a hundred years."

Hildebrand-Burke's eyes narrowed on Atticus. "You seem to disagree with my idea. I'm curious as to why, Mr Wolfe."

"You seem convinced there must be a socialist affiliation." Atticus spoke carefully. "I respectfully disagree."

"May I enquire why?" With the room's attention, Hildebrand-Burke's arrogance grew. "I say, you're new here, I'll explain it to you. That's just how socialists work. They get them young, impressionable. They bore into their brains like a woodworm."

It took all Atticus's strength not to groan out loud. Hildebrand-Burke seemed so set in his ways, they all did. He was clearly referring to the Cambridge Five—although Atticus wasn't sure they'd earned that particular moniker just yet—who'd been recruited during their early education, when they were suggestible. It was a long-term strategy that, in reality, was far removed from the norm. If this room was any indication, MI6 was suffering from a terminal case of groupthink. The scars from the recent past seemed to be clouding their judgement.

"No, not always, they don't." Atticus shook his head once more, this time with intent. "The vast majority are cultivated by a technique far more nefarious than that. And simple. They find those prone to blackmail, bribery, someone with a particularly interesting fetish or skeleton in their closet to exploit. Do they have a mistress? Did they drunkenly run down someone in the middle of the night? Were they the president of the Milli Vanilli fan club?" Realising what he'd said, Atticus could have kicked himself. Only minutes before, he'd told himself to be more careful. He moved on before anyone could question his nonsensical comment. "The Soviets call it компрометирующий материал. More specifically, they have one word for it: *Kompromat*. In English, compromising material. They'll use any damaging information they can find. It's far easier than cultivating a fellow traveller over years or even decades."

"Yes, of course, we all know that." Hildebrand-Burke shifted uncomfortably in his chair, suggesting he didn't. "But I don't know who the hell you think you are. This is an MI6 problem. You stick to boats and semen and leave the spy stuff to us, alright, boy?"

"That's enough, Hildebrand-Burke." Rathdowne seethed. "You'd better learn some respect. He'll be heading up the investigation."

The entire room was struck dumb, none more than Atticus.

"I will?"

With a slanted smile, Rathdowne bowed his head in agreement. "You will. Who better to find a mole than a man who has no skin in the game?"

"It's the colour of it that's got me worried."

Thankfully Atticus couldn't see who had slung the insult. There were a few sniggers throughout the room, but Atticus also heard grunts of protest and a few "Steady on, there's. He wasn't without support, if it could generously be called such a thing.

"Vincent, watch your tone or you'll be counting penguins in the Antarctic, got me?"

Lucky for Vincent, whoever he was, he didn't respond, so Atticus couldn't pick him out of the crowd.

"Now wait a moment, this department doesn't need outside help," Pillar protested. "We don't need some iron-glove approach from an outsider causing a ruckus. That's all I'm saying."

"Oh, I'm sorry, I thought we were spies here." Atticus leaned back and folded his arms. "You're worried about a ruckus? We're talking about finding a potential traitor. Did I walk into the wrong room? Is this the knitting circle?"

Beside him, Oliver sniggered.

"Steady on, old chap, there's some cheek." Pillar's cheeks grew red.

"Am I wrong?"

"It's the impertinence I resent..."

"Am I wrong?" Atticus's eyes didn't flicker from the polo-club toff.

It was as if all the air had been siphoned from the room. No one moved.

Atticus inhaled slowly, trying to keep emotion from his tenor. "Spy craft isn't about making friends, it's not about playing nice. It is a dirty, bloody business. It's about being better than the other side." There were grunts of agreement in the room. It was good to know he hadn't alienated all of MI6. "Catching a double agent isn't about making friends. It's about preventing more losses like our man Jayne. I'm terribly sorry if it causes you some minor inconvenience, but you can't play nice when hunting traitors, unless you want more deaths on your watch."

It had been a bad habit of Atticus's from school onward. He came out swinging in all aspects of his life. Those who weathered the initial stages of his need to attack things head-on eventually saw his softer side, his genuine and caring side. They were the ones who stayed for the long haul.

Atticus was once again reminded how alone he was in this world. He had no such network of friends here, no allies, no support. He was starting from scratch, and as impressions went, he wasn't rallying many to his side.

"Listen up." Rathdowne raised his voice to silence the

growing chatter. "Everyone in this room will have their nose to the grindstone and their balls to the wall and any other contortion you can think of finding out what the hell is going on after Friday. Might I remind everyone the head of a superpower has been murdered. And just to add a cherry on top, this hasn't been released yet, but Oswald once lived in the Soviet Union." There were grumbles and moans. They all knew the implications that would carry. "Quiet down! So, as you can imagine, the Prime Minister is thinking this might be some kind of prelude to a communist attack on the West. The disappearance of an MI6 field agent hasn't helped his constitution one bit, either. You all have your assignments. This meeting isn't about any of that—at least, we don't think so. Wolfe is in charge of this investigation because if we have a mole the rest of you will be up to your armpits trying to find Jayne and, if you can find the time, prevent World War Three. I'll hear no more about it."

It was a definitive statement that quelled discontent.

For about three seconds.

"Look here, Rathdowne, this just isn't cricket." Hildebrand-Burke took a long drag of his cigarette for dramatic effect. "We minister to our own, here. Your predecessor wouldn't have stood for this. He would have—"

"Let Philby leave in the middle of the night on a Soviet freighter?" Once again, Rathdowne silenced them. He may not have been the most popular man in the room, but he knew how to control it in the face of hostility.

Atticus wouldn't let him fight these men alone. He spoke up. "If Philby wasn't tipped off by a member of this organisation he would currently be enjoying several lifetimes at Her Majesty's pleasure. Instead, they're building statues in his honour the wrong side of the Iron Curtain."

Atticus took a long sweep of the room. "So, you tell me, how has looking after our own worked out for us lately?"

A whistle emanated from the doorway and all heads turned in that direction. A fit man in his fifties with intense blue eyes commanded the room. Atticus knew the face—it was Dick White, the Chief of the Secret Intelligence Service. He was the only man to have held the top job at both MI5 and MI6.

He turned to the front of the room. "If you don't put that man in charge, I bloody will, you hear me, Rathdowne?"

"Loud and clear, sir."

The Chief gave Atticus a nod of appreciation. Rathdowne positively beamed. That settled it. Atticus was on a mole hunt.

SEVEN

Half an hour later the meeting broke up and its members went their separate ways. Only Oliver and Atticus remained. Once again, Atticus was reminded how junior Oliver seemed. He had hardly contributed to the meeting, offering only the occasional suggestion, most of which were lost amongst the chatter only to be repeated several minutes later by someone else and met with rousing support. His station was completely at odds with the first impression he'd given in the hospital room. Atticus had yet to define exactly where Oliver's cog fit into the machine. They walked out of the room towards the elevator.

Oliver stuffed his hands deep into his pockets, his mood melancholy. "You do know you're now a target, yes?"

"A target for what?"

"You're the new blood and suddenly you've been given a high-profile assignment." Oliver's face was downcast. "You sink or swim on this, you understand that, surely?" He scrutinised Atticus's face. "It's all on you now. If there is a mole and he isn't what you said, your career is over before it begins. Everyone in that room wants you to fail, surely you see it?"

"Not Rathdowne."

"Possibly," Oliver shrugged, "but he's been given an out, don't you see? Now that the Chief has given you his blessing, Rathdowne's hands are clean. He has his fall guy, which unfortunately is you, Muggins. I'm afraid you're on your own on this one. You better not fail, is all I'm saying." He patted Atticus on the shoulder. "No pressure."

It seemed office politics weren't confined to the twenty-first century.

Trying his best to appear reassuring, Oliver gave a half-hearted smile. "But the boss said you have all the resources you need. So, that's something."

"You're right, it is." Atticus rubbed his eyes. "I only have a vague idea what that would look like. In my time, sure, but here I don't even know where to begin. I have to figure out what departments do what, what their capabilities are, where I obtain data and intelligence. I'm on the back foot here."

Oliver poked him with an elbow. "If only you had someone who knew how all that worked, hey?"

"If only." Atticus cracked his knuckles. "I have a team in mind, I just need to know how to make it happen."

"Already?" Oliver frowned in confusion. "You already have a team? You only just got here."

Atticus winked. "I work fast."

His colleague bobbed his head in agreement, not quite understanding. "Before we begin, I have one important question." Oliver's expression was grave. "What's a Milli Vanilli?"

~

"YOU'RE NOT ACTUALLY SERIOUS?"

Atticus gave Rathdowne a slanted grin. "I absolutely am, I assure you."

"They're not exactly a First Division attacking midfield, are they?" Rathdowne exhaled heavily. "I'd be hard-pressed to call them bench warmers for the Isthmian League if I'm completely honest." He pursed his lips together. "I'm beginning to wonder if I've made a grave mistake giving you this assignment." He glanced into the nothingness of distance.

"If it's good enough for Dick White..." Atticus knew it was an audacious move to throw that one down, but he wasn't overly concerned.

"You're bloody bold as brass, you are." Rathdowne threw his hands up in defeat. "Fine, but it's on your head." He hesitated a moment. "You're sure about Preston? He's Jewish, you know?" he said, addressing the top of the desk, then he gazed up with a hangdog expression. "I'm not sure if that's a problem."

It took all of Atticus's strength not to react. In his day such blatant discrimination would have resulted in a meeting with Human Resources and instant dismissal. But his new boss seemed so comfortable with such flagrant bigotry he doubted anyone in the building could even spell HR. It seemed he had more to contend with in this time than he thought.

Rathdowne hadn't mentioned the homosexuality which had been implied in the meeting room. Either it was just a rumour, or Rathdowne wasn't aware of it.

"Why on earth would it be a problem?"

"I honestly don't know. I'm not sure how the Jews and the..." Rathdowne pointed at Atticus, "you know, your people, get along."

"I'm not sure. Why don't you ask Sammy Davis Junior?" Atticus was quite pleased he'd made a contemporary observation, even more impressed it was relevant. He was less satisfied with the bigotry. "I'm sure we'll work it out."

"What is it you want to do?"

Atticus shrugged his shoulders. "Rustle feathers and make some people really uncomfortable."

"You seem to have done that already."

"I haven't even started yet."

The fear on Rathdowne's face was priceless. He gave a dry cough, a feeble attempt at diversion. "I'll assign you a place to work. Somewhere out of the way, so you won't be disturbed."

Far away from this office, Atticus thought. A warm prickly feeling came over the back of his neck.

Rathdowne went on. "I don't have to tell you, this investigation must be above reproach. I've put a lot on the line for you, Wolfe." He flexed his hands, holding himself stiff. "You have my full support."

"I'd feel better if you said it to my face."

Rathdowne looked up and Atticus steamed. His whole neck was on fire now.

Stamping down his agitation, Atticus asked, "What was the name of Jayne's mission?"

"Operation Odysseus."

Atticus waited, and when nothing further was forthcoming, he asked, "What was he tasked with?"

Rathdowne cracked his neck. "Until we know if he's actually missing, the Minister's deemed that eyes-only top secret."

"I'm... I'm sorry?" Atticus couldn't hide the shock in his voice. "If I'm tasked with finding a mole, I need to know what the hell he was meant to be doing over there."

"No, you don't."

The two men glared at one another for what felt like an eternity. Without uttering another word, Atticus swivelled and exited. With each step his sense of unease grew. What was most troubling was that he didn't know which thing had him most concerned.

AN HOUR LATER, Atticus's team sat before him, somewhat bewildered. No room had been assigned yet, so the four sat in a circle of chairs in the now-familiar Room 503. Atticus was adamant there would be no power play desk games here. This was a ragtag team, untested and green. It was exactly what he needed.

Oliver sat upright, looking alarmed, as if he'd been summoned to the principal's office. If his back was any straighter Atticus could have used him as a ruler. Maggie Dunbar sat with her arms folded and a wry, if somewhat baffled, smile on her face. She'd tied her hair in a bun, which Atticus took to indicate she meant business. He did note that it showed off her long, slender, flawless neck. Henry Morton, the lift operator, seemed the most confused of all. His bewildered expression was somewhere between a startled rabbit and a prisoner on their last death-row march.

"I guess you're all wondering why I invited you here?"

Maggie snorted. "Because there's been a murder in the manor house?"

"There's no manor house." Atticus raised an eyebrow.

"A murder though?"

Atticus waited a dramatic beat. "Probably."

There was no longer a smile on Maggie's face. She and

Henry exchanged urgent glances. Oliver remained rigidly upright, like head boy awaiting orders. Atticus marvelled at the speed with which the two of them had switched roles.

Henry filled his cheeks and blew out slowly. "Can I ask why we're here?"

"What I want..." Atticus shook his head. "What we're *going* to do is find a traitor."

Maggie's wryness returned. "Okay, I'll play along like a pillock. Where is this traitor?"

"Somewhere in this building."

"Bloody hell." If anything, Henry appeared more petrified.

Atticus quickly gave them a rundown of Alistair Jayne's kidnap in East Berlin. He didn't censor the details. When he was done, they all knew the ramifications.

"Are we one hundred per cent sure there's a mole?"

"No." Atticus inhaled. "This could be an elaborate deception, a mistake by either side, but..."

"You don't think so?" Maggie held his gaze. "You think there's an actual mole?"

Atticus nodded. "It's mostly a hunch right now, but whatever the other side were searching for likely came from this office. The reason he was sent there came from this office. The information he was carrying, this office. Therefore," he paused for effect, "the answers, lady and gentlemen, are in this office."

They all motioned their agreement. Each member of his team was smart, they all had abilities Atticus needed for this to work. Maggie was clever enough to earn a position in Signals, but her gender kept her from being a trusted member of her own department.

Henry's itinerant role made him far more aware of the organisation's inner workings than even he realised. As part of the agreement with Rathdowne, Henry would work part-time with the team but continue his role as lift operator, as apparently the notion of him leaving the MI6 staff to use the lift themselves during peak times was "abhorrent".

Oliver was across the entire spectrum of the organisation, knew how it truly operated, but wasn't trusted enough to be in any particular clique. He, of course, was also the only member of the team who knew Atticus's truth.

Atticus hadn't told them he already had a name for the group: The Outcasts.

There was something else he hadn't mentioned to the newly formed team, something he never could: they were all suspects.

As elevator operator, Henry was privy to snippets of highly confidential intelligence on an hourly basis. Oliver skirted around the periphery of the organisation, ignored, derided and barely recognised—an ideal situation for a double agent, able to breeze in and out at will. Then there was Maggie. What better way to take revenge on an organisation that neither supported nor respected her?

Every one of them could have come across the information on Jayne. Any one of them could be a Soviet Spy. In the background, one of Atticus's first tasks would be to eliminate members of The Outcasts as the mole. From there, he only had the entire organisation to deal with.

"Okay." Atticus cracked his knuckles; a bad habit he'd picked up from an equally bad father. "We need to know everything about Alistair Jayne." He blew out a lengthy lungful of air and scrutinised the room. "We need a whiteboard."

Maggie sniggered. "You mean blackboard, genius?"

"Uh, yeah, that." Atticus realised no matter how hard he

tried, he was always going to trip up on something. He forged on. "We need to know every facet of Jayne's life. Where he lived, who he lived with. Who he worked with, who he met. I want to know if he had a cat, what its name was, how many fleas it had and where those fleas went to school. We interview the landlord, his neighbours, his neighbour's first cousin's former roommate's childhood imaginary friend—everyone. I want to know what he had for breakfast three months ago. I want to know when he goes to the toilet does he scrunch or fold. Does he read? If so, what books are in his bookshelves? We need to scrutinise his bank account details, how he gets paid, everything."

"We all get paid by cheque." Maggie gave him the smallest of head shakes. "We won't have any bank details on file. I doubt we'd have the ability to..."

Damn. This was harder than he thought. "I meant, trace the cheques to an account. If we need MI5's help to shake the information loose, I'm sure Dick White can grease those wheels for us."

Their faces told him they understood what he was after.

"A mole." Henry was in a daze, deep in thought. "What kind of person would actually *do* that? Betray their country?"

"Sociopaths, mainly." Atticus was greeted by blank expressions. He went into explanation mode. "A double agent is usually on their way to becoming a sociopath, if they're not already there yet. They need, whether for duplicitous requirements or due to their own psychological issues, people to like them. How do they *do* it, Henry? It's simple. A sociopath doesn't feel guilt or remorse, it's just not in their make-up. Outwardly they appear friendly and engaging, and they'll make you feel like the most important person in the room, right up until you're not. You'll generally know when that is by the knife in your back. We've all had a boss who is all sweetness and light until they throw you to the wolves, right? Most sociopaths aren't murderers, they're out in the general populous. It's the rare few who take it too far—to likely murderous ends, in our mole's case."

Not wanting to appear like a lecturer, Atticus let that sit with them for a moment. Henry gave him an understanding bob of his head.

To complicate matters even further, Atticus was about to throw something else into the mix. His head swum at the number of plates spinning in the air.

After a few moments, Atticus spoke again. "Maggie, I have your first job, if that's alright?"

"Shoot." Her pencil hovered over a notepad.

"I need you to search for the name Omar Ganim." He spelled it out. "It may be nothing, but it came up in passing during the meeting."

Oliver eyed him curiously, knowing no such name had been mentioned in the meeting. He said nothing.

Atticus was thankful to have a team. When faced with a problem his first instinct was to google it. He had no idea how to get anything done without a computer. How did people even communicate with one another? Twice in the last hour he'd had to stop himself from asking for something to be emailed to him.

"I'd like you to check hospitals, police stations, hotels, anything in the central London area. See if they've had any trace of him in the last seventy-two hours."

"I can check with key rental agencies as well." Maggie's eyes grew wide at the magnitude of the task. "Right." She tucked a pencil behind her ear after making a note. "On it."

"And Henry?"

"Yes, Môn Capitan?"

"First of all, don't call me that." Atticus's eyes twinkled, letting him know the response was good-natured.

"Oh, right. Sorry, boss."

"Atticus is fine," he interjected with a smile. "I need you to go find a quiet place, somewhere without distraction. I want you to think about any conversations you might have overheard about East Berlin, East Germany, Jayne or newly deployed spies."

"But... but I don't eavesdrop."

Everyone in the room snickered.

"Right." Atticus gave him a friendly pat on the arm. "Maybe you took it in subconsciously, yeah? Write down anything at all, no matter how insignificant. Try and recall who was having the discussion. I can show you some breathing techniques to put you into a deeper meditative state which should help."

"Meditat-terwhatery?"

Atticus chuckled. "I'll walk you through it later. It works, I assure you." He turned to the last of the three. "Oliver, I need you to gather all the names and departments who were aware of Jayne's deployment. Not just the principals in the meeting, but the notetakers, secretaries, caretakers taking out the rubbish, anyone. Okay?"

"Got it. You'll have the information ASAP."

"Thanks." He turned to each of them in succession. "Alright team, let's get to it. We meet again at seventeen hundred hours."

Henry and Maggie left with springs in their steps. Oliver remained behind. Atticus was sure he was going to ask about Ganim.

"Rathdowne must have a lot of faith in you to give you

this assignment." There was no malice in Oliver's words, and his tone wasn't one of jealousy.

"He does." Atticus stood. He needed to stretch. "He has a lot of faith I'm going to fail."

Oliver baulked. "What? Why would you say that?"

"He's withholding information, for one. But mainly, the fact that he's assigned the reputation of the entire organisation to a man who walked through the door not five hours ago and who he doesn't really like, let alone know anything about. Doesn't that seem awfully odd to you? He wants us to fail."

Confusion creased every wrinkle on Oliver's face. "Why on earth would he want a mole to stay hidden?"

Atticus placed his hand on Oliver's shoulder. "That, my friend, is exactly what we're going to find out."

CHAPTER
EIGHT

The streets of Covent Garden were surprisingly busy for eight o'clock on a Monday night. Atticus wasn't quite sure what he'd expected, but it certainly wasn't this bustling nightlife, with old and young alike darting in and out of pubs, restaurants and still-open shops beneath bright neon lights. This wasn't the staid, conservative London he'd anticipated. This city bristled with life.

By contrast, his flat was as lifeless as an unused cemetery plot. There were only two TV channels, BBC and ITV. At first Atticus thought his set was faulty, but the afternoon paper's TV guide confirmed his lack of options. It seemed even BBC2 didn't exist yet. His choices were a documentary on cheese or an unfunny sitcom which seemed to primarily consist of exaggerated eye rolls, an annoying laugh track and a clichéd portrayal of homosexuality. If Oliver was indeed gay, it was no wonder he found it difficult to gain any traction or earn respect. Much of this society seemed to view being gay as either an amoral affront or a comedic cliché. Given the time, that shouldn't have been a surprise to Atticus, but it was still disappointing.

Alone in the flat, Atticus was once again reminded that he was exactly that. Alone. He had no friends to call. No one to make plans with. There was no one to make him feel better. The realisation only compounded his helpless sense of isolation.

It didn't help that his mobile phone was almost out of charge. He had a few things on it he could watch, but without a charger his entertainment would be short-lived. He'd love to read the books he'd downloaded, most of which were non-fiction. He really wanted fiction, though; reading a history book about the time he was stuck in was not what he needed right now. He required distraction, not reminders.

Like the first night in the flat with Oliver, Atticus felt the pangs of an existential crisis closing in. He felt trapped, restless, and more than anything, helpless. The walls seemed closer by the second.

Was this to be his life now? During the day he could distract himself with work. Work he knew, work he loved. But night offered no such distraction. Would he fall into this pit of depression every night? Was this his life now? No friends, no respite. A waking nightmare every evening. Dinner, desert and the black dog of depression lurking in the shadows every night?

Atticus shook his head. Keep the dog at bay. Think about something else.

Once he had money in his pocket he'd be sure to make some purchases. He'd invite his old friends Duke Ellington, Miles Davis, Ella Fitzgerald, Raymond Chandler and Dashiell Hammett to come stay. Something familiar, to ground him.

He'd also need some new clothes. The conservative suit Oliver had provided felt heavy, ill-fitting and unfashionable. Maggie said they were paid by cheque. How often was that? Would he need a bank account? Did he need ID for that?

Distraction wasn't working, his skin began to itch. He could have sworn the whole flat had become even smaller again.

Needing more diversion, Atticus extracting the strange keypad that had been found next to him on his arrival in this time. He flipped it over several times. Its once bright light display was dark and lifeless. He had no idea how it worked, nor where to even start finding out. The device seemed to be mocking him. There was no way it could get him home. The thought only depressed him more. He went to the cupboard and placed it in the tiny alcove he'd discovered there. It fit snugly in its new hidey hole.

None of the distractions had worked. The flat seemed half the size it had before. Atticus paced aimlessly, his brain overflowing with thoughts, none of them positive. He had to leave the confines of the shrinking flat and get some air.

As he aimlessly walked the familiar yet alien streets of London, Atticus mulled over his first day at MI6. He'd spent time with Henry walking him through some mindfulness techniques to shake loose any of those "snippets" he'd overheard. It wasn't hypnosis, which had been discredited as a preferred technique, but more of a closed-eye focused meditation, which had garnered results for Atticus's informants in the past. Henry had taken to it far more quickly than Atticus had anticipated. Utilising a subtle cognitive interview technique, he'd gently prodded Henry, leading to the recollection of several overheard conversations and observations which could prove useful. Then again, they might not.

Oliver had produced reams of paper detailing anything he could find on meetings remotely related to Jayne or the Berlin station in recent months. Right now, it was a series of names and times which meant nothing to Atticus. He had a significant learning curve ahead of him if he was going to be able to decipher it into anything meaningful.

Oliver had offered to take Atticus to dinner but he'd politely refused. He had so much to process, he needed time alone to do so. If he was destined to be marooned in this time, he needed to find his own feet and make his own way. Oliver seemed mildly put out, but brightened when Atticus promised to take him up on the offer later in the week.

Most frustrating had been Maggie's dead ends in finding any trace of Ganim. If he was in London, there seemed to be no trace of him in any official register. At least, not yet. Atticus's one flimsy tether to his own time seemed to have eluded him so far; he just hoped the terrorist's luck wouldn't hold. That is, if the man was even in this time. For all Atticus knew he could have stayed in their original era, or he might be dining with a T-rex. Thinking about it bent his brain.

Atticus went for a walk. The shape of the streets were familiar, but none of the stores resembled anything he remembered. Hardware, grocery and appliance stores permeated the streetscape. Where one day they would be replaced with soulless franchises and bulk-buy stores, here, the quaint family-owned shops dominated. He passed stores with names as strange as he felt. There was Levy's, J.W. Pullen, Three Star Drapery Dealers, Betts' butcher's shop, Anderson's Cards and Gifts. At least there was still a Boots chemist. Not everything had changed.

He also noted the lack of CCTV cameras. The London he knew was the world capital of surveillance cameras. But here, not one building sprouted the item so ubiquitous in Atticus's time that Londoners no longer paid them any mind. At least there were still a multitude of pubs to choose from. As enticing as the thought was, Atticus didn't stop for a pint. He was too full of restless energy; he needed to walk it off if he was going to have any chance at sleep. That, and he didn't have any money yet. He marched on.

Mind swirling, he crossed the Thames. Halfway across the bridge he realised where he was. Vauxhall Bridge. It was a crossing he'd made a thousand times, sometimes at a leisurely stroll, more often a fast-paced scramble. There was nothing for him at the far end of the bridge now. The south embankment was a construction site. An ugly rectangular office building was being erected, mounds of dirt and building rubble strewn everywhere. This was not the place Atticus recalled at all. The future site of the imposing SIS headquarters was nothing but another reminder he didn't belong here. He was an intruder, an anathema to this era. Atticus stuffed his hands in his pockets and kept moving, averting his eyes from the place that was so familiar yet wouldn't exist for another thirty years.

Trudging through the streets he noted an overabundance of cigarette billboards, not a health warning to be seen. He also noted the lack of high rises in this part of the city. One pervasive aspect Atticus wasn't expecting was the abundance of dirt. Most surfaces seemed to have a thin film of grime. Piles of bricks and broken wooden crates frequently interrupted his ambling route. Any flashes of colour and life were seemingly doomed to be dragged back down into the grime once more. There was a general feeling of decay, rather than the thriving metropolis he recalled.

Distracted by a red Mini driving up the road, Atticus's mind churned through images of the city he thought he knew. Several seconds after the car passed, his head whipped around. It was a Mini, but not a 1960s Mini. It was a modern, twenty-first century version, twice the size of its older counterpart. As the modern taillights disappeared around the corner, Atticus broke into pursuit. Arms and legs pumping, he skidded around the corner.

The street was bereft of moving vehicles. Not a Mini in sight, old or new. *Did I just imagine that?* Atticus folded over and put his hands on his knees and wheezed. Was he going insane?

"You alright, mate?" A young man with slicked-back hair and a woman on his arm looked on, concerned.

Atticus waved them off, unable to speak. He racked his brain, trying to decide if he'd truly seen the car or had imagined it in some hallucinogenic spectre that his unfocused mind had conjured. The realness of it made it difficult to dismiss.

He resumed his course, trudged on, doing his best to dismiss the illogical apparition as merely that. But as hard as he tried, the memory of it was still there, like a splinter in his mind.

Bringing his mind back to the present, Atticus wondered if it was safe to walk these particular streets. What here were slums generated ridiculous prices for gentrified homes in his time.

After he'd been walking aimlessly for about an hour, Atticus realised he'd unknowingly walked to the one place he'd actively wanted to avoid. He stopped dead at Stansfield Road, not wanting to take another step further.

Whatever he did, he needed to avoid Brixton.

It was the place of his birth, the area that held such fond memories of his youth. Yet he knew he couldn't set foot there. Unlike the rest of London, with its melange of memories and the unexpected, Brixton held something else entirely: his past. And that was certainly something he had to avoid at all costs.

Growing up, Atticus remembered becoming aware of his family's reputation. He distinctly recalled the moment, he couldn't have been older than seven or eight, when he realised other kids weren't ushered to the front of store queues like he was. Other kids his age weren't shown favouritism by local teachers. Atticus was the only kid he knew who never had to pay for his bus ticket. He confronted his grandmother with the observation and soon learned the truth. Like his father before him, Atticus was the son of a gangster. And not just any old gangster.

His naivety shattered, he learned his own history. His father took up the mantle from his father, the notorious "Sledgehammer Joe", who even the Kray Brothers referred to as "fucken' mental, mate". His grandfather Joe was known as "The King of Brixton". He gave back to the community who venerated him as the black Robin Hood. Even after his death, Atticus's grandfather was referred to in hushed tones, either out of reverence or fear.

Atticus's father, "The Prince", was just as feared, but nowhere near as revered. More formidable but also more unpredictable than his father, Thomas Wolfe was also not as altruistic as his predecessor. The crime lord was an oppressive force in Brixton when Atticus was young. He saw it in people's eyes—but only their eyes, for no one would dare speak it out loud, especially not to the son who was expected to take his family's formidable mantle.

Atticus's mother, Angela, was a pacifist with a filthy temper. She always seemed ashamed of her son, a reminder of her dalliance with the devil. She'd left in the middle of the night when Atticus was nine, never to return. He received a letter on his fifteenth birthday telling him his mother had died in a car accident in Tunisia.

For most of his life, Atticus had been raised by his redoubtable but loving grandmother, Eliza. With no mother and his male role models in and out of jail, she was the rock who moulded him to be the man he would become.

Eliza Wolfe, the most important person in Atticus's life, was the reason he had to stay out of Brixton. She would be a young woman now, married to the King of Brixton, a force of nature herself. There were good reasons to avoid the place of his birth. Not for the painful personal memories but because Atticus knew if he saw his late grandmother in the flesh, he'd find it hard not to embrace her and cling to the only evidence of his former life. That was something he couldn't afford to do. How could he explain his presence here to the most important person in his life? He couldn't even explain it to himself.

Atticus turned and walked back the way he'd come, towards his flat with its two channels and no music. The ghosts of his past would have to wait for another day.

CHAPTER
NINE

Atticus sat alone in The Outsiders' office, reading through the endless piles of meeting notes Oliver had gathered. Although calling it an office was somewhat generous. It was more like a glorified broom closet.

He checked his smart watch - well, without wi-fi or a mobile network it was basically just a watch. He'd had to change the settings so the screen remained a watch face. He fought the urge to continually check for emails or messages. There wouldn't be any for another fifty years.

Oliver and Henry were two floors below, literally knee-deep in paperwork. They were searching for more references to Alistair Jayne, his assignments, as well as any and all connections to the East Berlin mission. They'd taken his directive from yesterday to heart and were scrutinising every facet of the spy's life. If there was a missing school report from his grade three physical education class, they'd find it. They'd leapt at the task with admirable gusto; Atticus was impressed with their shared enthusiasm.

Unfortunately, none of what they'd found so far was relevant to Operation Odysseus.

Alone in the office, Atticus rubbed his eyes. Another night of restless sleep. He'd love a cup of coffee, but he'd yet to find anything remotely worthy of the title. He needed to get out of the office. He picked up his little spiral notepad and opened it to the appropriate page. About to stand, Maggie bounded in, carrying a piece of paper, her face beaming.

"You always seem so pleased with yourself."

She fluttered her eyes. "Look, when you're this fabulous it's hard to be anything else."

"Ha, okay, I'll bite, what've you got?"

Dancing over, she elaborately placed the piece of paper before him and raised an eyebrow.

"And this is?"

"A piece of paper." She comically placed her outstretched palms beside her face in mock-shock, then her expression turned serious. "One of my mates downstairs decrypted a message from Teufelsberg." She paused, apparently revelling in the dramatic tension. "It uses the words 'entführen' and 'MI6'."

"Entführen. Kidnapped?"

She nodded. "The rest of the message was undecipherable, but it is kind of critical, right?"

Atticus scratched his chin. They potentially had their link. An East German mentioning kidnapping and MI6 together. It was no coincidence. There *was* a mole.

Atticus turned the paper over several times. "What happened to this once it came in?"

"That's the thing." Maggie sat on the corner of the desk. "The indigo memo package went upstairs, marked urgent."

Atticus waited for the rest of the story. Apparently, that was it. He shrugged his shoulders, as if to say, *and?*

"This all occurred yesterday. The secure memo envelope was sent back to be destroyed, marked complete."

"Complete?" Atticus shook his head. "And it didn't get to the team actually searching for a mole."

"Hence why we're having this conversation. Seem strange to you?"

Atticus was used to the ruthless efficiency of his MI6, but he highly doubted that even in this time something so crucial could have been accidentally missed. This wasn't an oversight; this was deliberate sabotage.

"It really does." Atticus was no longer tired. "Can your friend find out who had access to the memo circulation?"

"She's already on it. I've asked her to do it in secrecy."

"You're a natural agent."

This required further investigation. Were The Outsiders being hobbled before they'd even started? Why did it seem like a deliberate act of sabotage? Once again, Atticus was reminded there was far more going on than he was aware of. It only strengthened his resolve. If they thought leaving him out of the loop on a memo would slow him down, they didn't know Atticus Wolfe.

He tapped the page with a knuckle and nodded his thanks. "Better get your coat."

Maggie tilted her head in confusion.

"Get your coat, time for some field work."

She grimaced. "Now you're making fun of me."

"No, I'm actually not." He lifted the spiral pad. "I have Jayne's address here, I was going to check it out. You up for an adventure?"

She practically jumped up and down on the spot. "Yes, I am!"

"By adventure," he tried to sound all business, "I mean entering someone's flat, poking around and coming back to work. Not what one would call particularly exciting."

"That's the most exciting this job has ever gotten!"

Atticus grinned. "It's a flat in Soho, not a parachute drop into the middle of the Kremlin."

Waving a finger, Maggie squinted. "Don't short-change this. The closest I've ever come to field work is the time I took three letters to the GPO four years ago. This is big for me."

"Guess what, Maggie Dunbar? You're a field agent now."

She did a little shimmy as she reached for her coat, and Atticus was sure he heard her give an excited squeal.

He was about to make a crack about how Jayne could afford to live in Soho, then realised he was living in Covent Garden. In his time, both areas were pretty much exclusively reserved for the rich. Atticus didn't know if Soho was as prohibitively expensive in 1963, but it did seem an odd choice for a spy's address. He reached for his coat.

"I have to make one stop first before we head out, if that's okay?"

She shrugged. "You're the boss."

Downstairs on the ground floor, Atticus asked Maggie to wait outside, explaining that he had something to ask Mrs Abernathy. Behind her eyes he could see there was a war going on. Maggie seemed inquisitive as to why he had to speak to Mrs Abernathy, but chose to say nothing. He expected she was deeply interested, but feared jinxing her invite.

Atticus approached the pleasant, but apparently deadly, receptionist, who sat rigidly behind her desk.

"I hear, as well as being the most marvellous receptionist, and a snappy dresser, you're also the resident armourer."

Recent experiences had reinforced Atticus's belief that he needed to be armed even when he least expected to need it. The confrontation with Omar Ganim in the street was the first example that came to mind. Atticus wasn't willing to take any chances.

Mrs Abernathy shook her head and issued a wry smile. "My, aren't you a smooth one." She hefted an eyebrow. "But also, you're correct about all those things."

"Excellent. I need a gun."

Her pleasant demeanour soured. "What, may I ask, for?"

"I'm not sure, entirely. Perhaps shoot a thing, if it comes to that. I hear guns are suitable for such activities."

"What activities might they be?"

"Indeterminate. Could be a number of troubles. Maybe nothing."

"That's rather vague."

"We live in a vague world."

"You have no target in mind?"

"No. But I can't say the same for the other side."

"So, there's no direct threat to your person?"

"No, not directly, but we live in dangerous times."

"So, you're not aiming to do anyone in particular harm?"

"I wasn't planning to. Do *you* have anyone in mind? If I may say so, for an armourer you seem rather reluctant to issue a firearm."

"Just performing my responsibilities as designated. It is my sworn duty to protect the citizenry of the British Empire, from the street beggar to the Prime Minister."

"I wasn't planning on murdering any beggars."

"What about the Prime Minister?"

"Why on Earth would I assassinate the leader of our nation?"

"There's a lot of it going about."

"So I hear."

The two plastered on pleasant expressions and eyeballed one another across the desk. Somewhat reluctantly, Mrs Abernathy opened a drawer and pulled out a Browning Hi-Power and two 9mm Parabellum cartridges and placed them on the centre of the desk.

The choice of weapon was quaint. The Browning was reliable as hell but had a tendency to "bite" the web of the shooter's hand, between the thumb and forefinger. Atticus had fired one on the range years ago, more for the novelty than anything else.

He went to pick up the pistol, but Mrs Abernathy slapped his hand with a clipboard.

"Sign here, please." Her demeanour was devoid of any of her previous amusement.

"Certainly." Atticus signed. "I shall return it in two shakes of a lamb's tail."

Her narrowed eyes didn't leave Atticus until he was through the front door. Despite her gruffness, he quite liked Mrs Abernathy's cold efficiency. He had little doubt she was capable of living up to her deadly reputation.

Outside, the wind was biting. Atticus folded the overcoat Oliver had given him around his torso. The oversized coat didn't fit particularly well, and it was coarse and heavy. It felt more like a horse blanket than a stylish overcoat. He really hoped he would get paid soon.

Maggie greeted him beaming. She positively danced down the street, she was so excited. She was less pleased when she eyed his coat, however. Thankfully, she kept her opinion to herself, her expression as dispassionate as an Egyptian sphynx.

As they entered St. James's Park tube station Atticus felt suddenly ill at ease. He'd walked home the night before and to work that morning. The first time on the underground, Oliver had handed him the ticket and he'd been too wrapped up in the novelty of the experience to pay much attention to the practicalities of it all. How did he pay for tickets? Was there an inspector like there was on a bus? He couldn't afford to have Maggie see him floundering over what to do. He'd done that enough already. But there was no way he could convincingly talk her into walking to Soho. He'd have to bluff his way through and hope for the best.

Nearing the platform, he instinctively wanted to pull out his Oyster card and tap on. An ingrained force of habit. For a fleeting second, he wondered if he lived for another forty years if he could use the remainder of his balance. The meandering thought was soon dismissed by a far more pressing matter.

A uniformed transit officer approached with a pleasant demeanour, all humorous eyes and rosy cheeks. He had thick grey muttonchop sideburns. "Ticket, love?"

In Atticus's time, anyone calling someone "love" would likely soon be at the receiving end of a tirade, but Maggie returned his humorous manner, opened her purse and flashed a grey cardboard ticket. The man gave her a polite grin and turned to Atticus, face expectant.

Fighting the urge to tug at his collar, he sighed. "I, uh, need to buy a ticket."

"Right you are, sir." The man fiddled with the silver mechanism strapped to his belt. "Where to, then?"

"Oxford Circus. Return, I guess."

It was then Atticus realised the situation was graver

than he first thought. Oliver hadn't given him his own money. All he had was a wallet full of plastic banknotes and microchipped credit cards; not exactly helpful in 1963.

"I, ah, left my money in my old wallet."

Tilting her head to the side, Maggie gave him a playful shake of her head, as if saying, *you're useless*. From her purse, she stuffed a handful of coins in his palm.

Atticus gaped at the unfamiliar coins, then at the transit officer, then at Maggie and then back to the coins again.

The bridge of Maggie's nose crinkled in mixture of amusement and confusion. "Just give him three and six for a weekly. That'll get you through. Fix me up later."

Atticus contemplated her blankly. Sweat flowed from everywhere. Why did being around Maggie make him far more nervous than anyone else? Trying to get his head back in the game, he attempted to focus, and racked his brain on how old money worked. He recalled something about the pre-decimal pound being divided into 20 shillings and each shilling into 12 pence, making 240 pence to the pound. Or was it the other way around? *How the hell was anyone meant to make sense of that?*

As the uncomfortable pause was meandering into outright awkwardness, Maggie noted his hesitation. "You right there?"

Atticus threw her his best charming smile and held the coins aloft. "It's, uh, I haven't used the Tube in a while."

She crinkled her face as if he'd just said, *I forgot how to walk.* Maggie rolled her eyes, took a few coins from his collection and handed them to the blue-coated officer. The two exchanged pitying expressions as the older man handed Atticus the cardboard ticket.

"There you are, squire. Enjoy the journey."

Atticus's mouth was dry. He thanked the transit officer

with a nod and strode as quickly as he could to the platform. At least he knew which line to take to get to Soho. Or at least, he thought he did. For all he knew he could end up in Thamesmead.

Thankfully, travelling on the Tube was the same as he'd always experienced. Hardly anyone spoke. He and Maggie stood together in the swaying carriage not talking. Instead of heads buried in phones, commuters buried their heads in newspapers and paperback novels. A few stared blankly at nothing at all, but all were lost in their own little self-contained bubbles. Nothing much had changed there.

The two exited the station and walked side by side. They ambled down the recognisable streets of Soho—at least, the layout of streets was recognisable. On the corner was where his favourite sushi joint was. Or would be. Atticus was having trouble keeping track of his tenses. Further down was where he bought his moisturiser. He once went on an unsuccessful blind date where there was now a family-owned hardware store. Atticus couldn't remember if in his era there was a single hardware store in the greater London area that wasn't a chain store.

They strolled quietly for a few minutes. Maggie twitched and placed her hands in her pockets, then out, then in again. It was as if someone had asked her how to walk and she was self-consciously trying not to appear like she wasn't overthinking it.

Atticus smirked. "Stop fidgeting." He pointed to her hands. "A field agent makes as few movements as possible. You're like a junkie with Parkinson's."

"Easy for you to say, Mr Cool-as-a-Cucumber." She blew a stray hair which fell across her face. "Take my mind off it then." Maggie went to pull her hands out of her pockets, but stopped. "Is there a Mrs Wolfe?"

"No, no Mrs Wolfe."

"Girlfriend?'

"No." Atticus wasn't sure why, but the question stung. He'd recently gone out with a lovely young advertising executive who he'd hoped to see again, but it would be a good thirty years before she'd be born.

If this was his time, the next question would have been if Maggie had a boyfriend or husband. But he was all too aware that this wasn't his time. "I guess my work makes it difficult. I have a lot of friends to hang out with when I'm in town, they look after me."

Atticus was overcome with pangs of homesickness. Memories flooded in. Nights out in Soho with friends at the hip new Tibetan restaurant where you just turned up because they didn't accept bookings and you drank over-priced cocktails in the packed waiting area while praying for the next available table. Good times he wouldn't have again. Friends he'd never see again. A life he'd never get back.

With a growing sense of unease, he realised how pitiful the life he currently led in this timeline was. He currently had no friends to speak of. The ones he remembered hadn't even been born yet. In this time, at best he had work colleagues, but he'd only known those for a couple of days. He admired the camaraderie Maggie and Oliver shared, but he'd yet to attain it himself. His association with Oliver was one of necessity rather than genuine friendship. Once again, Atticus was reminded how companionless he was. The memory of his little sojourn to Brixton the night before rammed the point down his throat all too well.

Strolling around the familiar/unfamiliar Soho, Atticus wondered if you could be homesick when you were actually home, walking the exact same streets you so desperately longed for.

"You seem a million miles away there. You alright?"

Atticus turned to Maggie. Her forehead was crinkled in concern. He gave her a reassuring smile. At least she'd stopped fidgeting.

"What about you?" He scanned her hand. "No ring, so not married. Boyfriend? Let me guess, you're dating the prettiest Mod boy."

Scowling, Maggie shook her head. "Oh, god no. No woman in her right mind dates a Mod boy."

"Why not?"

"Well, they dress beautifully, of course, loads better than the birds. But they love their stuff, you know, purple hearts, French blues, black bombers," she jutted out her elbow, "you know. They're way too hopped up for any respectable dolly girl."

Atticus thought she most probably meant amphetamines, speed.

"Most care more about their clothes and outdoing their mates than spending quality time with birds. Plus, on the stuff they don't have the, uh, drive, and their thing don't work." She turned suddenly coy but moved on quickly. "Nah, Mod boys are good friends, but useless for anything else."

He didn't have anything to add. As they walked on quietly, Atticus vigilantly scanned the streets. Suddenly, a figure out the corner of his eye caught his attention. He turned his head to see Omar Ganim standing on the other side of the street. No fanfare, no dramatic sting. The terrorist simply stood there, leaning against a brick wall, gazing blankly in Atticus's direction. He raised a hand to wave as a double decker bus sped by. When the bus had passed, the wall he'd been leaning against was blank, no sign of Ganim. Atticus stepped forward to give chase, but there was nothing to pursue. There was no door or way he could have disappeared from view. There was only one possible explanation.

Atticus stopped walking and stood rigidly still. He was definitely going insane.

He was there, I know he was there. Atticus did his best to show no outward sign of panic, though he surely failed. The vision had been fleeting but seemed so real. Combined with the phantom Mini from the night before, Atticus wondered if he might actually be losing his mind. Something else to add to the list.

Concern seeping from every pore, Maggie touched his sleeve. "Are you alright?"

Not sure he could accurately answer, Atticus motioned that they should keep walking. Forehead wrinkled with worry, Maggie did just that, albeit reluctantly. As they went, Atticus couldn't help looking back at where the realistic apparition had appeared. His chest tightened. *What is going on?*

He swallowed hard, concentrating on the task at hand. He looked towards the next corner, doing his best to hide how rattled he truly was. "We're here."

They turned off Brewer Street onto Golden Square. Jayne's flat was in sight. Third floor, overlooking Golden Square park. Not bad. Not bad at all. If Jayne didn't come from old money, Atticus was becoming increasingly suspicious of the missing spy.

With something to focus on rather than a phantom criminal, Atticus's mood improved. The closer he came to the building, the more Atticus felt back on familiar ground. More than that, it felt like home. For the first time in days, Atticus felt like he was finally back at work. *His* work.

Feeling warm from the recognisable rush of adrenaline, he took off his coat, scanning the streets for surveillance vans or anyone taking a more than casual glimpse in their direction. The street seemed clear, but his years of experience told him one could never be certain.

Looking him up and down, Maggie shook her head. "I'm pretty sure my grandad has that exact same suit."

Atticus glanced down at his ill-fitting attire. She was right. Even an off-the-rack suit would be better than what he was wearing, especially compared to his normal tailored ensembles. Oliver had warned him repeatedly not to wear the suit he arrived in as he deemed it too "futuristic".

"At the Admiralty I wore naval uniforms, so I'm a bit out of the loop, unfortunately. When I get a second, I'll go shopping." As lies went, it was pretty convincing. "Until then," he did a little twirl, "I guess I'm the ambassador for grandpa fashion."

She issued him a curious look, as if she wasn't quite sure what to make of him. Atticus put his game face on. It was time to go to work.

Carefully entering the airy carpeted foyer, Atticus eyed every door with suspicion. The paintwork was blemish free and the mailboxes weren't worn from years of use. The whole scene gave a high-end impression. They slowly made their way to the third-floor landing.

From the rear of his unfashionable suit Atticus extracted the Browning. Maggie's eyes went wide at the sight. Her mouth opened in a gasp, but to her credit she made no sound.

In a hushed tone, he asked, "Do you know how to use this?"

"It's not usual training for the secretary pool, I'm afraid." Her voice was frail, unsure.

Atticus flicked the safety off and handed it to her. "Pretty straightforward, just point and shoot. Unless you actually want to kill someone, keep your finger out of the guard and rest it like this." He gently moved her delicate finger to the side of the pistol. "Try not to shoot anything unless I tell you to, alright?"

Pale at the thought, Maggie gulped. "Alright." Even as a whisper, her voice broke.

Leaning down, Atticus inspected the door's lock. He extracted a small leather pouch from his jacket pocket and selected his favourite two silver implements. The lock picks were MI6-issued, like the Browning, but these were from his own time. Atticus never went anywhere without his trusty lockpicking kit. Thankfully it had been in his pocket when he'd been transported back in time. He was pleased to discover a Yale lock was still a Yale lock.

As he leaned in and slid in the Bogota rake, Atticus half turned to Maggie. He spoke in a low whisper. "See, some folks think it's all about the raking action. But it's the tension wrench that's the unsung hero of lockpicking. Too much tension and the pins will not be able to set correctly; too little, same result."

Maggie skewed her soft lips to the side of her mouth. "Are you trying to impress me, Mr Wolfe?"

"Why would I be doing that?"

"I'm asking myself the same thing, actually."

Atticus hadn't been. At least, he didn't think so.

The lock snapped into place and the door slid open silently. Seemingly against her better judgement, Maggie gave an amused smirk. Pocketing his tools, he tenderly took back the gun from her with a wink. Jerking his head towards the flat, he softly pointed the gun inside, indicating that he'd go first. In reply Maggie clenched her fists. Their communication was silent but assured.

Atticus Wolfe stepped into the flat, gun skyward, eyes scanning for threats. The hallway was clear, silent. A couple of framed Matisse prints gave the entrance a sophisticated air. Stepping quietly on the sides of his feet, he entered the lounge room. It was light-filled, but small. The furniture was more modern than his Covent Garden flat. Minimal clutter. It seemed Alistair Jayne kept an orderly flat. No one was at home.

"Seems Jayne is a loner."

Maggie closed the front door silently. She hefted her top lip into a playful sneer. "What, because he keeps a tidy room?"

"More than that. I can tell a lot about the man by simply standing here. There's minimal seating—he doesn't expect extra guests. Same goes for lack of cushions; it's not about making people feel welcome. The uncluttered bookshelf, lack of personal effects. The organised setting signifies a Type A personality who values the way things appear over the way they function."

A wry smile crossed Maggie's red lips. "It could be that an MI6 field agent doesn't care about home comforts. Thought of that, Mr Everything-has-a-meaning?"

"Believe me, he cares. When all is said and done this would be his sanctuary. Travelling the world, risking your life, you want something familiar and comforting when you come home. You want something more personal than endless hotel rooms."

"And what would you know, sailor boy?"

Realising he had no comeback, Atticus remained mute.

With a nudge, Maggie rolled her eyes. "You like being the smartest guy in the room, don't you?"

About to retort, Atticus stopped.

There was a noise, a faint *creak* of a floorboard. It wasn't from either of them. They weren't alone in the flat.

Motioning for Maggie to remain where she stood, he edged slowly towards the large arch to the left of the lounge, to what Atticus could only assume was the kitchen. Rounding the corner, Atticus aimed his pistol at the new target.

Standing at the centre of the kitchen was a solidly built man in his forties. He had salt and pepper hair and a tartan suit. He stood over a collection of papers which had been poured onto the kitchen table. In his hand was a soft brown leather chequebook that he seemed particularly interested in.

He turned as Atticus entered and issued a friendly wave. "Oh, hello."

"May I ask you who you are?" Atticus didn't lower his weapon.

"Jenkins. The landlord." His accent was all London. No Russian twang.

In his peripheral vision, Atticus saw Maggie's shoulders sag in apparent relief. Atticus wished there was a way he could convey to her not to. In fact, she should be doing the exact opposite.

"Is that right?" Atticus didn't move. "Awful lot of papers there."

"I was just thinkin' the same thing."

"Is it usual for landlords to go through their tenants' chequebooks?"

"'onestly can't speak for other landlords, mate."

Atticus had to concede the point. "Owned the place

long?"

"Sp'ose going on five years or so, I reckon."

"Own many properties?"

"Oh, enough to keep me busy, not enough to make me rich."

"May I ask you something, Jenkins?"

"Sure, guv. It's a free country, innit?"

"You don't seem particularly perturbed that a man entered your flat armed with a gun. In fact, you didn't feel the need to even mention it."

"I thought that was more your concern."

Atticus did his best not to smile at the response. *This guy is good.*

It was the shoulders. The move was tiny, almost imperceptible, but it was there. The right shoulder tilted slightly forward. His right hand issued the tiniest of twitches. His gun hand. Probably-not-Jenkins was readying himself for a crouch or to reach for his weapon, which was creating a slight bulge under the left side of his jacket.

"Well," Jenkins scratched the back of his neck with a sigh, "I guess we should be gettin' on with it then?"

"I guess we should at that." Without turning, Atticus leaned his head back and spoke towards the lounge. "Maggie, best you leave now."

"W-why?"

Jenkins wiped his nose with the back of his hand. "He means to say there's gonna be a gunfight, love."

"A wha—"

In a lightning-fast move, Jenkins hefted his knee to kick up the table, flinging it into the air, and with it the pile of papers. In the same instant, he reached under his jacket and extracted a pistol.

Atticus and Jenkins fired at the same time.

CHAPTER
TEN

The first shot Atticus fired took a chunk out of the table, which was still in mid-air. Luckily, Probably-not-Jenkins' first bullet also went wide.

Both men dove for their lives: Atticus backwards and to the left into the lounge; Not-Jenkins out of the direct firing line and behind the solid brick archway. Maggie fell to the floor, covering her head. Deadly silence enveloped the flat for a few seconds, during which Atticus heard nothing but his own heavy breathing.

Atticus motioned for Maggie to get behind the couch, the only cover nearby. She didn't need to asked twice. Atticus hung by the front entrance, ensuring he'd have ample warning if Not-Jenkins made a move. The only problem was, the opposite was equally true.

From the kitchen came a calm voice. "I usually know the names of those I'm goin' to 'ave the pleasure of killing. You're a geezer I don't know from Adam, mate."

Jesus, this guy is stone cold.

"I could say the exact same back to you, friend."

"That right?"

"Seems so. You're the one outnumbered and cornered here. I'm willing to hear your terms of surrender."

"What if I don't wanna give you none?"

"Then I'll accept your last confession." Atticus pulled back the hammer of his Browning. "Anything you wish to confess before the end, my child?"

Open-mouthed, Maggie shook her head at Atticus. The expression on her face practically screamed, *who the hell are you?*

Keeping her head low behind the cover of the couch, Maggie seemed to be weighing up the situation. Apparently coming to a conclusion, she leaned over and loudly whispered, "We charge him."

Atticus raised his palms questioningly. "With what?"

"What?"

"What... what?" Atticus shrugged. "We charge him with what?"

"No, charge him." Maggie made a lunging move with her hands. "You know."

With a shake of his head, Atticus frowned. "That's a terrible idea."

From behind the brick archway, Not-Jenkins raised his voice. "If anyone cares, I think it's a terrible idea, too."

"Nobody asked you."

"Right you are. Carry on."

Ignoring Not-Jenkins, Maggie addressed Atticus. "Faute de mieux. It means—"

In spite of the situation Atticus couldn't keep the humour out of his voice. "I know what it means."

"I don't." Not-Jenkins' self-assured tone hadn't diminished. "Anyone gonna enlighten me?"

Maggie's French phrase meant *for want of anything*

better. But Atticus was sure there was more to be done before mounting an ill-fated full-frontal assault.

"Now I'm intrigued as to what agency you belong to." Atticus wasn't sure Not-Jenkins was as authentic an East Londoner as he seemed. In the twenty-first century, regional accents were slowly disappearing with a more transient population and the all-encompassing prevalence of TV and movies. Most polished the rougher edges of their pronunciation. This guy sounded pure Cockney, but Atticus wasn't completely convinced. "Why were you rifling through a missing man's effects?"

"Oh, is this where I confess everythin' and give away my dastardly scheme an' all?"

"It would make everything a lot easier if you did."

Not-Jenkins chuckled. "I'll answer if ya tell me why *you're* 'ere."

"I'll show you mine if you show me yours?"

The man in the kitchen tutted. "That's no way ta speak in fron' of a lady, guv."

"I'm no lady." Maggie's voice carried more confidence than her face portrayed.

Atticus had to admire her bravado. Not everyone could be so composed under such circumstances, especially when she had started her day expecting paperwork, not a shootout. Perhaps she had what it took to be a field agent after all.

Crouched low, Maggie narrowed her eyes towards the white baseboard. Head tilted, she glared at Atticus, then back at the baseboard, then back to Atticus. The expression on her face cried, *this is important*. It may well have been, but Atticus had more urgent matters to attend to.

"Whatever, mate." Not-Jenkins' tone was casual. Atticus knew he was stalling. He just didn't know what for.

"Seems one of is goin' to have to make the first move, yeah?"

"Seems that way."

The gunshots echoed through the tiny flat, delivering a deafening cacophony that assaulted their eardrums. Atticus pushed himself against the wall, gun raised and ready. Maggie buried herself lower, as if trying to burrow through the floorboards.

Anticipating a hail of bullets that never came, Atticus raised his head. No shots hit anything in the lounge. Furniture and human alike remained unscathed.

From the other side of the flat came the sound of smashed glass and rustling. Stifled grunts told Atticus all he needed to know. He dove forward, rolling under the archway, gun scanning the kitchen.

It was empty.

The broken glass of the small kitchen window told the tale. Atticus rushed to the shattered frame. Blood trickled down a shard still embedded in the bottom. Beyond the fragmented window, the building's awning was two floors below. Not-Jenkins had fired on the window and hurled himself through, leaping to the tin roof of the awning.

Atticus made it to the window in time to see his quarry roll off the canopy onto the ground. Someone on the street shrieked. Atticus turned and sped into the lounge.

Maggie lurched from behind the couch on all fours, pale as a Nazi curling team. Stifling a belch, she waved a finger. "I'm going to throw up."

"We don't have time." Atticus was already at the front door. "He's on foot and injured. We need to question him. Come on."

Without waiting for a response, he flung the front door open and bounded down the stairs, five at a time. To his surprise, he heard clomping footsteps vaulting behind him. His co-worker was a tough unit. Her fortitude only garnered more respect.

In seconds he reached the front door and threw it open. The street seemed positively average. No Not-Jenkins in sight. Running in any direction could just as equally lead them further away from or closer to their prey.

Maggie charged through the front entrance, panting. Like Atticus, she scanned the street, which appeared normal.

"Is that parachute drop into the Kremlin still an option?"

Atticus gave her an amused shake of his head. She was fine. He closed his eyes, listening to the soundscape of London's streets.

"Wha—"

Atticus held up a finger and Maggie stopped, allowing him to concentrate on the sounds, listening for anything that could point them towards their prey.

There.

Far in the distance, to the right, someone squealed in alarm. It was all Atticus needed. He broke into a run. Arms and legs working in unison like steam pistons, he sprinted towards the sound. Along the way he noticed small, shiny pools of red liquid. The trail of blood fired him to sprint faster.

Atticus instinctively reached into his pocket for his phone. His hand only got halfway before he chastised himself for the fruitless habitual gesture. His phone wasn't there, not that it would have served any purpose if it was. This was all on him. He corrected himself; *almost* all on him.

Behind him, Maggie ran. For someone unfamiliar with recreational running she was surprisingly fast. Streaking across Beak Street, he dodged a Vespa and halted on the far side of the road. There was no sign of Not-Jenkins. No blood, no sounds.

Taking a solitary intake of air to steady his mind, Atticus went with his gut. The crowds were thicker at the end of Carnaby Street. If Atticus wanted to get away, he'd pick the place with the largest crowd to avoid detection. He ran into Carnaby Street, ignoring the bothered shouts of locals as he sprinted down the centre of the narrow road.

Store names flashed by: *Lady Jane. Cranks. The John Stephen Trouser Bar. Mod Male.* Atticus did his best to ignore the brightly painted edifices overflowing with equally vibrant clothing. The crowded street was far more outlandish than any he'd seen in this era; the stylishly dressed Londoners gawped at Atticus sprinting down the centre of their fashionable street.

He assumed his target wouldn't want to hide out in one of the shops. Again, it was wholly reflex on his behalf, but honed with years of experience. No one being pursued wanted to be cornered. It was pure animal instinct; fight or flight in action. Once flight was triggered, the unconscious compulsion was to get as far away as possible from that which means you harm. Atticus ran on.

His theory soon bore fruit. Caught in glimpses between the crowd, he spied flashes of salt and pepper hair and the garish tartan suit. Atticus was closing the gap with every stride. *Let's dance, you fucker.*

Still, he had to be careful. This wasn't an American movie. One doesn't spray the street with bullets when chasing a subject. That was far more likely to result in the injury of an innocent bystander or, just as bad, to kill the suspect. Interrogating a dead suspect rarely garnered results. Atticus ran on.

He'd lost Maggie somewhere behind him but he couldn't afford to slow down. Bounding towards his target, he assessed vectors of attack, methods of disarmament and techniques to subdue an opponent. It was unfortunate that the one aspect he didn't consider was that he'd already been spotted.

Not-Jenkins stopped dead and leapt behind a clump of brightly coloured teens. Atticus stopped running and reached for his gun.

A shot rang out as Atticus nosedived into a rack of military jackets and careened into the ground with an unceremonious thud. Not-Jenkins wrapped his arm around a terrified teen in a bright yellow woollen dress and trained his gun at Atticus. The girl screamed as her friends bolted for the nearest cover. Startled shoppers did likewise, leaving Not-Jenkins and the teen alone in the street. The MI6 agent ducked below a stack of suitcases displaying multi-coloured scarves. Hardly bulletproof cover.

Atticus desperately scanned the street for an advantage, something he could use to defuse the situation. "Let the kid go! She's got nothing to do with this."

"Oh, sure, I'll just let go of the one thing preventing you from shooting me. Bollocks to that."

"I'm not going to shoot you."

"The gun in your hand says otherwise, guv."

The teen in Not-Jenkins' clutches screamed and twisted in an attempt to escape. He held firm and swung his pistol in all directions as a warning to anyone crazy enough to approach a wild man with a gun.

"Oi, what d'you think you're up to, mate!"

Atticus looked up to see a bearded man wearing thick black-rimmed glasses and a garish pink fur-lined suit storm out of the store. Evidently, this was the owner of the clothing Atticus was currently tangled up in, and he was oblivious to the hostage situation taking place. Before he could say more, Not-Jenkins fired another round, sending the proto-hipster scurrying for cover.

Pinned down, Atticus had few options. Even if he could quickly untangle himself from the jackets, his options were severely limited. Not-Jenkins had the advantage; Atticus would be seen as soon as he raised his head. Atticus could try to leap out with gun blazing, but the likelihood of him hitting the teen was high; too high. He had to think.

"Oi, twat!"

Glancing over the suitcases, Atticus saw a sudden, and if he were completely honest, astounding sight. Careening towards Not-Jenkins, Maggie's brilliant eyes were aflame as she wielded a cricket bat emblazoned with the Union Jack. She struck the impromptu weapon brutally downward as Not-Jenkins lifted his arm defensively. The excruciating crack reverberated off the surrounding buildings and blended perfectly with his agonised scream. He relinquished his stranglehold on the teen, who scrambled away, her fear-streaked face laced with hope.

Maggie wielded her scimitar in an upward strike, dislodging Not-Jenkins' pistol. To finish, she pulled the cricket bat back and gave him a final blow, the flat of the bat smacking his forehead, sending him whirling backwards and landing sprawled on his back, unarmed and vanquished. Hoisting the bat on her shoulder, Maggie stood above him triumphantly and blew a stray strand of hair out of her face.

She turned to Atticus with a triumphant grin. "Oh hey. Is this how you play cricket? Always been a bit vague on the rules."

Stumbling to his feet, Atticus disentangled himself from

the jackets and gave Maggie an appreciative dip of his head. In reply she doffed the cricket bat at him, a fierce warrior queen of the British Empire. There was no masking the air of smug satisfaction at her own actions. *Rightly so, too.*

As he approached, Atticus shook his head. "That's the most English thing I've seen in my life."

"I nicked it from *Lady Jane*." Maggie twirled the Union Jack-adorned implement, her face contemplative "Come to think of it, they didn't even say anything when I ran in and nicked it."

"An officer of The Service never nicks," he corrected her, "one simply appropriates for Queen and Country."

Screwing her face up impishly, she gave a heavy sigh. "Seems like I have a lot to learn."

Atticus watched Not-Jenkins writhe on the ground in pain. "Far less than I would have thought, as it turns out."

He picked up the pistol before a member of the public was alarmed by the sight of it. Atticus tucked it under his jacket alongside the other and stood next to Maggie, looking down at the moaning Not-Jenkins. The teens sped away, no doubt trying to put as much distance between them and the traumatic confrontation as they could. The teen in the yellow dress gave a frail yell of, "Thank you" over her shoulder as she scuttled away with her friends.

As they were about to discuss their next steps, Maggie glimpsed something over Atticus's shoulder. Her eyes went wide. Something poked into the centre of his back. He sighed and raised his hands.

"I'll have both of those shooters, thanks, guv. Nice and slow, yeah? We don't want to startle the civilians, now do we?" The accent was pure Cockney, the same as Not-Jenkins.

Doing as instructed, Atticus slowly uncoupled the

pistols and held them by the barrel. The man behind him relinquished him of both weapons. How quickly the tables had turned. Atticus wanted to slap himself. Not-Jenkins hadn't been running from them. He'd been running to something. An accomplice. The faceless man behind Atticus now held all the cards.

Maggie stepped forward, cricket bat held ready in a baseball stance. Atticus gave her a slight shake of his head. *No. We can't win this one. Let it go.*

With a grunt of pain, Not-Jenkins pushed himself up, holding his broken arm gingerly. The fist of his good arm clenched as he zeroed in on Maggie. Atticus tensed his body, ready to leap between the two.

The man behind Atticus stepped forward, allowing himself to be seen for the first time. Older than his partner, he was less loudly dressed, in a double-breasted suit. He seemed completely at peace with the situation. He tsk-tsked as he gave a tiny shake of his head. The message was clear: *stand down.*

"She bloody well broke my fucken' arm!" Not-Jenkins winced as he took a step forward.

The newcomer placed a hand on Not-Jenkins' chest, halting his advance. "Well then, you need to be more careful, don'tcha?"

That put paid to Not-Jenkins' thoughts of revenge. There was little doubt who was in charge. The injured man cowed next to the newcomer, giving Maggie the stink-eye.

The new man turned to Atticus. "I don't believe we've had the pleasure, me old china?"

"Something tells me we'll have ample opportunity to get to know one another, friend."

The new man folded one lip over the other without offering a response. He flicked his head from Not-Jenkins to a bright green Austin Healey roadster that was double-parked by the side of the road. Not-Jenkins flopped into the passenger seat with a grunt.

Hand deep in his jacket and eyes not moving from Atticus, the newcomer opened the car's door and gave an elaborate bow to Maggie before sliding behind the wheel. Within seconds he'd started the engine and accelerated away.

Again, Atticus reached into his pocket for a non-existent mobile phone. *Fuck.* "We need to find a phone, target CCTV, call in satellite surveillance."

Maggie scoffed. "Right, do you have the direct number for Sputnik, then?" She shrugged. "What are you on about?"

"Nothing... I..." It was unusual for Atticus Wolfe to feel helpless. He ran his hand over his sweaty scalp as they watched the roadster disappear in the distance. Silence swirled around them.

Staring at the road where the Austin Healey had sat, Atticus had an uncomfortable thought. He'd lost the Browning. He didn't particularly relish the idea of informing Mrs Abernathy that he'd lost the first gun she'd given him. Atticus had a feeling she was going to be a more formidable foe than Not-Jenkins. He gulped.

As a distraction from thoughts of the confrontation to come, he turned to Maggie. "Thank you. You wield a mean cricket bat, Ms Dunbar."

She stared wide-eyed at nowhere in particular. "I've never done anything like that in my life."

"How did it feel?"

Her eyes went wide as she beamed. "It was a total flashkick."

"A... a what?"

"Flashkick, you Square." Maggie rolled her eyes. "A flashkick is a thrill, excitement. You've heard of teenagers doing things for kicks, right? They're flashkickers. Got it?"

Unsure how to respond, Atticus just nodded. "Thanks for helping back there."

"No problem." She studied his face. "You don't have to do all this alone, you know?"

She was more right than she knew.

ELEVEN

"Wait, wait... wait." Henry held up his hand. "Just... wait."

Atticus was reasonably sure the want-to-be-Beatle was having an aneurysm of some description.

Henry rubbed his temples. "You lot were in a gunfight?"

"A small one." Maggie waggled her shoulders, not trying to hide her self-satisfied expression. "But we absolutely were."

Now the shock had worn off, Maggie had come to appreciate her own efforts, literally, under fire.

"Well, get a paint tin and colour me green." Henry threw his hands in the air. "That is probably the coolest thing I've ever heard in the entirety of my life or anyone else's." He whistled.

They had all arrived at Jayne's flat at the same time. It had taken only a couple of minutes to bring Oliver and Henry up to speed.

"Let's not forget someone could have been killed, shall we?" Oliver was the least impressed of the group. In fact, his demeanour was decidedly sour. "I wouldn't exactly classify the encounter as cool." He turned to Atticus. "This is not how one conduct's oneself as a member of Her Majesty's Secret Service in propriety nor in adherence to the legally sanctioned directives. Might I remind you we are not cowboys. We're not the CIA, we don't go around shooting everything in sight. Remember when I said you need to keep a low profile?"

Behind Oliver, Maggie's head slumped backwards, and her mouth flapped open like a teen being scolded by her mother. Henry turned away so Oliver couldn't see him roll his eyes.

Under his breath he mumbled, "Sure thing, grandpa."

Maggie's hand shot to her mouth to cover her snigger. Atticus jumped in before Oliver could react.

"No one was injured. I think the most pressing consideration is who they were."

"Soviets?" Henry asked. There was an element of glee in his question.

"They had the thickest Cockney accent of any Russian in history." Maggie threw up her hands. "I grew up in the East. If those blokes were Soviet, they have the best ear for accents I've ever come across. Those lads were born within earshot of the Bow Bell. I'd bet my balls on it."

It was Henry's turn to snigger. Oliver tutted.

Maggie's face turned serious. "Why would Cockneys be rummaging around in a missing spy's flat?"

"If Jayne was offed in revenge for shagging some bloke's bird, I'm going to be bloody disappointed." Henry poked the bookshelf as if it might give him an immediate answer.

"Well, whatever it is, those gentlemen were willing to kill for what's here." Atticus righted the overturned table and started to straighten the dislodged papers. "We need to secure these, and search the rest of the flat thoroughly for anything else he hadn't got to yet."

"Oooh! The thing!" All eyes turned to Maggie. "The fucking thing!" She dropped to the floor and crawled.

"Is this one of those new dance craze things?" Oliver's eyes narrowed. "Let me guess, the cockroach? No, the flounder. The epileptic spider?"

After giving Oliver the two-finger salute Maggie clambered to the corner of the lounge and clawed at the baseboard. Tongue firmly planted in the corner of her mouth, she tore at the white wood. It refused to budge. In frustration she hit it with a balled fist and it smoothly creaked open. It was as if the whole mechanism was on a hinge.

"That's how you spy, me ol' muckers!" Maggie reached into the dark cavity and rummaged about. Triumphantly, she hefted aloft a brown paper package bound in string. "I saw it when I was cowering on the floor. My foot hit it and it sounded weird. Got a bit distracted when the bullets started flying, though." She stood and threw the package to Oliver. "If Jayne wanted it hidden, I kind of think we'd want to investigate it, yeah?"

Oliver harrumphed. "Indeed."

The four reverently kept their eyes on the package as Oliver carried it to the now-righted kitchen table. Carefully cutting the string, Oliver cautiously unwrapped the waxy brown paper. Inside were a series of letters in a woman's hand, the envelopes pockmarked with love hearts and hand-drawn red lips.

More importantly, it also contained another chequebook. It was the same brown leather as the one Atticus had observed Not-Jenkins thumbing through. Oliver placed the seemingly identical chequebooks side by side. Henry picked up the letters, all addressed to Jayne. They were open and seemingly well thumbed.

"They're..." Oliver flipped through the cheque stubs of both books. "They're the same dates, same cheques, well, most of them. This one," he motioned to the one on the left, the original unhidden one, "has more entries. Curious." He glanced up to see Henry wide-eyed and flipping through the pages of handwritten letters. "Henry, what have you..." He waved a hand in front of Henry's intense, unblinking gaze.

"This is some... woah, this is some steamy stuff, guys. I wish," he baulked in shock, "I really wish a woman had written me something like thi—" His eyes went even wider. "She did not just say that! Can, can she even do that?" Henry embarrassedly raised his head, as if suddenly realising he was speaking out loud. He waved the pile of letters at the other three. "I might need to take these home for further analysis."

Oliver gently took the letters from Henry's sweaty grasp. "Please don't become sexually aroused by evidence, Henry. It's ungentlemanly."

Atticus pondered what these additional pieces meant. It could be everything or nothing. Without further information, they were merely a couple of pieces of curiosity. Time would tell if they fit the puzzle to form anything of substance.

"Maggie, maybe we could put you in charge of finding out who's the author of these steamy communiqués and what connection there is to Jayne." In the corner of his eye Atticus could see Henry's shoulders slump in despair. "It might make for, ah, less complications that way."

With a yawn, Maggie gave him a knowing grin. "Probably for the best." She wrinkled her nose at Henry. "Sorry, me old mucker, think this one's mine."

Henry folded his arms and strained his neck as Maggie tucked the letters into her purse. Oliver gave Henry an amused shake of his head before turning his attention to the other two.

He assessed Atticus and Maggie. "You both appear exhausted. Go home, Henry and I have this. We'll see if there are any more little hidey holes. How about you go home and freshen up? Are you still fine for dinner, Atticus?"

If Atticus were honest, he'd completely forgotten about their dinner plans. "Sure, not a problem." It was a complete lie. The rush of adrenaline that had been propelling him was suddenly washed away by admitting its existence, replaced by sheer exhaustion. His limbs felt heavy and awkward.

"See you tonight. Looking forward to it." His head felt like it was filled with concrete.

Bidding the other two goodbye, the pair made their way downstairs and outside. The wind had an extra chill and the afternoon sun was lower in the sky.

Atticus sucked in the colder air and it partially revived him. His uncomfortable couch and two channels suddenly seemed very appealing.

Maggie playfully poked Atticus in the ribs with her newly acquired cricket bat. "What now?"

"To be honest, I was planning on going home and crashing."

She vehemently shook her head. "I'm too hyper to go home. Feel like someone's slipped me a French blue."

Atticus bobbed his head. He'd been there, wired from an assignment. "What do you suggest?"

Like Oliver had done only moments before, Maggie

looked him up and down. The added waggle of eyebrows was all her own, however. There was no escaping the tractor beam of her impish smile.

∼

"Well," Atticus fell backward, completely spent. "If I wasn't knackered before, I bloody well am now." He inhaled deeply, trying to catch his breath. "You're a machine, you know that?"

Maggie fluttered her eyelids. "A girl tries."

Using the palm of his hand, he wiped sweat from his brow. Had he expected this when he'd gotten up this morning? Absolutely not. Was he delighted? With a heaving sigh, he had to admit, he totally was.

Maggie's glowing face hovered above his. "Want to go again?"

Atticus issued a guttural grunt. "Are you trying to kill me, woman?"

She laughed a deep, hearty laugh and tucked a stray hair behind her ear. "Come on, you've got one more left in you, surely?"

Atticus groaned as she took his hand and hauled him up. The shopping bags were heavy in his other hand.

"I've never had a chance to shop at Lord John. We need to find you a jacket, one to wear on a night out. I'm sure you're rather dashing in your naval uniform, but it's time to gab up like you actually live in the sixties, okay?"

"Gab up?"

"Seriously, I thought you were more hip than Oliver. To gab up, get dressed, wear the latest thing, yeah?"

Atticus had to agree. He definitely needed new clothes. Maggie the Mod was only too pleased to oblige. Under the initial pretext of the returning the Union Jack cricket bat, she dragged him around Carnaby Street making him try on all the latest suits to update his image. Despite the fact that the image she was "updating" him to was a good sixty years out of date, she chose well. The slimline suits fit his physique perfectly, and he felt far more comfortable than he had in the baggy grandfatherly suit Oliver had supplied.

She agreed to spot him until payday. He only hoped when he was paid he'd be able to cover it. Atticus hadn't discussed wage with Rathdowne because he'd feared his new boss would ask for a number. Given that he struggled with guineas and shillings, that conversation was probably best avoided.

Over the last hour he and Maggie had shopped, joked and had fun. She had boundless reserves of energy. She strolled into stores with all the authority she lacked in the work environment. Enthusiastically engaging the staff, she had them racing around trying to please Atticus like he was royalty. It was like she was a different woman—more energetic, more alive. He very much liked this Maggie.

After they'd secured him a purple velvet jacket, they rested at the far end of the street enjoying an ice-cream.

"Can I ask you something?"

"Right now, you can ask me anything." She beamed in the sunlight.

"When we first met, you said you had a reason for joining MI6. I'm kind of intrigued as to what that was."

Her joyous demeanour fell as heavy as an iron curtain. The transformation was as stark as it was sudden.

Atticus realised he'd crossed some unknown boundary. "I'm sorry, I didn't mean to—"

She held up a hand, appearing to fight back tears. "It's

okay. It's fine." Her smile was as convincing as a real estate agent's greeting.

"You don't have to—"

"My mother."

Atticus furrowed his brow. "Your mother wanted you to join?"

She shook her head sadly. Atticus realised it was best to let her tell the story.

"My mother worked for The Service, during the war. She was fluent in French, German and Italian, so they sent her on missions. At least, that's what my father thought— he was never entirely sure. Near the end of the war two men in uniform turned up in the middle of the night and took her away in a town car. Said she had a mission to complete, that she'd be back in a few days. I never saw her again. No one ever told us why or even where she had gone. My father died a widower, never knowing what happened to the woman he loved."

She stood and threw her dripping ice-cream in the bin, seemingly having lost her appetite. Silence enveloped them for a time.

"I'm sorry if I brought up a painful topic, I didn't mean to bring the mood down so suddenly."

"Oh, so you meant to bring down the mood, though?"

"I... I..."

"At ease, sailor. I'm just taking the piss." She tapped his knee. "You weren't to know. It's okay, really. We can talk about it, I've had a lifetime wrestling with it, believe me."

"I'm wondering, if your mother died a spy, why do you..."

"Because if I don't, then what did she die for? Hmmm?" The melancholy she carried was old and heavy. "She died protecting this country, fighting men who were trying awfully hard to remove our freedoms, our way of life. I'm not going to stand by and let what she died for simply wither away because it was hard."

And no doubt you also hope to come across what really happened to your mother. He left it unsaid; she'd likely deny it, and besides, he didn't know Maggie well enough to call her on it. Some things a friendship had to earn. Despite the change in mood, Atticus was pleased to realise they'd made exactly that: a friendship.

Another realisation occurred to him. He and Maggie were both doing the exact same thing. They were working for MI6 with an ulterior motive. For her, it was to uncover the truth of her mother's death. For Atticus, it was to find any trace of Omar Ganim. It was odd that the two of them had found one another.

Maggie suddenly stood. "Enough of this maudlin drivel. We can probably get you a cravat before everything shuts."

Atticus stood rigidly straight. "I draw the line at cravats."

"Don't be such a square!"

Having regained her previous effervescence, she dragged him down the street. She skipped a few feet ahead, practically dancing. Atticus wasn't sure how much of it was an act to cover the deeply personal nature of their conversation.

A group of youths approached, five in all, walking the other way. They wore white t-shirts, jeans, motorcycle boots; a few donned leather caps. Their hair was uniformly worn in an exaggerated pompadour hairstyle, slick with Brylcreem. They prowled the streets as if they owned them. The lead blonde whistled at Maggie as she approached.

"Hey darlin', what'cho doing tonight, then? Wanna have some fun with me and the boys?"

"Rockers aren't my bag, sorry fellas."

The blonde sized Atticus up and spat on the footpath. "Nah, you got shadier taste, doncha?"

Atticus stepped forward and the leader of the group recoiled a step. "I think she has other plans, thank you."

"'right, 'right, mate. Don't get your panties in a wad, yeah." He snickered and wiped his nose on the back of his hand.

They strode on. Once they'd passed, the leader threw a cigarette at Atticus and bolted; his mates followed suit.

Over his shoulder, he yelled, "Oi, love, you should have left yer golliwog boyfriend on the boat!"

The cackles of his mates echoed down the street as they sprinted away. Atticus shook his head. They were never a threat. Just young kids letting off steam, thinking they knew better, thumbing their nose at anyone older than they were. That wasn't exclusive to this or any other time period.

About to make light of it, he turned back to Maggie only to see that her face was deadly serious. She gazed deep into Atticus's eyes, as if reaching into his very soul. For some reason Atticus thought her expression was as if she'd locked eyes on him for the first time.

Her hand dashed to her mouth in alarm. "I'm terribly sorry, Mr Wolfe, I have to go."

With that, she pivoted on the spot and sped away in the opposite direction from where the youths had run. Atticus stood in the middle of the street holding the shopping bags.

What the hell was that about?

CHAPTER

TWELVE

"Nice jacket."

Atticus gave the white-gloved footman a nod of thanks for guiding him to the table, then turned his attention to his dinner companion. "Thanks. Maggie bought it for me. I'll fix her up when we get paid."

He sat opposite Oliver in the members' dining room of White's private club in St. James's. Oliver had been rather insistent on the venue and Atticus had only agreed reluctantly. The old establishment still existed in the twenty-first century, but wasn't a place he'd ever been. Gentlemen's clubs were a bit too quaint for his liking, but the main reason he'd never gone was White's distinctly non-twenty-first century insistence on continuing to exclude women. The thick gilded wallpaper, Edwardian furniture and lush red carpets weren't doing much to dispel Atticus's apprehension.

"Oh." Oliver's face was splashed with pained surprise. "You move fast." He traced circles on the tablecloth. "She's a nice girl."

Atticus frowned in reply. "It's not like that."

Oliver lifted an eyebrow. "Are you sure?"

It had been several hours since Maggie's mysterious disappearing act and Atticus still didn't know what to make of it. Was it because the Rocker's racially charged comments meant she'd suddenly realised she was associating in public with a man of colour? The reasoning didn't sit right with Atticus. He'd thought they were forming a friendship. Perhaps the thought of anything more than that had horrified her? Either way, she'd made her leave so suddenly.

Rubbing his hands together as he didn't quite know what else to do, he took a deep breath. "Oh, I'm sure."

Thankfully, a waiter wafted over and asked for the newcomer's drink order. Atticus was sure the elderly gentleman with the waxed moustache had been eavesdropping and cut in at the opportune moment.

"Old fashioned. Rye whiskey, easy on the fruit."

"Very good, sir." The waiter's tuxedo tails swooshed as he trotted away.

Atticus stretched, taking in the opulent room. "Can I ask how you afford this?"

Oliver sipped a martini. "The final bequeath from my late father. Pretty much the only thing he had left." A sadness descended across his features. "He was a merchant, imports mainly. In sixty years he went from penniless panhandler to respected self-made man, working seven days a week. But in the end, all he had to show for it was mounting debt, three mistresses and his lifetime membership here. He used it to schmooze clients. I use it for the free meals."

"And they let him join, with his, ah, heritage?"

Oliver bobbed his head in acknowledgement. "Yes.

Took him a few years—he was nothing if not persistent; some would say pig-headed—but they eventually let a lowly Jew join. It's funny how often money trumps bigotry. It's not hypocrisy when someone else is writing the cheques."

Atticus didn't mention his own trepidation when entering, wondering if they'd let him in. "This isn't the thirteenth century. The Edict of Expulsion is so 1290."

Oliver chuckled. "I keep forgetting you have history in the future."

"Where I come from Cliff Richard is ancient history."

The waiter served Atticus's drink with a flourish. *Not bad.* They ordered entrees and mains. After his second drink, he finally managed to relax.

Over canapés, Oliver circled the conversation back around. "So, there's nothing between you and Maggie, then?"

"Is that jealousy I hear?"

"Over Maggie? Hardly."

But Atticus wasn't talking about Maggie. There was no missing Oliver's longing gazes in Atticus's direction. Not that Atticus minded. He just wasn't wired that way. It wouldn't be the first time he'd been the focus of another man's affections. In college there'd been a few who had tried to sway his attention. He'd politely explained his preference for women. It had taken his friend Alex a while to get over it, but the two had remained firm friends ever since.

That it was the second time Oliver had raised Maggie was telling. It was time he brought Oliver's feelings out in the open. Atticus tried to approach it with as much tact as he could muster.

"Oliver, I'm straight."

"Straight what?"

Atticus couldn't help but smile. "As in, I prefer women, not men."

Oliver shifted uncomfortably in his seat. "Ah, so do I."

"No," Atticus did his best to keep a friendly, but firm tone, "you don't. I'm not saying this to make you uncomfortable, Oliver, I'm saying it to let you know I'm completely fine with it. It's nothing out of the ordinary where I come from. I just thought you needed to hear it."

"Oh." Oliver's voice sounded smaller, but his face soon brightened. "Thank you for, ah, being *straight* with me." The term seemed to amuse him. "It actually means a lot." He uncurled his back. "Now we have that sorted, let's talk business."

Over the next half hour they discussed the case. After Atticus and Maggie left, Oliver and Henry had rummaged around the flat, searching for further clues. Behind another skirting board they'd hit paydirt. From his jacket pocket, Oliver extracted an Australian passport and tossed it to Atticus. The picture was of Jayne, but the name on the passport was James Phelan. Atticus glanced across the table, confused.

"We didn't issue it." Oliver snorted. "Inferior. Look here," he ran his thumb along the edges, "the photo, the stamp quality, see the lack of clean lines? This is amateur-hour stuff. You could get this from any back room down the docks."

"Why would a spy need his own backup passport?"

"That, sir, is an excellent question."

Plates were cleared and their mains delivered by a small army of waiters. The menu was primarily game, which was not to Atticus's mainly vegetarian sensibilities. He'd chosen the pork belly for its abundant sides.

As he ate around the slab of meat at the centre of his

plate, Atticus brought up a topic that had been plaguing him for some time. "I've been racking my brain and I just can't remember an agent being kidnapped or killed in East Germany."

Oliver waggled his head from side to side contemplatively before slicing into his venison. "Now isn't the time for another stuff-up. Perhaps The Service swept it under the carpet. It certainly seems like they're trying to do that already. Like you said, Rathdowne apparently wants you to fail. Perhaps there's a reason."

"Maybe. But what if my appearance in this time somehow made it happen?"

Oliver tapped his thumbs on his lips contemplatively. "You turn up one day and a chap in East Berlin is kidnapped? I can't see how they're connected."

"To be honest, neither can I." Atticus rubbed the back of his neck. "I really hope I don't make us lose the Cold War now."

"I would very much like to know how we defeated the other side."

Atticus smirked. Of course he would. Any spy would. If his co-workers wouldn't give him respect, Oliver could ensure it forever by foretelling events for the next sixty years. It would be too much power for anyone. His own disruptive existence was one thing, but the ability to rewrite the future was something else entirely.

"Sorry, I'm not giving you a history lesson, Oliver. I think I've caused enough of a butterfly effect by merely being here, let alone telling someone who can actually influence events. No, sorry my friend, everything needs to unfold as it should."

Oliver gave a sad of tilt of his head in acquiescence. "Is there anything you can give me advice on?"

With a shrug, Atticus inhaled thoughtfully. "Don't spend too much time on your MySpace profile, don't buy a Hypercolor t-shirt no matter how rad you think it is, and don't call your kid Karen."

Oliver pursed his lips. "I'm sure that's terribly clever in your time."

"Not really."

"I still find it difficult to believe we prevail in the Cold War, to be honest. For my entire life there has been one absolute truth: this uneasy truce cannot hold. Someone has to flinch. I always assumed it would be us."

Placing his knife and fork down, Atticus finished his drink. "To be honest, I'm still coming to terms with the fact that I'm actually living through it. In my time, the threat of nuclear annihilation is academic at best. Here, I see it in the eyes of shopkeepers, ticket collectors, everyone. There's an undercurrent of fear, everyone is so sure war is coming."

"That's because we're a species of violence. We always have been, from the first caveman with a club to now. It's only the weapons that change. Ever since Mesopotamia we've warred nation against nation, it's the one certainty of humanity. Oh, you can pretend otherwise by pointing at Michelangelo or Degas or Van Gogh, but you can't put a plaster over the festering wound of the truth. We're a vicious and violent species; war is in our nature. We didn't learn from the so-called War to End All Wars because it wasn't. We didn't learn from the next one, either. We are as powerful as we are stupid. Now we finally have weapons to end us all. Until I met you I was sure the next war was coming, as certain as the dawn. It wasn't a matter of if humanity would be wiped out, only when."

"Aren't you a little ray of sunshine?" Atticus used jazz hands to emphasise the point. "But mutually assured destruction changes that. For the first time, we invented weapons so powerful we were scared to use them."

"Nagasaki and Hiroshima would argue otherwise."

"I mean on a global scale. You've seen it. The Cuban Missile Crisis proved that the major powers were terrified of their own creations. I've seen it. We survive this."

"But who is to say *your* future still exists? Your presence here could alter your history. Have you considered that, my friend? The future you're so sure of may no longer exist."

Leaning back, Atticus clasped his hands together and placed his index fingers on his lips. "Are you saying I cause a nuclear holocaust?"

"Please don't say holocaust to a Jewish person."

The two chuckled good-naturedly as waiters cleared their plates. They ordered desserts. Atticus ordered the treacle tart. Oliver ordered the spotted dick, which amused Atticus no end. They ordered wine. When the bottle of Chateau Mouton Rothschild arrived, Oliver shooed the waiter away and uncorked the bottle himself. When he handed the glass to Atticus it sloshed over the side; it seemed he'd had a few too many already.

"Have you considered that perhaps you're in a coma?"

"Maybe." It was a topic Atticus had spent significant time contemplating himself. "And this is my brain's way of coping, do you think?" The spectral appearances of the modern Mini and Omar Ganim hadn't dispelled the possibility in Atticus's mind. "It's possible. That would mean you're not real. Do you feel real?"

Oliver felt his own arm and looked up, amusement dancing across his features. "Pretty real."

"If it is all in my mind, why would I imagine all this?" Atticus waved vaguely about the room. "I didn't know much of this stuff, this era. It's far too detailed for my mind to make up, surely. Plus, if it is my mind, why didn't it pick something more stimulating, like," Atticus waved his finger and sat up, suddenly animated, "like the time I met a Swedish girl in Majorca. We were totally wired and spent seven blissful days in a bed overlooking the Mediterranean. I could live there for quite some time, believe me."

Oliver picked up the cork and threw it at Atticus's head. It bounced off his forehead, and a passing waiter caught it in mid-air, not even breaking stride. He disappeared into the kitchen, never glancing back once.

"Ow." Atticus rubbed his temple. "What was that for?"

"Did it hurt?"

Atticus smirked. "Yeah, it did."

"Probably not a coma, then. Ah, here comes dessert."

Atticus and Oliver talked over sweets, their conversation unhurried, like they had all the time in the world. They turned over words like soil, tilling their thoughts over and over again.

The more time Atticus spent in Oliver's company, the more relaxed he felt. It seemed Atticus was making a genuine friend. Not for the first time, he felt perhaps he could not only survive in this time, but truly live in it. Initially his only thought had been to use MI6 to find Ganim and somehow get back home. But with every passing day that dream seemed increasingly far-fetched and improbable. He had to start a life, a new life in this time. As tasted the last blissful bite of the delicious tart, the warm haze of alcohol enveloping him, Atticus decided there were worse places to do just that.

∽

Outside, the wind sliced through his skin like blades of ice. The night was freezing, but Atticus was sure the alcohol consumption added to his shivering. The thought of his bed was appealing, but so was the idea of hitting up a bar. Maybe getting a kebab.

That last thought confirmed two things. Firstly, it was going to take a long time before Atticus kicked the habit of thinking like he was still in the twenty-first century. Late-night kebab joints probably weren't yet a thing. Secondly, he was most definitely drunk.

"What now? Another bar?"

Oliver checked his watch. "Past ten. Pubs are closed, I'm afraid. Unless we head down to Billingsgate, where all the shift workers are, and I have to say it wouldn't be my first recommendation. There's some coffee houses, but they play that modern music racket, can't stand it."

"So that's it then?"

Atticus was surprised to realise he genuinely wanted to spend more time with Oliver. He was enjoying his company.

"I know a place, but—"

"But?"

"It's not really for straight people." Oliver seemed to enjoy the new meaning of the word. "It's a bit hidden away."

"Let's go there."

"Are you sure?" Oliver seemed surprised but delighted.

"To see a seedy underground sixties watering hole? Bring it."

When Oliver said "underground", he'd meant it literally. The subterranean bar had no sign on the street, nothing to indicate it was a bar at all from the outside. It didn't even have a name. To access it, Oliver led Atticus through a darkened series of interconnected tunnels, each seedier and damper than the last.

Atticus knew that well below the thriving streets of London, an entirely different city existed. Composed of hidden tunnels, rivers, sewers, train tubes, deep shelters and government citadels, the streets above concealed a disused, forgotten world below—forgotten by all except those few privileged enough to know its secrets. In Atticus' time urban explorers accessed neglected and hidden areas under an oblivious city. It seemed Oliver's destination was equally veiled from the unknowing world above.

When they finally arrived at the bar itself it was suitably dark, but elegant in its own way. Mismatched Persian rugs rested below battered velvet couches shoved against one another, surrounding an art deco mahogany bar. Everything seemed to have been transported in from another era. The underground space branched off to a dozen other doors, each likely to hold its own secrets.

With no one single point of entry, patrons could leave via a different egress. Atticus thought this place would make a fine MI6 headquarters. Better than the dingy fire extinguisher company, at least.

Noting his friend's glances at the various doors, Oliver winked. "In case of a raid. Plenty of escape routes."

Atticus took in more of the cavernous space. Candlelight illuminated groups of men, their chatter low and intimate. A smoke haze only added to the ambience.

In a low voice, Atticus said, "I hope people don't think I'm a tourist."

"A tourist from where?"

"I mean, someone who doesn't belong and is just here to look."

Oliver grinned. "We like to keep to ourselves and leave

judgement to others." He jutted his head towards a clump of five men in the far corner. "My friends. We call ourselves The Coven."

"Isn't a coven normally reserved for—"

"Yes, but we named it after some joke none of us can remember now. It somehow stuck."

A tall lanky man from The Coven waved in their direction. "Thumper!"

Gesturing in reply, Oliver jerked his head to Atticus. Introductions were made, of sorts. Nobody used their real name. Besides Oliver's Thumper, there was Raven, Stockholm, Worm and Chaucer. The tall lanky fellow was Lancelot. Atticus was introduced as Milli Vanilli.

On the way to the bar, Oliver had described it as the only place his kind could feel safe. Now inside, Atticus could understand why. They were far below the accusatory glare of those above. Atticus understood the need for a secretive place when even the slightest hint of homosexuality meant, at best, expulsion, at worst, criminal charges, jail and a life ruined. It was underground in more ways than one.

Between small talk, Worm ordered a round of absinthe for the table. The group were welcoming but didn't ask personal questions. They spoke of art and literature, and issued wise, if world-weary, observations. Atticus liked them.

When the absinthe arrived, Oliver declared, "I'll be mother". As he tinkered with the silver fountain, absinthe spoons and reservoir glasses, he jutted his chin towards Atticus. "Our new friend is a science fiction writer." Atticus didn't respond, unsure where Oliver was going with the statement. Oliver dripped the water, creating a milky opalescence in the glasses.

"He's writing a novel set in the future, about our kind."

All eyes turned to Atticus, who felt suddenly quite warm. "That's right. I am."

Lancelot frowned, seemingly impressed. "So tell me, Mr Milli Vanilli, what does our collective future have in store for us, then?" He scanned the group with an amused, expectant eye. "For our kind, I mean."

"Over the next, say, fifty or sixty years progress is slow, but progress we do. There are famous people who come out, making it less hidden away. There's acceptance and embracing. It's not easy by any measure, but it happens. The eighties are particularly rough, but over time it becomes accepted and mainstream."

To his surprise the men shook their heads and scoffed. Chaucer waggled a finger at him. "Rubbish. Nobody's going to read it, mate. That's not science fiction, it's fantasy."

"Oh, don't get me wrong," Atticus went on, "it wasn't painless. It happened, in the story, far more slowly than it should have, but it does happen." They appeared unconvinced. "I went to many... I mean, I wrote a scene that was set at a wedding. I was going to say gay wedding, but that sounds like one is better than the other, right? Love is love."

"A gay wedding. Ha." Raven shook his head and chortled. "Can't see the Archbishop of Canterbury blessing that one. Not in a hundred years."

"Less than that." Atticus smiled. "It'll happen. Eat your vegetables, look after yourself, work out. It will happen in your lifetime, believe me. Send me an invite."

The faces around the table were sceptical. Oliver shot Atticus a quizzical expression. In reply, Atticus waggled his eyebrows to confirm the fact.

With a surprised shake of his head, Oliver whispered,

"Well, I'll be."

"Your book character, what's he called?" Lancelot asked.

"Freddy Prinze Junior."

Oliver pursed his lips, knowing somehow it was a joke that he'd get some time in the future. "I wonder what advice Freddy Prinze Junior would give us now?"

Atticus grinned. "Oh, that's easy. Buy bitcoin, don't buy a Zune. Don't get too attached to *Firefly*." The blank faces told Atticus he'd lost them, but he couldn't help but go on. "Never learn the Macarena, or Lambada, or line dancing for that matter. And lastly, no matter what you're told, don't freak out about Y2K."

A bemused silence swirled around them. Some were amused by his nonsensical words, others bewildered.

Lancelot let out a bawdy laugh and shook his head. "I have to say, you do have quite an imagination Mr Vanilli." He jutted out his chin. "Let me know when it's published. I'll give it a read."

AN HOUR and several absinthes later, Atticus watched the room spin and decided it was time to pull up stumps. The cold night air would sober him up. He had work in the morning. Oliver's friends tried to persuade him to stay, which he appreciated, but he thought it best to leave them to the rest of their night.

After bidding them farewell, Atticus stood unsteadily and realised he had no idea which of the myriad of doors to use. The place was a maze.

Thankfully Oliver walked him to the right exit. "Thank you for this evening. You're the first person to ever... travel from one of my worlds to the other. Quite apt for a science fiction writer, I would say."

"That was pretty well done, the whole writer thing. We'll make a spy of you yet."

Oliver chuckled and opened the large metal door. "See you in the morning." He handed Atticus a torch. "Keep going left. It's a disused tunnel on the City & South railway, comes out at Borough. You can make your way home from there. Not much of a walk."

And walk he did, although it wasn't home. In an effort to sober up, Atticus walked aimlessly for a time, concentrating on keeping one foot in front of the other, not blindly walking onto the road or down an open manhole cover.

As he fought the cold, he tried to focus his mind on something, anything, to stop his swirling intoxicated thoughts, and especially to half all thoughts of kebabs. The focus came when he began dissecting the mole case, and in particular, his part in it. He had yet to identify the true reason Rathdowne had assigned him. Yes, it was to set him up for failure, but why? Why would a senior member of MI6 not want to catch a mole? Rathdowne had been avoiding Atticus, he was certain. He knew other staff members had managed to make an appointment with him long after Atticus had been told there were no more for the week. The next morning he'd camp out in Rathdowne's office until the two had an enlightened chat. All Atticus had to do was sober up first.

Unsure how long he'd walked the streets, Atticus decided his frozen limbs weren't getting any warmer and his sobriety wasn't improving. It was time to head home and gulp several litres of water. Getting his bearings, Atticus stopped dead and swore at himself. He'd done it again.

He was standing on Brixton Road, the one place he'd vowed to keep away from. For the second time in a week he'd gravitated to something familiar, the closest thing he had to call home. *Idiot. What are you trying to achieve?*

It was late, but not late enough for random groups of revellers to be marauding down the streets, whooping it up. That was one thing Brixton always had in abundance: life. Atticus was just turning in the direction of Covent Garden when a group of five people noisily exited a darkened pub. It was well after closing time, so the rowdy group must have been part of a lock-in, where patrons are "locked" into a pub after closing to continue drinking. It had been a few years since Atticus had had an old-fashioned lock-in, and he was slightly jealous of the group as they danced and sang their way up the street ahead of him.

He watched the three men and two women as they sang some song Atticus had never heard. What they lacked in talent they made up for in volume. Their jubilation was infectious; Atticus couldn't help smiling. The men all appeared to be of Caribbean descent. The two women had dark hair, though one had far shorter hair than the other, and a skirt to match.

The woman with the longer hair called out, "Mary Quant is tone deaf!" and the entire group laughed, including the other woman, who Atticus assumed was Mary.

There was something familiar in the taller woman's voice. The long dark-haired woman strode alongside the group with familiar ease, and was hooked arm in arm with the tallest male. When the two turned to kiss, the rest of the group groaned affectionately. It was then Atticus saw the face of the woman.

It seemed Maggie was as acquainted with Brixton as he

was. The exuberant group peeled off a side street, changing to a song which they all seemed to have different lyrics for, though that didn't halt their rowdy rendition. They disappeared into the night.

Atticus had to stop walking to process what he'd just seen. Maggie Dunbar was dating a black man from Brixton. He had to admit he hadn't seen that one coming. After all his confusion stemming from Maggie's sudden disappearance, he could certainly cross one possibility off the list. It seemed safe to assume Maggie wasn't racist.

Ramming his hands into his pockets, Atticus strolled on, his mind even more stuffed full of confusion than before. His walk didn't seem to have alleviated his meandering thoughts, only multiplied them.

By the time he reached the Flower Market he'd sobered up enough for bed. Possibly. He still felt tipsy. The magnitude of the night suddenly weighing on him, Atticus's feet dragged the last block before his own. Reaching for his key, he halted. There was a Vauxhall parked across the road from his building with one occupant. The figure sat upright, alert, head turned towards Atticus's door.

Not having passed the car, Atticus was reasonably sure the occupant hadn't seen him. He stepped into the shadow of a shopfront. Quietly observing the male shape in the car, he wondered what the person was there for. No matter what time period it was, it wasn't common for someone to be parked in an empty street, just sitting in their car, after midnight on a weeknight.

The angle of the car shielded Atticus from view. It was possible the man in the car had expected him to come from the opposite direction. Perhaps he was an amateur. Atticus couldn't assume the latter was true. Having lost his pistol in the afternoon scuffle, he was unarmed. Perhaps one of the Cockneys had returned, and his compatriot wasn't far away. Confronting one was a challenge at the best of times, let alone two—especially in his current state.

Sticking to the shadows, Atticus slunk back the way he'd come. Thankfully he spied a bobby casually strolling along the opposite side of the street, whistling a tuneless melody. Atticus waved him down.

The surprised officer scanned Atticus from the ground up. "Can I help you?"

"Yes, thank you officer. There's a man in a car across from my flat, number seventy-two A. He's been there some time. I think he's casing the place, there may be another one nearby. I'm pretty sure he's waiting for me to come home. If you could possibly—"

"Been drinking, have we, sir?"

"What? No—well, yes, but that's got nothing to do with—"

"Out awfully late, sir, wouldn't you say?"

Atticus did his best to quell his simmering anger. "That's hardly the point."

"I'll decide what is and isn't the point, if you don't mind... sir."

"Actually, I do mind. There's a man on a stakeout in front of my place, possibly one already inside. I would have thought the police would have been interested in someone who's about to be attacked in their own home."

"Oh, we've suddenly escalated to an attack now, have we? My, what an eventful life you must lead."

"I don't like your condescending tone."

"I don't like your flights of fancy, mate." His jaw hardened. "I'll see some identification, please."

Atticus didn't have time for this, but the way the police officer's eyes narrowed made it clear this guy wasn't going anywhere anytime soon. Atticus could knock out the bobby, but it wasn't his style to attack a member of law enforcement, no matter how rude they were. Plus, he'd stupidly given out his address. First things first.

"I'm not the one you need to be talking to." Atticus clenched his jaw, doing his best to mask his annoyance. "I haven't broken any laws."

"Again, sir," the police officer unholstered his truncheon, tapping it on his leg, "I'll be the judge of that."

"What the hell are you going to do, arrest me for reporting a crime?" Atticus threw his hands in the air. "Are you that fucking stupid?"

~

"WELL, it seems he was, to use your words," Oliver tapped the cell bars, "that fucking stupid." He tilted his head for effect.

In spite of the situation, Atticus chuckled. "You're enjoying this, aren't you?"

"Which bit would that be? The part where my star recruit was arrested for drunk and disorderly? Or the part where I was telephoned in the middle of the night to report the fact that said drunkard was in custody? I'm having a whale of a time."

"I wasn't arrested, I was detained."

Oliver eyed the burly police officer as he unlocked the cell door. "Big difference."

The officer glared at Atticus and hefted a thumb. "Out you get. You're lucky you got friends in high places, mate." He was clearly displeased. "Your type usually spends days in 'ere to learn you a lesson."

Oliver bristled. "Your type?"

He scowled. "You heard. Off you pop before I chuck the both of you in."

Exhausted, Atticus just wanted to sleep. He grabbed Oliver by the arm. "Let's go. It's not worth it."

The two strode through the dingy Bow Street Police Station in silence. Atticus was more than happy to see the back of the piss-yellow tiles of the claustrophobic holding cell.

They passed through the huge heavy oak entrance and out into the silent, cold morning. The street was empty bar a couple of stray dogs scurrying about in the half light of the pre-dawn.

"Friends in high places?"

Looking at his wallet, Oliver shook his head in mock-seriousness. "I may have accidentally brought some identification that indicated I was from the Foreign Office. Not sure how I could have accidentally made such an error. Quite irresponsible of me, what?"

"Totally irresponsible." Atticus gave a tired chuckle. "Thank you."

"My pleasure." Oliver stretched his back and flattened his messy bed hair. "I suppose being locked up just because you're black stops happening in the future too?"

Atticus sighed, every cell of his body exhausted. "It really doesn't."

AFTER A SHOWER, a shave and an awful cup of industrial-strength instant coffee, Atticus almost felt human. Alone in the cell, he'd had plenty of time to contemplate the spinning plates of the mole hunt. He woke the napping Oliver, who was asleep in an armchair. He was eager to get stuck in. The case was becoming more complex by the day; and personal. Atticus was sure the man outside his flat had been there for him. He was gone when Atticus and Oliver arrived home as dawn broke over Covent Garden.

Did he mean him harm? It was likely. Well-wishes generally came via letter or singing telegram, not a beefy bloke in a black Vauxhall. What did it all mean?

The answer didn't come on the way to the office. Atticus opened the door to the Minimax Fire Extinguisher Company with some reluctance. He wasn't relishing the thought of advising Mrs Abernathy he'd lost his weapon. He needn't have worried.

Instead of the usual vacant ground floor with the straight-backed Mrs Abernathy and her judgemental eye, the reception area was packed shoulder to shoulder. Members of MI6 milled about, as confused as Oliver and Atticus. It was clear something was up, but nobody was quite sure what that something was.

Pushing their way through the sea of bodies, the two made their way through to the reception desk. There they found Maggie with her arms around a distraught Mrs Abernathy. It was clear the hard-as-nails woman had been crying. Atticus's first thought was that something must be gravely wrong if the formidable woman was so disturbed.

In spite of her troubled state, on seeing Atticus, Mrs Abernathy jutted out her chin. "How's the Prime Minister?"

"Safe for another day," Atticus answered with sympathy in his voice.

"I'm glad to hear it." Her expression was weary, but there was the tiniest hint of humour behind her eyes. "Wasn't looking forward to the paperwork otherwise."

He gave Maggie a quizzical tilt of his head. In reply she gave a slight shake of her own; she didn't know what had upset the redoubtable Mrs Abernathy either. Maggie gave Atticus a sad smile, as if she were pleased to see him. In return, he gave her a wink. Her face lit up before she returned to consoling Mrs Abernathy.

The exchange wasn't lost on Oliver. Mumbling, he said, "Oh, it's totally not like that."

From the back of the room came a posh voice. "What's going on? Why's everyone standing around like dock workers?"

That set Mrs Abernathy off once again. She broke down and buried her head in Maggie's shoulder. Between sobs, only certain words were distinguishable. The most frequent was "Elevator".

Leaving the distraught woman, Atticus strode to the elevator. He had to elbow past Hildebrand-Burke and Pillar, who grunted at the Herculean task of moving slightly to let him though. A crisp white sheet of paper was taped to the door, a single word scrawled hastily across it: "Don't!"

Atticus hit the up button, and heard the hydraulic thunk of the ancient door mechanism.

From behind him, Mrs Abernathy screamed, "No, please!"

The elevator shuddered open with a clunk. The scene inside drew gasps and screams. A body hung slumped against the back wall. The face was pallid and lifeless with an ugly red weeping sore around the neck. Atticus reluctantly stepped in and saw the apparatus of death. The end of the thin black tie was fastened to the floor lever.

Atticus redundantly checked for a pulse, but there was no need. Henry was already dead; strangled by his Beatles tie.

CHAPTER
THIRTEEN

"Get an ambulance!" someone shouted. Nobody moved.

Atticus stepped out of the lift, but not before pressing the button to close the doors. He sighed with all the heaviness he felt in his soul. "There's no need." He found it difficult to speak. His feet were made of concrete, his mouth full of ash. "He's been dead for hours."

"And how would you know?" If Hildebrand-Burke's nose was any higher in the air it would be a hazard to aviation.

In no mood for confrontation, Atticus answered with all the exhaustion he felt. "The petechial haemorrhaging." On seeing Hildebrand-Burke's blank expression he added, "The pin-head collection of blood in the eyes indicates acute blood pressure to the head. That means hanging. The placement of the tie confirms it. He's cold, he's been gone for hours."

Atticus was doing his best to retain a professional bearing. He was sure he was failing. Henry was dead. He'd been a trusted colleague, well on the way to being a friend. Now

Atticus would never have the chance to get to know him at all. His short life was over before it had truly begun. He wouldn't experience any of what should have been ahead of him. There would be no *Revolver*, no *Sgt. Pepper's Lonely Hearts Club Band*, no *White Album* to blow his mind.

The poor kid didn't deserve the horrific scene in the elevator. Few did. Millions of thoughts bombarded Atticus's mind. First and foremost was an unrestrained compulsion to rip the city apart to track down the murderous bastard responsible for the death of Henry Morton.

Several people deep, the toff Pillar clapped his hands to garner attention. "I say, do we need everyone milling about like this?"

Actively avoiding Atticus's gaze, Hildebrand-Burke spoke up. "Right you are. There's no need for you lot to stand around like you're waiting for the coronation. Everyone push off home until this afternoon when we'll—"

"No." Atticus was surprised at the harshness of his tone. "Nobody leaves until we've taken statements."

"Who put you in charge, Wolfe?"

Atticus sidled up to Hildebrand-Burke with barely contained rage. With a growl inaudible to anyone else, he eyed the chinless wonder with every ounce of the disdain he felt. "Your incompetence did."

Stepping back, Hildebrand-Burke glowered at Atticus with a mixture of contempt and fear. His flabby lower lip trembled, but he remained mute.

"I say old boy, at least send the women home," Pillar chimed in, unaware of the exchange and still on topic. "They don't need to be present for such horrors."

"Fuck off." Maggie's head shot up, as if realising she'd just spoken. Alarmed, she hunched her shoulders and added, "Fuck off... sir?"

Thankfully, before Pillar could react, Rathdowne barged through the doors, stopping short when he saw the amassed crowd. It took all of a minute for him to be brought up to speed.

"Nobody leaves until we have a testimonial from all and sundry stating their whereabouts last evening. I don't care if you play squash with the Queen's corgi groomer, everyone stays put until we have your statement. Do I make myself clear?"

Hildebrand-Burke bore the brunt of Rathdowne's glare. He gulped and gave a hangdog dip of his head. "Yes, sir."

"We also need to search the place before anyone leaves," Atticus added.

Rathdowne blinked at Atticus. "We do?"

Atticus nodded. "The murderer could be hiding. Or they might have hidden something of importance. We need to search the elevator shaft. Cupboards, closets, ventilator shafts, everything. No corner of this building can be left untouched. If we find anything suspicious in someone's desk, we need to question them here and now."

Rathdowne thought it over, then gave an agreeable bow of affirmation. "Two teams, one on statements, the other on the search. No one searches alone, I want teams of two or more, and we mix departments to keep us all honest." He planted his fists on his hips. "Well, let's bloody get on with it, then."

Before the first question had been asked, Atticus already knew a few things for sure. Both of the remaining Outsiders, Oliver and Maggie, had an alibi for the previous night. In both cases, that alibi was Atticus himself. He, of course, had been out, arrested and then spent the rest of the evening with Oliver. Likewise, Oliver's movements were beyond reproach. Atticus had spied Maggie roaming the streets of Brixton, and going by the way she'd hung off the man she was with, Atticus was certain she'd have a witness to account for her whereabouts throughout the night.

That just left the rest of MI6 as suspects.

~

HENRY WAS DEAD. The finality of the statement was as personal as it was gut-wrenching. The exuberant young man with the rest of his life ahead of him had been murdered.

As Atticus slumped back in the chair in their empty office, he stared at the smoke-scarred ceiling and came to one inevitable and chilling conclusion.

It was his fault Henry was dead.

Since arriving in this time period, he'd seen some unsettling events unfold. The Kennedy assassination had occurred just as he'd recalled, but then Jayne went missing soon after Atticus arrived. Was it a coincidence? Perhaps, perhaps not. He didn't recall ever hearing about a Jayne, or an agent who had disappeared behind the Iron Curtain at the same time as Lee Harvey Oswald had stunned the world at Dealey Plaza.

It wasn't like MI6 broadcast each and every one of their past mistakes. It was possible Jayne would turn up, and there was no mysteriously missing MI6 agent affair to be remembered. Then again, maybe not. Either way, the whole Jayne incident could be unconnected to Atticus.

But there was one thing he was certain of: no one from MI6 had ever been murdered in the confines of their own headquarters. That gruesome fact led to one inevitable and painful conclusion. His presence had unilaterally changed the past as he knew it. And not for the better. Dread gripped him from all sides. Atticus Wolfe had altered history, and good people were dying because of it.

Instinct told him to walk away, to protect the timeline at all costs. But then there was the other, more forceful part of his personality. The one that was screaming for vengeance. For now, the latter was winning, and by a large margin.

Turning his attention to the scrawled notes on the desk, Atticus tried to centre his chaotic thoughts. The killer must have had access to the MI6 building. The only logical conclusion was that the mole was real.

The floor-to-floor search had yet to uncover anything of importance, apart from a few prohibited bottles of alcohol, a couple of pornographic magazines and some amphetamines. Everyone had been checked for scratches or rope-type burns to their hands. Everyone came up clean. On top of all that, everyone was scared. One of their own had been murdered, virtually under their noses, in the most heinous of ways.

Death happens in espionage; it is an accepted and unwelcome fact of the job. But it occurs in far off lands, where the mind can concoct heroic deeds preceding the unfortunate loss of life. This was not just close to home, it *was* home. It was shocking. It was personal.

Atticus checked the wall clock. He had a meeting to go to. Making his way two floors up via the rickety wooden stairs, he entered the meeting room and took a seat near the back. Conscious he hadn't been with the organisation a week and had been throwing his weight around enough already, Atticus vowed to keep to himself as much as he could for the duration of the meeting.

He was sure Oliver would have laughed out loud at the absurdity of his optimism.

Within minutes room 503 was packed. During his first meeting in the room Atticus had detected fear following the Kennedy assassination; that was nothing compared to the panic in the eyes of those present now. Terror gripped the chain-smoking men of MI6. It was no longer academic; this was real, this was close, and worst of all, it was unseen. There was no affable backslapping this time. Every one of them had their game faces on.

Like the previous meeting, Rathdowne thundered through the doors in a fog of harried frenzy and slammed down a manila folder. "If anyone still harbours any doubts as to the existence of a mole, I'd like to hear them." Without pausing for an answer, he went on. "Didn't think so. Henderson, report."

Henderson stood and ran his hand over his slicked back hair. "The poor unfortunate Mrs Abernathy discovered Morton's body in the elevator just before 8 am. The coroner believes time of death to be between 4 and 6 am, or thereabouts."

"Why was he even here at that hour?" Hildebrand-Burke asked.

It was a good question. Atticus could have kicked himself for not thinking of it himself. There was no part of their investigation requiring Henry to be at MI6 at 5 am. So, why was he even in the building? One possible explanation was that he'd been lured there. Perhaps there had been some forceful reason to compel him to be at MI6 at that ungodly hour. It wouldn't have been urgent lift business, therefore it must have been to do with their investigation, which again came back to the mole. If Atticus could find out why Henry was there, he'd be well on his way to finding the killer.

"I'll direct that question to the lead on the mole investigation." Rathdowne pivoted his palm in Atticus's direction. "Mr Wolfe?"

Atticus gave the smallest of grunts. *Thanks for throwing me under the bus.* Walking to the front of the room, he felt every eye on him. "Yesterday was paperwork and securing Jayne's flat." He briefly thought back to the two Cockneys, but failed to see a connection. "Neither of which would compel Henry to be in the office outside of hours. Therefore, this leads to several suppositions, none of which carry substantial weight at this time. One, he was lured here by persons unknown offering a false promise of information, which led to his unfortunate demise. Alternatively, he may have had some reason to come into the office which he believed couldn't wait until morning, and in doing so disturbed someone, likely the mole, who then murdered him, believing they'd been compromised." Atticus blew out a frustrated breath, sliding his hand down his exhausted face. "Then again, it could be completely unrelated to the mole at all."

"But you don't think so?" Rathdowne tilted his head inquisitively.

"Right now, I'm not willing to take anything off the table. But my gut says this is him. It has to be."

"Has to be." The contempt in Hildebrand-Burke's voice would have shamed a surly teenager. "On that," he lit his pipe to give a theatrical pause, "I have an observation. Does it strike anyone as odd that Wolfe turns up and people start dying? I mean no disrespect, far be it for one member of Her Majesty's Secret Service to accuse another, of course, but a man we know nothing about appears out of thin air and suddenly all hell breaks loose. Granted, I'm just a lowly Associate Director, but I just thought I'd mention that it does seem somewhat irregular, wouldn't you say?"

"If you have an accusation to make, I'd appreciate it if you had the balls to say it to my face."

"I'm merely summarising the facts. I do believe that is what we're here for, is it not?" Hildebrand-Burke gave a shrug with the innocence of a used-car salesman. "Or are you perturbed by candour? You seem reluctant to speak plainly with your new colleagues." He gestured theatrically to the room. "Now, I wonder why that would be?"

In no time at all the conversation had somehow descended into a witch hunt, and for the wrong target. Given Atticus's gossamer thin existence in this time period, it wasn't a place he particularly wished to dwell.

Atticus knew from experience that sometimes the best form of defence was attack. Why was Hildebrand-Burke so keen to pin anything on Atticus? Did he himself have something, or potentially everything, to hide? It was a distinct possibility. Then again, he could simply be as he appeared, an entitled pretentious prick. It was a margin call.

"I say," Pillar poked a cigarette in Atticus's direction, "if you think this whole ballyhoo is related to your mole chap, then why not tell us what you know so far? You've been at this for days. What have you actually achieved?"

"I bought a new suit." Atticus rocked on his heels and thumbed his lapels. "Do you like it?"

Hands were thrown into the air. Hildebrand-Burke and Pillar huffed, and were joined in their exasperated clamour by a large portion of the room. There were far more utterances of, "I say" than Atticus would have liked.

It was time for him to take charge of the room once more. "The murderer is most likely in this building as we speak, potentially even in this room. I'm disinclined to discuss my investigation in the presence of the actual traitor." He took a moment to survey the room, and his gaze quelled the growing discontent. "If that inconveniences you, I suggest you lodge a formal complaint with the nearest embassy of the USSR, because you're sure as shit getting nothing from me." He turned to Hildebrand-Burke and glared. "Especially not with that superior, condescending tone. Is that plain enough, or you want me to write it down in crayon for you?"

Rathdowne shook his head and motioned for Atticus to take a seat. "I think you've made your point, thank you."

For once Atticus was pleased to wield such bluntness. It enabled him to hide the fact that he hadn't achieved anything. His hunt for the mole had turned up little of substance, let alone anything that pointed to the perpetrator. Granted, they'd only just started, but it stung. Henry deserved better. The more that time wore on, the more despondent Atticus became. And the further he traversed that darkened path of thought, the gloomier it all seemed.

As Atticus took his seat, Rathdowne went on. "In the short history of this organisation we have never faced a crisis such as this. Not wanting to put too fine a point on it, but this must be your first and foremost priority. Your careers, and the lives of every fellow in MI6, rest in your hands. The Prime Minister was already after our hides after the Philby, Maclean and Burgess debacles; this has put all our heads well and truly on the chopping block. It didn't help that we were blindsided by the American mess, then Jayne. But the death of poor unfortunate Henry Morton has brought us well and truly under the microscope. Make no mistake, gentlemen, the future of our organisation is at stake. We must find this mole and we must do so very, very quickly. Do I make myself clear?"

Atticus could feel the heat of a thousand eyes boring

into him. Rathdowne had essentially said the future of MI6 rested on his shoulders. No pressure, then.

If he failed in his task, would he be responsible for the destruction of his beloved organisation? It seemed increasingly likely, and the worst thing was, Atticus had no idea how to prevent it.

"THE FUNERAL WILL BE TUESDAY."

Oliver's statement was met with sombre vacant stares from Atticus and Maggie. It was late in an emotionally tumultuous day. The minimal grey light that shone through the tiny window had faded into darkness. They were all exhausted, and should have been home, but they stayed because leaving would have meant a delay in finding Henry's murderer. They stayed because they had nowhere else to be.

Atticus was hunched over, elbows on his knees, contemplating the floor. Maggie paced nervously in the small confines of their tiny office. Receiving no reply to his statement, Oliver slumped onto the hard wooden chair in the corner. With nothing to say, all three went back to their collective brooding.

Atticus studied Maggie's pretty and despondent face as she prowled the room. He had chosen to say nothing of his almost-encounter with her and her friends the previous evening. How could he? Confessing stalker traits rarely ingratiated oneself to another.

As he was about to pick something random to break the uncomfortable silence, Maggie beat him to it. She sat on the other side of the table and looked him in the eye. "Susan Palinosky."

"I'm sorry?"

Maggie pointed to the letters found in Jayne's flat. "The woman who wrote these. One had a return name and address." She shrugged. "You two were gallivanting about with all the important manly meetings, I thought I'd make myself useful."

"We should give her a call."

"I did. She wasn't very talkative."

"Why not?"

"Because she's dead."

Her delivery was deadpan, there was none of her customary snark. The subject of death was too close to home to make light of now.

Atticus scratched his head. "It would make for a one-sided conversation."

"Henry would have been disappointed, he quite liked her racy prose." Oliver seemed surprised he'd spoken. "Sorry, that was insensitive."

"No, it wasn't." Maggie reached over and sympathetically rubbed his shoulder. "Henry would have appreciated it, so it's okay, I think." She absentmindedly flipped through the letters on the table before her. "I spoke to her parents. They didn't know who Jayne was, said their daughter never had a boyfriend. I think it's safe to assume their affair, or at the very least, their correspondence, was a secret. The letters were only a year or so old, and she died six months ago. Horse-riding accident at a friend's estate."

In the absence of anything else to do, Oliver and Atticus exchanged shrugs. It seemed the letters were unrelated to their investigation, a keepsake of a relationship that was no more. Mere sentimentality, rather than a piece of critical geopolitical spy craft.

"Maggie, are you alright?" Atticus wanted to reach out

and touch her hand, but knew it would be inappropriate in any time period.

In response, she folded her arms. "I'm perfectly fine, thank you, Mr Wolfe."

Mr Wolfe.

It was a substantial change from the merriment of their shopping spree the day before. The fun they'd had darting in and out of shops on Carnaby Street, their fits of laughter and their adventures seemed a million years ago. It was even a marked difference from the sad smile he'd received when he arrived that morning. Even the arbitrary distance of grief wouldn't explain her sudden cooling. Henry's death was horrific and had taken its toll on them all, but this seemed different, aimed at Atticus in particular. It wasn't exactly the cold shoulder, but it certainly wasn't warm. Perhaps tepid was the best temperature gauge. She was definitely giving him the tepid shoulder.

Something else had changed. Henry's death, obviously, but would that affect their fledgling friendship? Her interactions with him were perfunctory and decorous.

In search of an answer, Atticus turned to Oliver, who shrugged and gave him a *damned if I know* look. He seemed to find Maggie's mood towards Atticus out of place as well. Instead of mourning as a team, united in their grief, Maggie had singled him out. Did she blame him for Henry's death? She wouldn't be the only one. Atticus did too, but for different reasons. And even that it were the case, it still didn't explain her sudden vanishing act the day before.

Before Atticus could pull his various strains of thought together, Maggie moved the letters aside and rummaged around in the small cardboard box. Extracting the two leather chequebooks, she plopped them on the table. "The fake chequebook is the real one."

"What's that?" Oliver seemed thankful for something else to talk about.

"The hidden one, the one without the bookie debts, that's the real chequebook."

"When... how?"

A genuine smile crossed her lips for the first time. "Like I said, you two were off having your meeting, I needed distraction. I needed to do... something." She motioned to the two practically identical chequebooks.

"I went to visit the various businesses, slipped into the accent of the old neighbourhood and told them I was working for the Kray twins."

"You what?" Oliver seemed half aghast and half impressed at her audacity.

Maggie gave her best innocent shrug. "Nobody wants to be put down as messing with Ronnie and Reggie. It's amazing how quickly a shopkeeper decides to help after I drop their names. What was it Roosevelt said? Speak softly and carry a big stick and you'll go far. Well, I went as far as Romford. The amounts and dates matched the cheques. At least, they did in this one." She lifted the one that had been hidden. Henry had marked it with a white dot to ensure the two weren't mixed up. "By the fifth stub I had my shit down. It's amazing how cooperative people are when they think the boys will be paying them a visit." She gave an amused shrug.

Maggie went on to explain that the entries in the hidden book matched day-to-day transactions. Groceries, car repairs, dry-cleaning and the like. The various businesses confirmed the payments. A couple of businesses hadn't cashed the cheques yet, so she was able to verify the cheque numbers, not just the amounts. The now-apparently-fake book had the same dates and values, but the cheque numbers didn't match. Furthermore, the additional entries, which appeared to be payments of gambling debts, were to bookies who didn't seem to exist.

"My uncle's a... let's say he persuades individuals to honour their debts if they like functioning and unbroken appendages. He told me he'd never heard of any of these blokes. Uncle Lenny's been working this business for thirty years; he knows anyone who's anyone. He's sure there's no one by these names working within five hundred miles of London." She seemed buoyed by Oliver and Atticus's rapt attention. "Cheques from this one," she held up the unmarked book, "are as fake as Uncle Lenny's *authentic* Rolexes."

The only logical explanation for the fake chequebook was that it had been left there deliberately. But to what end? Fake gambling debts? Why would a spy need fake gambling debts?

Oliver shook his head. "What does it all mean?"

No one had an answer. A theory began to develop in the back of Atticus's mind, but it wasn't fully formed yet. The three descended into quietness once more. Atticus's thoughts turned to Henry's face in the elevator. The silence was as ominous as it was claustrophobic.

Rathdowne entered the room, shattering the sombre mood, although in less of a flurry than his usual agitated pace. For once he seemed to read the room, and matched their solemn dispositions.

"I'm sorry for Henry's passing. We may not have seen eye to eye, but the lad was a good egg."

They waited for more, but there was none. That was apparently the sum total of the heartfelt condolence Rathdowne had to offer.

Atticus stepped in before the gap in conversation

became uncomfortable for all. "What's the protocol for MI6 funerals? Is there some sort of security concern with everyone being in the one place?"

"That won't really be your concern, Wolfe."

Gripped by trepidation, Atticus reluctantly asked, "Why's that?"

"You won't be there."

Am I being fired? Before Atticus could verbalise his shock, Rathdowne went on.

"None of you will." He gestured to the equally surprised Oliver and Maggie.

"I don't understand."

"In four hours' time you'll all be on a flight to Germany. Orders from upstairs." Rathdowne's face was as serious as Atticus had ever seen it. He took three plane tickets from his breast pocket. "The Berlin station just received a dead drop to one of our fronts." No one dared make a sound. He went on, aware of their rapt attention. "It's from Jayne. He needs extraction, but he's alive."

"Or someone claiming to be Jayne." No matter the time period, Atticus exercised caution when it came to espionage.

"Exactly." Rathdowne waggled his finger in agreement. "Although the code checks out. Also, the flag codeword wasn't used, so he's apparently not compromised."

Oliver frowned, coming up to speed on the sudden change in events. "Even so, still smells fishy. It's likely a trap."

Rathdowne scowled. "I wouldn't say likely."

"What would you say?"

"Probable?"

Maggie folded her arms. "Oh, that's well different."

"You're sending us into an ambush?" Atticus was

reminded once more of the possibility that Rathdowne was setting them up for failure.

"I'm sending you in as the second team, for if or when Jayne shows up. It's bloody dubious you'll be fighting off the Stasi hand to hand."

"But you're not ruling it out."

Their boss shrugged. "I'm also not ruling out Turkish-wresting Khrushchev while Chairman Mao plays *O Come All Ye Faithful* on a banjo."

All three stared at him, stunned.

"Did you—did you just make a joke, Rathdowne?"

He held up a palm. "It happens."

Atticus gave a slight shake of his head. "Not in my experience."

Maggie slowly shook her head. "Mine either."

Oliver scratched his chin. "I recall there was something about a vicar and a fish pie at last year's Christmas party."

That seemed to quell the conversation for the moment. Each of them drifted off into their own thoughts. Atticus stared at the plane tickets. Jayne was alive and in West Berlin. Now all they had to do was get to him.

FOURTEEN

"The sky's blue."

Flashes of vivid sky flitted between the tall stone buildings as the BMW sedan sped through the early morning streets of West Berlin.

"What?"

"The sky. It's blue," Maggie continued, gazing up. "In all the movies, Berlin is always grey, overcast, depressing. This is... you know, like normal."

"I'm pretty sure weather patterns don't stop at the Iron Curtain." Atticus's amused tone was aimed at reviving the group after an arduous journey. "I've seen Saint Petersburg and I can assure you they have clear blue skies like everyone else."

"You mean Leningrad?" Maggie turned to him and scowled. "You've been there?"

He had, several times. Once as a tourist, twice on MI6 business. Covering his tracks, Atticus replied casually, "On film, I mean. Standard intelligence work for the Navy. After all, that's where their naval headquarters is." Atticus hoped that was true. In the twenty-first century it was, but he wasn't so sure where the Soviet Navy called home in this time period.

The response seemed to satisfy Maggie. "It's prettier than I thought, too. Look at that flower market, glorious. Don't you think it's a glorious city, Oliver?"

In the front seat with his arms folded, Oliver grunted. "I suppose."

"Why are you so grumpy?" She leaned forward and poked his arm. "You've been complaining forever about wanting to spread your wings with some real field work. How many lunches have you spent banging on about being on the front line? Well, here you are in Berlin." she splayed her hands and motioned out the window for effect. "You couldn't get more front line than this. There're spies everywhere." She pointed to the street. "That guy's probably a spy. Or that old lady. Oooh, the dachshund, he's right shifty." She leaned forward. "So why are you acting like someone poured sauerkraut down your long johns?"

Staring blankly at the windscreen, arms folded, Oliver sighed. "I'm not sure, why don't you ask my three aunts who got marched off to the showers and never came back? I'm sure they'd have no issue with me popping over to Germany for a lark." He turned to Maggie sharply, his expression even more aghast than hers. "Oh, my lord, that was utterly uncalled for. I'm a heel."

"It's... it's fine, really. *I'm* sorry, I didn't even think." Maggie slumped back in her seat. "I should have..."

"Tosh," he interrupted with a wave of his hand. "I'm an insensitive twat who should learn to think before he opens his trap. I'm terribly sorry, love."

In reply, Maggie screwed up her nose, rolled her eyes and shook her head. It translated to, *don't be silly*. Tensions eased, they returned to watching the streets once more.

In retrospect, Atticus shouldn't have been surprised at Oliver's outburst. After Henry's passing and the lack of sleep, they were all on edge. If it hadn't been Henry, it could quite easily have been any of them. If they were wound any tighter they'd snap. The little group had been through so much in such a short period of time.

Maggie gazed out the window wistfully. "It's like they're just getting on with their lives, as if ten thousand tanks weren't encircling their tiny little city. Are they mad or ignorant?"

"They're just people." Oliver didn't take his eyes off the street. "No different to everyone else. They just want to live their lives. Watch TV, shop, get drunk, screw."

"Oliver!" Maggie exclaimed in mock offence. "I'm shocked you could use such language in front of a lady."

"Oh, I'm sorry," he turned to Maggie with a grin, "I wasn't aware we'd stopped to pick one up."

The Royal Marine driver beside Oliver did his best to stifle a chuckle. Maggie playfully hit Oliver on the shoulder. The moment of levity was a welcome one. On top of their loss and lack of sleep, the uncomfortable flight to Berlin certainly hadn't helped their mood.

After a delay, the BOAC DC-7 had arrived on the cold windy tarmac after midnight. The freezing passengers filed in one by one. Maggie had made a point of taking the single seat on the opposite side of the aisle, forcing Oliver and Atticus to sit together. She was asleep before wheels up. Oliver and Atticus soon followed suit.

Atticus awoke somewhere over the Netherlands, a frightening thought interrupting his much-needed sleep. What if they weren't headed towards answers, but away from them? What if Rathdowne, or whoever wanted them off the scent, had orchestrated a distraction from the real goings on? It seemed overly convoluted if it were true. Regardless, Atticus couldn't sleep after that. Mind whirling, his thoughts were jumbled.

Back in the car he glanced up at the blue sky and asked himself why he was so invested in the mission. To a man of his time, this was all history. The mainly silent battles of the Cold War had been fought well before he was born. He didn't even remember the Berlin Wall falling, although his grandmother swore she'd sat Atticus in front of the TV, telling him how momentous it was.

Was he taking the mission so seriously because it was his natural default to do so? If given a task he had to drive hard to see it through, and damn the consequences. Or was it, as he highly suspected, more personal? The vision of Henry's face haunted him. He was plagued not only by the loss of his friend, but also by the irrefutable fact that it was Atticus's presence in this timeline that had caused his demise in the first place.

In the back of the car, Atticus flipped through the briefing papers for the fourth time.

At 13:23, East Berlin time, a chalk mark had been detected on a mailbox across the road from Glänzend Putzerei dry cleaners. An MI6 front. The mark was an infinity symbol with a horizontal line beneath; Jayne's signal. On seeing the mark, the owner immediately shut up shop and made his way to Städtischer Friedhof, a graveyard in nearby Lichtenberg. At a designated plot in a quiet corner of the park-like cemetery, the dry cleaner/MI6 operative picked up a seemingly discarded camera film canister. Inside was a piece of paper containing a series of letters and numbers, code; more precisely, Jayne's code. Taking it back to his shop, he decoded the short message. It simply read: *Mission compromised. Captured by Stasi, escaped. Extraction required.* He then gave a location and a time. It was hours from now.

The three of them were on their way to wait for the extraction team, who would escort Jayne across the treacherous border from East to West Berlin. Escape across the Berlin Wall was always hazardous. Since the Wall's brutal construction in 1961, many had died trying.

The plan, such as it was, wasn't the best strategy Atticus had ever heard. Three men, posing as Canadian Army officers, would enter East Germany via Checkpoint Charlie, the main entrance point for foreigners. It was the location where only two years previously, American and Soviet tanks had faced each other, threatening to ignite World War Three. Since that tense standoff it had been tacitly recognised that Allied officials and military personnel would have unimpeded access to the East German capital.

It was common for military and diplomats to cross the border to attend cultural events, operas and museums. The cover story was that the three men would attend an art exhibition on the Eastern side of the wall. One of the men would spend the morning taking pictures of the modern art installations in case they were stopped and interrogated later. The other two would meet Jayne at the designated rendezvous point. One would swap identities with Jayne and cross the border later that night under another name at a different checkpoint. Three men, now including Jayne, would cross the gate in a Canadian consulate vehicle at approximately 5 pm, rush hour at the checkpoint, in the hope they'd be missed in the crush.

Atticus checked his watch. Just past 8 am. It would be a long day.

The plan depended almost entirely on the scrutiny, or

lack thereof, of the East German border guards. Atticus's keen spy experience told him it was reckless and impulsive. The plan was fraught with too many uncontrollable elements. He understood the need to extract their man immediately, rather than hide him from elements who had captured him once already, but this was foolhardy at best.

The man had escaped the Stasi, surely they would be on the lookout for him at all border crossings, especially in Berlin. If this were Atticus's operation, he would have found another crossing, preferably in another country, where they wouldn't be expecting it. If Jayne had escaped as he'd claimed, then the authorities would be on high alert.

That was another complication to throw into the mix. *As he'd claimed.* Jayne had been compromised awfully quickly on arrival in East Berlin. It had never quite added up. Any self-respecting spy agency would have observed a known foreign agent on their turf to garner any additional intelligence, rather than kidnapping them virtually on arrival. Or, alternatively, refuse his entry from the outset and avoid a confrontation altogether. Then there was what they'd discovered in the man's flat. The multiple cheque-books and the seemingly fake bookie entries. Then there were the Cockney thugs. Where did they fit into events unfolding six hundred miles away?

The BMW rolled to a stop outside the Berlin Hilton. It was a checkerboard twelve-storey hotel with a well-mani-cured, if somewhat quaint, garden out the front. It seemed modern compared to the scant remaining buildings of old Berlin, and in stark contrast to the numerous vacant lots still dotting the city, no doubt empty since the war. The passenger side door was opened by a sharp-suited young man who clicked his heels with German efficiency.

Within half an hour they'd checked in, dropped off their

bags and assembled in the near-deserted hotel restaurant to meet their contact. The freshly painted surrounds seemed both curiously antiquated and contemporary. Retro fifties modern was an apt title, if a somewhat confounding one.

A man entered on the far side of the room, noticed their presence and marched towards them. Marched was an apt word. He wore his suit like a military uniform. The walrus moustache added to the overall impression. He seemed to have come directly from a Boer War battlefield.

Quick introductions were made. Captain Montgomery was Head Security Officer for Berlin. He shook Oliver's hand first, then with reluctance he accepted Atticus's. He ignored Maggie entirely, while she stood her ground defiantly.

Finally acknowledging her existence, he harrumphed. "If these uncultured swine have Earl Grey get me one of those. No sugar, no milk. No airs and graces, me. There's a good girlie."

Atticus had never seen Oliver move so fast. He stepped in between Montgomery and the rapidly reddening Maggie, who was in the process of balling her fists. "They'll come and take your order, sir, but Maggie here is from Signals and part of our team."

Montgomery frowned while scanning Maggie slowly enough that it aired on the side on lecherous. He sat with military precision. The frown remained.

"I assure you, sir, she's a vital and effective part of our little squad." Oliver's tone had a ring of desperation. "She speaks fluent Russian and German."

"And Mod," Atticus added under his breath.

That earned a grin from Maggie, whose shoulders eased. She sat and folded her arms. If the daggers she shot

Montgomery were real he'd be sliced into a thousand pieces.

Clicking his fingers at a passing waiter, Montgomery asked, "What's a Mod?"

The trio ignored the question and ordered beverages. Even without Montgomery's outburst, the mood around the table would have been tense. And it wasn't solely about Jayne's extraction.

"You spotted us quickly." Oliver's tone was chipper. He seemed eager to keep the peace.

"Right-o. Not many..." he gazed sideways at Atticus, "... fellows like him in Germany, with, er, your swarthy complexion, what?" He seemed quite pleased with himself for being so PC. "Wasn't difficult at all."

Atticus was ready to help Maggie wring his neck. Oliver glared at him wide eyed, as if saying, *I know, but please don't murder him*. What really eased the tension was when Maggie reached across the table and touched Atticus's hand. That was all, a mere touch, and all his anger dissipated. She gave him a tiny sympathetic smile. It was one of the few signs of their friendship since Carnaby Street. He was again confounded by her wildly inconsistent attitude towards him, but the thought soon passed. There were more pressing matters.

It was going to be a long wait until after 5 pm. A hundred things could go wrong. None of them they had any control over any of them. The impotency was not lost on Atticus. He was used to running the operation, not waiting patiently while others put their lives at risk and hoping for the best. Their drinks arrived and Atticus stirred in sugar as he ground his teeth.

"Careful, you'll break it." Oliver pointed at Atticus's

coffee. "The spoon, looks like you're about to snap it in two."

"I'm practising to be the next Uri Geller."

"The who now?"

Not wanting to explain the spoon-bending crackpot from the seventies, Atticus moved on. "When do we get to speak to Jayne?"

"All in good time." Montgomery sipped his tea loudly, and despite being a man with apparently no airs or graces, he stuck out his pinkie as he did so. "The Station Chief will want a debrief after my initial one, of course. Then his handler. He'll need to rest up, recover. Could be a few days."

All three newcomers exchanged horrified looks. They'd raced across the continent in the wake of the loss of one of their own only to be told there was no hurry at all. Atticus was ready to break more than spoons.

On seeing the frustration on Atticus's face, Montgomery leaned forward with a condescending air. "No use getting all hot and bothered, my good man. There are protocols to these things. Procedures to follow, etiquette. I'm sure you understand."

"People are dying." The weight of his own words hit Atticus hard. He forged on. "We don't have time for protocols, let alone fucking etiquette." He ignored the squirming Oliver to his left. "The organisation, *your* organisation is on the brink of collapse, rotting from the inside. There's no time for what is *usually* done, the proper thing. We need to talk to him as soon as he's over the wall. Lives could depend on it."

Montgomery appeared unmoved by the words. "I'll see what I can do."

Bureaucracy 101. *I'll see what I can do* always translated to the exact same outcome: nothing. Bristling at the brush-off, Atticus realised there was little he could do about it right now. They had a long wait before Jayne emerged; that is, if he managed to make it across at all.

The assembled MI6 team disinterestedly pushed food around their plates. Oliver, Maggie and Atticus drank coffee to shake off their collective fatigue. Montgomery did little to keep them energised.

"Any of you military men?" The question was aimed at Oliver, and even then, only half-heartedly.

Atticus had done two tours of Afghanistan, but thought it best to keep that to himself. More out of boredom than anything, he replied, "I am."

"Oh, really?" Montgomery straightened his back ever so slightly. "Which branch?"

"Navy."

His face crumpled into a scowl. "Oh, I'm terribly sorry to hear it."

Rubbing his eyes from exhaustion, Atticus wondered if there was time for a nap. If it was going to be a long day, he'd need to be alert. His yawn didn't bode well. He definitely needed rack time before the extraction.

Before Montgomery could express more disappointment, he was interrupted by muffled words coming from the tinny cloth-covered loudspeaker. The words were interspersed with static; Atticus had to strain to hear. Oddly, it was all in English. "... Doctor Quaid to emergency, Doctor Quaid... Trauma call, room fifteen..."

Atticus stood up so suddenly that everyone else at the table recoiled. "Did you hear that?"

Their blank stares told him they hadn't.

"Some bugger has a telephone call?" Montgomery smoothed out his moustache. "I don't see how..."

Not waiting for him to finish, Atticus bolted for reception, startling guests as he sprinted across the vast room. Within seconds he'd reached the desk. The prim middle-aged woman behind the reception desk flinched slightly, but kept her cool.

"Kann ich Ihnen helfen?"

"Do you speak English?"

"Of course, sir. How may I help you?"

"The loudspeaker... there was..." Atticus gathered himself to prevent him sounding mad. "There was something over the speakers, like announcements in a hospital?"

Ruffled, but retaining her composure, she replied, "There is a call for a Mr Nathan Farrugia, sir. I can transfer you to booth number two to your right if you would—"

"There was something about a doctor, and, uh..." Atticus's resolve was fading. Had he imagined the whole thing?

"I'm sorry, sir, the name is Farrugia. *Mister*, not a doctor."

Atticus blinked several times. There were only three possibilities. One: someone was playing games with him. Two: he was so tired he was hearing things. The final alternative seemed the most likely: he was going crazy.

He grimaced apologetically to the receptionist and left without a word. Trudging back to the table, he did his best to dismiss the mounting feeling of helplessness. *What the hell is going on?* He shook his head. Now wasn't the time for distractions. He needed all his wits about him. Jayne was the priority. All his concentration had to be focused on the mission.

If only it were that simple.

ATTICUS IMMEDIATELY KNEW something was wrong.

He'd seen enough operations go south to know the mission had gone awry practically instantly. Sitting by the window in a stuffy room above Cafe Adler watching events unfold via binoculars, Atticus instinctively wanted to call the TOC team to abort the mission. But there was no TOC. There was no team. No one to call. All he could do was watch powerlessly as events unfolded.

Seventy metres away, Checkpoint Charlie managed the trudging flow of citizenry, government officials and military personnel between either side of the Iron Curtain. Tensions were already at breaking point in the wake of the Kennedy assassination. Half the Western world expected an attack from the Soviets. No one knew who was really behind the assassination attempt. Oswald was dead, the Warren Commission report was a year away. A week after the assassination tensions were still high, distrust and hysteria even higher.

In his time, the real Checkpoint Charlie had been torn down and a replica built down the road for tourists, next to a McDonald's. It was quite apparent from the faces of those nearby that the leisurely sightseeing days of the future were the last thing on anyone's mind.

For an hour, Atticus had watched the tense faces on either side of the checkpoint eye one another off, expecting the worst. Then there he was. As soon as Atticus spotted Jayne in the flesh, he knew the operation was blown.

It was the eyes that gave it away. Magnified by the binoculars, intimately close, Atticus saw fear in Jayne's eyes. No, fear was the wrong word—panic. It was more than the dread of having to pass through the checkpoint. His constant backwards glances only reinforced that something was drastically amiss.

First of all, he was on foot. No sign of the Canadian

consulate car the three agents were supposed to come back in. Instead of the two agents accompanying him, there was only one, and he appeared white as a sheet. The two joined the crowd, conspicuous amongst a sea of bored faces, their angst clearly apparent. Unable to stand by himself, Jayne held the other man upright as he coughed and spluttered, clutching his side. If Atticus were to hazard a guess, he'd say the man had been shot or stabbed in the side.

Instinctively, Atticus stood, wanting to sprint towards the men and help them across. It would have been suicide. Between him and Jayne were forty metres of machinegun nests, barbed wire and soldiers with itchy trigger fingers. No, Atticus had to watch helplessly as events glacially unfolded.

"Oh shit." Maggie wasn't watching the street below, her eyes were on Atticus. "This is bad, isn't it?"

Oliver had been unable to squeeze into a vantage point so absentmindedly flipped through magazines on the other side of the room. Like Atticus, he was now on his feet, although he didn't know why. Atticus quickly explained the situation without taking his eyes off Jayne.

"Oh," Oliver strained, trying to see out the small window, "as Maggie so eloquently put it, shit."

Without the extra authority the consular vehicle afforded, the two men would face extra scrutiny from the border guards. It was the last thing they needed while smuggling an injured man through to the West. Atticus was sure they'd fail.

As the painful minutes ticked by, the crowd of citizens and officials slowly proceeded through the checkpoint. As they moved closer to the front of the line, Jayne's offsider grew more and more pallid. At one point Atticus was sure he'd pass out. There was no way this would work.

It seemed Jayne's companion agreed. Without warning, he staggered away from Jayne, into another man in the line, shoving him hard. The man, who had a thick neck and a face like a slab of concrete, pushed back. Hard. It must have cost him every ounce of strength he had left, but Jayne's companion took a swing, which landed on the other man's jaw with enough force that he staggered back a few steps. His surprise didn't last long, and then it was on. The crowd made way for the impromptu title fight. The melee attracted the attention of the East German soldiers, too, who unslung their rifles and bellowed orders.

To his credit, Jayne acted professionally. He knew what his companion had done for him and repaid him in the only way a career spy could. He got on with the mission. At the front of the line he handed over his papers to a distracted guard, who was peering over Jayne's shoulder at the fracas. He stamped the paper and waved Jayne on.

The spy strode forward, head high, not glancing back. Atticus held his breath as he crossed no-man's land between the two fragments of the same city. That wasn't the act of a coward; it was the act of a professional performing his duty. He would ensure his companion's sacrifice was not in vain. Jayne getting across the border was the mission; he was going to make damn sure he made it.

In the crowd, a woman screamed. They'd discovered Jayne's companion's injury. Perhaps they'd assumed the worker had inflicted it in the fight. Whatever the guards thought, it earned Jayne enough time to make it across to the American side, where he was waved through. Montgomery met him with a curt nod and he was ushered into a town car and whisked away.

On the other side of the checkpoint, the other spy was

engulfed in a sea of uniforms. Jayne's companion soon disappeared from view, roughly dragged away by guards, as was the burly worker, still swinging haymakers.

As he raced down the back stairs to the waiting car, Atticus had no time to contemplate their fate. He had a more pressing mission. He had to talk to Jayne and find out what the hell was going on. More importantly, he had to find out who killed Henry and deviated the timeline, so Atticus could make it right once more.

As he burst into the back lane with Maggie and Oliver close behind, Atticus knew it wouldn't be that straight-forward.

Unfortunately, once again, he was right.

"ABSOLUTELY OUT OF THE QUESTION!" Montgomery stood in the front yard of the MI6 safe house, hands on his hips, moustache positively bristling with indignation. "No, I won't stand for it. Not on my watch. Under no circum-stances."

Atticus tilted his head. "So that's a maybe, then?"

Behind him, Maggie sniggered. Montgomery, however, turned beetroot red. As he was about to launch into a tirade, another member of MI6 came through the front door, diverting his attention. The two had a hushed conver-sation by the front entrance.

The villa was deep in the Grunewald Forest, an untamed woodland on the outskirts of Berlin. In Atticus's opinion it was a good place for the thatched-roofed safe-house. The surrounding woodland meant there were no neighbours, and the grassy areas surrounding the safe-house meant no one could sneak up unseen. The straight leafy driveway afforded an ample vista to observe approaching vehicles. There was a highway nearby, should a fast getaway be required. It was almost ideal, except for one minor point: none of the group were allowed inside.

They'd arrived knowing it would take several days before Montgomery would permit them to see Jayne. Finding that arrangement untenable, their little coterie turned up anyway. That move had the Head of Security brimming with ire and well on his way to infuriation.

After a brief chat with his offsider, Montgomery marched over in a huff. "You're still here?"

"Sir," Oliver started, "with all due respect—"

"In my experience," Montgomery interrupted, "the phrase 'with all due respect' is usually followed by a statement affording the exact opposite."

Oliver's jaw clenched. "With all due respect, we've come an exceedingly long way and we are on a mission to prevent even more deaths, sanctioned, I might add, by the Chief himself. This comes from the very top. I apologise if you deem it impertinent, but time is of the essence."

"Is it now?" Montgomery's features softened somewhat. "Well, protocol is of the essence to me. Last I heard, I was Head Security Officer at the Berlin Station, and not the Chief, nor the Foreign Secretary, nor even the almighty Royal Highness herself can tell me how to run my operation. We've already lost men on this mission. Our man from yesterday has disappeared off the map. There is absolutely no time for cock-ups. Everything will be done by the book from here on. That includes you lot, whether you like it or not." He huffed, as if punctuating his own words. "The three men inside is all I need. This is not a house party, a free-for-all with everyone doing the Twist or whatever the hell kids are doing nowadays. I will conduct this debrief as I see fit, and I certainly don't need you lot crowding up the place. I have well-established and effective methodologies that are incompatible with a lot of scruffy young 'uns breathing down my neck. I will state for the very last time, unequivocally, as it seems this has been difficult for you to grasp: you will be notified when I am good and ready. If I see any of you before such time, I will quite happily pack the lot of you off to London before you can say insubordination." He tugged the base of his vest. "Now, bugger off or I'll call the Chief myself and have you shipped off to the Australian desert to count grains of uranium before the week is out. Do I make myself clear?"

Clear it was. There was no use arguing with the man. He'd dug his heels in and no amount of rational discourse would dissuade him. Without another word, all three trudged towards the Mercedes Benz 220se parked halfway up the gravel drive. They sat in the car, deflated and silent, for several minutes, alone in their own thoughts.

Atticus's mind was busy generating possible approaches, each of which he instantly dismissed. It seemed like they'd not only burnt their bridges with Montgomery, but also blown them up for good measure. Atticus had to find a way, any way, to get to Jayne sooner. After ten minutes he had nothing but a headache.

Rubbing his eyes, he stared absentmindedly at the dark woodland. Berliners, especially Berliners of this time, loved their forests. Grunewald in particular, with its lakes, played an important role for all those trapped behind the Berlin Wall. Citizens of West Berlin no longer had access to the countryside surrounding the city, unless they particularly enjoyed tank shells entering their person. The forests were the only patches of accessible "nature" that didn't involve a plane ride or border controls. The dark foreboding woodland seemed like it had lain untouched for centuries. Atticus could imagine Goethe sitting amidst the chaotic forest, penning a poem of nihilistic romanticism.

As he idly scanned the trees, something caught his eye. It had only been a fraction of a second, but he'd definitely seen it. Low near the base of a mossy oak tree was a hunched shadow. He likely would have ignored the form if not for a flash of light. The kind you might see reflected from a camera lens. Or a sniper's scope. It had been aimed at them.

"Everyone needs to casually get out of the car."

"But Montgomery said—"

"We're not alone." Before it sunk in, Atticus quickly added, "Don't look around. Don't arouse suspicion. Keep up the bored expressions. Pretend to make tired small talk as we make our way back up the drive. We have to let them know."

"Know what?"

"We have company."

"Maybe they're his men?"

Atticus casually swept his gaze across the forest. *There you are.* "Remember, he mentioned there were only three of them. Montgomery's keeping the numbers low to minimise leaks. There's no one patrolling the grounds. Plus, I don't think they'd be lying in a forest. Montgomery's operation has been made. We need to tell them they've got company."

Atticus exited the car and casually put his arms above his head, as if he needed the stretch. The other two took his lead and moved casually, as if they were in no rush at all. At a meandering pace, they made their way towards the cottage.

At the garden near the villa, Atticus turned to Oliver.

"Stay here, have a cigarette. Don't look towards the woods, only from the corner of your eye, okay?"

"I... I don't have any. Cigarettes, that is."

"Here you go." Maggie handed him a silver case and a lighter, amusement dancing on her features. "Try not to cough up a lung."

"I can't promise anything." His hands shook as he brought a cigarette to his white lips.

Maggie and Atticus trudged up the remainder of the gravel drive.

"You okay?"

"I'm fine." It was an obvious lie. She was rattled, but doing her best to conceal it.

He let it slide. There was no use talking about it; there was little they could do but get on with it. Maggie or Oliver couldn't sit this one out. They were all in the centre of it now.

As they neared the villa, Montgomery stormed out the front door. He skidded to a halt a few feet away from Atticus, his face fiery red and furious.

"You again?" Montgomery furrowed his brow in frustration. "I thought I bloody told you to—"

He never finished the sentence.

Before Montgomery could utter another syllable a bullet entered his left eye socket and exploded out the back of his head. The man seemed to hover in mid-air, as if his body didn't quite believe it had been shot and stubbornly refused to fall.

Maggie screamed. Before the body collapsed, Atticus thrust his hand into the man's jacket, extracting his Webley Revolver, and grabbed the dead man's lapels.

"Get down!"

Maggie did exactly that as Atticus swivelled the dead

weight of Montgomery's body and hefted his sizeable mass onto his shoulder. It wasn't a noble act; Atticus needed a shield. He raised the dead man's weapon and stormed forward, scanning the trees for the target he'd spied moments before.

By the base of the oak, rifle raised, probably a Mauser bolt action, a man crouched on one knee. His second shot went wide. The third hit Montgomery in the back; a lethal blow, if he were still alive.

Breathing heavily and struggling to carry a dead weight and a weapon at the same time, Atticus awkwardly pressed on. He remembered his training. SASAS. Surprise, Aggression, Strength, Accuracy and Speed.

Struggling with half of those, Atticus zigzagged to infuriate his attacker. He skidded on the gravel when he halted his approach. The body slumped forward and Atticus grasped the sides of his jacket, preventing Montgomery from falling onto his back; he still needed cover. Using Montgomery's shoulder to steady his aim, Atticus fired three rapid bullets of his own. They were rushed, but the last two found their mark. The man fell face first into the dirt and didn't move.

Atticus stood, still aiming his revolver at the fallen man in the distance, and letting Montgomery slump to a final ignoble rest. Atticus scanned for other threats. Oliver scrambled up the drive and helped Maggie to her feet.

Flicking his thumb towards the house, Atticus spoke urgently. "In the house. I'll cover you."

"There's more, over on the right," Oliver's voice was high pitched. "They're running in our direction."

Putting his body between the new threats and his friends, Atticus ran with them. They left Montgomery where he lay. The man was dead, there was no use trying to recover the body now. The living were the priority if they were to stay that way.

Bursting through the front door, the bookish MI6 agent leapt to his feet in the front sitting room. "I say! Didn't Montgomery tell you lot to—"

"Montgomery's dead." That shut him up. Pulling the curtain aside, Atticus pointed out the window. "His assassin's dead over by the tree line. There's two running around in the woods fifty feet away. East side. Likely more nearby."

The man's lips flapped momentarily until his brain caught up. It was then he noticed the blood covering Atticus's shirt. In an instant he was all business. He advanced to an ornate bureau, extracted pistols and shotguns and handed them out to the newcomers. Atticus and Oliver checked the ammunition and cocked them. Maggie stared at the Remington in her hand in disbelief.

Another blond agent appeared from what Atticus assumed was the kitchen. He strode towards the telephone and lifted the receiver. After several seconds he slammed the handset down.

"The phone's out."

The two agents proceeded to close the curtains, shutting off the already dull afternoon light. The first man bounded towards the back door, ensuring it was locked. He came back and gave his compatriot a nod.

All five stared at one another. There was no doubting it: they were cut off and under siege.

CHAPTER
FIFTEEN

"They'll come after dark."

The remark by the blond agent, Brooker, cut through the silence that had floated heavily above them for several minutes. The other agent, Kent, was at the back door, nervously watching for any approach.

"Someone would have heard the shots and called the police, surely?" Maggie sat on the floor, her Remington pistol on the stool beside her. It hadn't been touched since it had been handed to her.

"Doubt it." Brooker's voice was calm, but there was an edge to it. "This forest is far from walking tracks or the lake. Plus, we're only a few miles from hunting lodges, where the local aristocrats hunt ducks pretty much all day long. Gunshots aren't exactly a rarity around here. Gave me the willies first few times, let me tell you."

His plastered-on smile did nothing to lift the sombre mood in the room. A veteran of MI6, he'd been stationed in Berlin for eight years. His offsider, five. They were experienced, war-hardened men. And they were scared. It was always the eyes that gave it away.

They were cut off, no communications, no backup. Their debrief of Jayne was to be conducted in secret, so no one knew which safehouse they'd use. No one would miss them for days. They didn't have days. They had hours at most.

Jayne was yet to appear. Brooker had gone to bring him out but after hearing the news of the siege he took that moment to have a shower. He'd advised Brooker that was when he had the most clarity of thought. Exactly what Jayne had to contemplate was unclear. The sound of running water had been going for ten minutes. The delay was infuriating. The reason they were all there seemed ominously absent from events of his making.

"Seems the men out there are very patient." Maggie turned to Atticus, fire in her eyes. "Just wondering, as you seem to know everything in advance, exactly what time are they going to bust in and shoot up the place. Do I have enough time for a tea or should I just lie down now to get it over with?"

Brooker turned to Atticus with a semi-amused eyebrow. He stretched. "I think I'll go check on Kent. He gets awfully lonely at times, you know."

Brooker slunk out of the room quietly, leaving the three of them alone. When Maggie turned away, Atticus gave Oliver a quizzical shrug. He returned the shrug and added a frown. *Buggered if I know.*

"Is there something on your mind, Maggie?" Atticus enquired as evenly as he could.

She turned to him and folded her arms. "No, why ever do you ask?"

"Well, if you think I know even remotely what's going on," Atticus pointed for effect, "out there, I think you do have something on your mind. Let's have it."

She squirmed, scrunching herself down as if trying to make herself smaller. This was a conversation she apparently didn't want to have, but the genie was out of the bottle now.

"Do you... do you know the men out there?" She seemed unsure of her words.

"No. Of course not." Atticus raised his palms inquisitively. "Did you miss the bit where we were being shot at? Or the part where I put a bullet in the gentleman's head?"

"I guess." She poked the carpet in front of her. "But you took out that man, who was armed with a rifle," she looked up; confusion creased her forehead, "with a pistol. That's hardly a thing they teach you in the Navy, now is it?"

She had him there. He was about to throw in a comment to steer the conversation away from this line of discussion, but Maggie cut him off. She gazed directly at him, her deep blue eyes unwavering. "You're not who you say you are, Atticus Wolfe."

He was speechless. Atticus knew there had been something on Maggie's mind for days, but he'd been expecting something else entirely. Instead, she seemed to have seen through him completely.

"What's that?" Atticus swallowed. "If I'm not me, who am I?" He kept his tone playful, hoping vainly he could make light of the situation.

Maggie's face remained porcelain still, not a flicker of merriment to be seen. "It seems a good place to start, I guess."

Start? This can't be good.

"Let's talk about that, shall we?" Animated, Maggie sat up, staring him down. "Your name. You said, and I remember this distinctly, that your mother chose it after reading *To Kill a Mockingbird*. That book came out three years ago. Either you're the most mature three-year-old in the history or you're full of it."

"That was a misunderstanding, I meant—"

"And what about before?" Cutting him off, her voice rose several octaves. "The way you shot that man," she pointed outside, "the way you moved. They don't teach you that on a boat. Or the bloke in Jayne's flat. You were bantering with him like you were doing a music hall act. You were cold and calculating, but most of all, it was all effortless for you. Like you'd done it a million times. It doesn't sit with Mr Naval Strategy guy. Nothing about you adds up. You're not who you say you are."

"Look," Oliver's voice nearly broke, "I think there's been some confusion, my dear. Atticus is—"

"Is a fraud. I know." Having started, she seemed unable to stop. "And then there's all this stuff you didn't even know. Basic stuff. Like how the Tube operates. I've seen children less confounded by a train station. Oh, and let's not forget you didn't even know how money worked. I've never seen a bloke so confused by shillings in my life." She waved a finger at him. "You wanted to call in satellites to find those Cockneys in the car, like, I don't know what. You didn't seem to know we don't have any satellites. Well, we had one but thanks to top British ingenuity it conked out. But the Soviets have plenty, don't they? Then you called the city Saint Petersburg, not Leningrad, told me you'd been there before, even." Her eyes narrowed. "It smells terribly Bolshy, if you ask me."

"Ah, I can explain all of that. Let's start at the top. My name—"

"Atticus." Oliver's voice was quiet, but forceful. "Tell her."

Atticus turned to him, aghast. "But..."

"She's too smart." He shook his head with a knowing grin. "She's already figured it out. We have to tell her."

Aghast, Atticus gave a slight shake of his head. "We can't."

"I'm frightfully sorry, old boy, but we don't have a choice." He pushed his glasses up. "She won't let this go, believe me. She'll make your life hell. When this woman knows she's right she can't let it go, ever. She'll hound you for the rest of your days. It is an undeniable and irrefutable fact."

"Tell me what?"

Both men stared at her blankly. *Where to start?*

"Maggie..." Atticus inhaled. "I'm... this is going to sound really dumb..." He closed his eyes and turned his face to the ceiling. "I still don't entirely believe it myself if I'm completely honest, but..." he took in a slow deep breath, "but I'm from the future. 2024, to be exact."

There was no reply. Atticus turned to Maggie, who stared at him, all expression eradicated from her face. She tilted her head, as if spinning the idea around in her mind. Atticus hoped she'd link the statement to her observations and find some tenuous link worthy of further exploration, and apply a robust scientific rigour to explore the possibility.

"Get fucked." Maggie pushed herself up. "Seriously. Both of you, get horse fucked." She stood and paced. "Do you expect me to believe... that's the dumbest piece of..." She turned to Oliver. "You're honestly going to back him up on this? He's a time traveller? *Really?*" Her arms flew up in disgust. "*That's* the best you came up with? Like the bloke from that inane kids' show that started the other night, *Doctor Who* or whatever it was? Stupid thing, if you ask me, won't last. Like you, Atticus Wolfe." She folded her arms. "If we survive the night, I'm walking into MI6 tomorrow and exposing you as the fraud you are."

"Maggie, dear, don't be——"

"Don't *dear* me, Oliver!" Her hands flailed. "This is beyond preposterous! A man from the future. With a brain like yours, that's what you went with? Hell, pretending he lost his memory after being hit in the head by a frypan is better than this." She shook her head. "I thought we were friends."

"Show her the watch."

Atticus sighed. He still wasn't sure, but nevertheless pulled back his sleeve.

"I've seen his stupidly large watch. Pretty, but pointless. Much like the man himself."

Ignoring the compliment, if that's what it was, Atticus pressed the button on the side of the watch to unlock it. Swiping the screen, the standard analogue watch face disappeared, replaced by icons for apps, most of which were useless without a network to connect to.

Maggie's face morphed from icy cold anger to intrigue. Her eyes darted to Oliver's in astonishment, and a flicker of possibility flashed across her face. Atticus swiped various screens across, searching for something, anything that would convince Maggie the device was not of this time. The screen alone seemed to have cracked her hard uncertainty, but he wanted to find something to force a definitive wedge, creating a gap wide enough to allow reality inside.

He chose a music playing app and selected the first song to appear. In seconds the annoying nineties earworm of *We Like to Party* filled the room. Maggie and Oliver stared at the device in awe. There was no room for a record on his wrist. No reel-to-reel tape. There was no current-day explanation for the annoyingly catchy and soulless Eurodance ditty filling their ears. He'd downloaded the song as an alarm to playfully annoy a co-worker months before and never got around to deleting it.

Atticus pressed stop. "That's why I mentioned the satellites when we wanted to catch those blokes, because where I come from, *when* I come from, they're ubiquitous. Everyone uses GPS, uh, global positioning systems, satellites, to navigate their cars, find shops, hell, you can track your pizza delivery." That last one garnered a surprised gasp from the other two. "I work for MI6... I did work for... I *will* work for MI6 in the future. We use satellites to track Tangos... the bad guys. Using devices like this, we can communicate with virtually anyone instantaneously, anywhere in the world."

Not taking her eyes off the watch, Maggie's lips were parted in wonder. "Fuck."

"Really, Maggie," Oliver tutted. "I don't think there's a need for that kind of language."

"What would you suggest?"

"Oh, I don't know, criminy?"

Atticus and Maggie glared at him incredulously.

Shaking her head slowly, Maggie blinked at Oliver. "No, I think I can honestly say that my current disposition can be encapsulated by the word fuck in a way criminy just doesn't seem to adequately capture." She turned to Atticus. "Can you... can you do video calls on it, like Dick Tracy?" Curiosity had replaced ire, but only by a small margin.

"You actually can, with the technology of my day— satellites and wi-fi. The world is a much different place, believe me."

"Tell me about it."

There was a breathless awe in her words, all traces of anger dissolved. She wasn't convinced though, not yet. She was far too intelligent for that, but she was listening. That alone was a breakthrough. Atticus carefully explained how he had been unceremoniously cast from his own time to this one. Well, as best he could without understanding exactly how it had happened himself.

"How is technology in the future? Is it like *The Jetsons*?" She kept her voice low, in case someone overheard their outlandish discussion.

"Well, kind of. Less flying cars, misogyny and robots, but there's a big reliance on computers, for sure."

"There's computers? People, regular people, have access to them?"

"Everyone carries one in their pocket."

Maggie blinked. "A computer... in your pocket?"

"My watch is one. I have a phone, a pocket computer in my flat, about the size of a pack of cards. It's a hundred thousand times more powerful than anything that will be developed this decade. We have access to every piece of human knowledge, and are able to communicate with anyone on the planet at any time."

Maggie's mouth opened in awe. "You must live in a time of marvels. Humankind must truly be better and enlightened in the future."

Atticus shrugged. "Not really, we just use computers to yell at strangers and send memes of goats."

Her face screwed up in confusion. "What's a meme?"

Atticus grinned. "Okay Boomer."

Maggie no longer regarded him with scorn. Her inquisitive nature, her intellect, meant she had to know more. If he succeeded, if in the end Maggie believed him, then he had to accept the unfortunate reality of the turnaround: his life, his continued freedom in this timeline had been secured, but not by his or Oliver's wily reasoned discourse. No, his fate had been saved by The Vengaboys.

AFTER AN HOUR, Kent and Brooker had established their patrols of the villa. They checked the perimeters to ensure all vantage points were covered, leaving the other three to their hushed but engrossed discourse. Even inside, the air had a chill to it; they could all feel the coldness of night encroaching. The dull sky hadn't shown signs of nightfall yet, but they could all feel it advancing on them like a predator. The stillness wouldn't last. They didn't have long.

There had been talk of sending a runner, or all of them leaving en masse, but those ideas were soon dismissed. There was nowhere nearby where safety was guaranteed, nor could they safely assume that the direction they chose to run to wouldn't be into the jaws of the enemy. They could just as easily get lost in the woods and later found by the enemy. They were in the unfortunate position where they had to wait for an attack, and defend their position as best they could.

The group had conducted a weapons inventory and their arms were meagre. They had five pistols, including the one Atticus had relieved from Montgomery, and two shotguns. It was hardly enough to ward off a legion of Spetsnaz shock troops. In all honesty, it was hardly enough to ward off a group of slightly annoyed girl scouts. On the plus side, they had some ammunition to replenish some of the weapons. Which sounded good in theory, but was rather pointless if no one was left alive to load it.

Silence descended on the house like fog. The inevitability of their fates cut down chatter. All but Atticus shared around cigarettes' he'd never been a smoker, and was likely to barf up a lung if he tried now. Even Oliver tentatively took a few shallow puffs. Without a word being uttered, the old adage smoke 'em if you got 'em was made manifest. Even in the twenty-first century, a soldier facing down a likely death appreciated the noxious fumes of a cigarette. Some things hadn't changed all that dramatically.

Putting his years as a tactical officer to use, Atticus roamed the house searching for architectural idiosyncrasies that could be used for some strategic advantage. Finding one near the fireplace, he explored the wooden trapdoor in the floor, where wood was stored. As Atticus crawled on his hands and knees in the dirt below the old villa, the first inklings of a plan began to formulate in his mind. Keeping the idea to himself until it was fully formed, he emerged and patted the grime from his knees.

On his return, Atticus noted that the mood had sagged even further. It was if the weight of the situation was crushing them all. There was no doubt they had little time left. Jayne had managed to make it through the wall but was about to be slain at his supposed safe haven. Maggie was the only one who seemed to have any spirit left. She bombarded Atticus with questions about the future, in part to allay lingering doubts about the truth of his claim, but also to fuel her insatiable inquisitiveness.

Maggie sat next to Atticus near the internal door of the lounge, while Oliver stood vigilant at the window.

"Does man live on the moon?"

"People."

"What?"

"Do *people* live on the moon. In my day, we don't say 'man' to represent our achievements because it's intrinsically sexist. We try and be far more inclusive."

Maggie's face advising she took in the new information. Despite that, she bounced on her chair. "Well, do we? Live there?"

Atticus smiled. "No, we don't live there, not yet. But humankind does make it to the moon. In 1969."

Maggie's mouth dropped open. "This decade? Bloody hell." Her bright eyes were wide. After a moment, her gleeful expression dissipated, and her gaze turned downward. "Was it the USSR?"

"No. They win the first few—first satellite, first person in space, first to land something on the moon and the like, but the Americans spend a fortune to make it there first. To be honest, I think the US loses its way a little after the achievement. They reach the pinnacle of human achievement and fail to figure out what should come next."

By the window, Oliver hardly stirred. He was actively listening to what was being said, but seemed preoccupied with what was outside the window. Atticus had to wonder why he was being aloof. Was it jealousy, either at the rekindled friendship between Atticus and Maggie, or another kind? Then again, he could have been all-consumed with his likely impending demise.

"What's it like for women in the future?" It seemed she had a million questions and was picking whatever came to mind. "You mentioned things are less sexist, so it gets better?"

"It really does. There's still a lot of work to do, a hell of a lot, but there's plenty more opportunities and equality than there is now." He tilted his head. "We even had a female Prime Minister."

"In England? You're joking!"

"No, I'm not. She served for all of the eighties."

"Wow. She must have been much loved."

Atticus pursed his lips. "No. Not really."

"Because she was a woman?"

"No, a whole mess of other reasons. Look, that one's a bit complicated."

She frowned, accepting the answer while not understanding it. "What's music like in the future?"

"Fractured." Atticus was happy to be on more comfortable ground. "Because everyone has access to pretty much any song in existence on their mobile phones, everyone listens to their own thing. But it's a positive—whatever you like is always at your fingertips."

With a shake of her head, Maggie tried to comprehend such a thing. Atticus guessed it would have taken a wild leap of imagination. In her time, she had access to a tiny sliver of recorded music, some of which had to be ordered from America. It could take months. What he was suggesting was pure science fiction.

"Do you think I'd like the music in the future?"

"Oh, no doubt. I'm just annoyed we're living in a time when MI6 doesn't conduct drug tests and we have to wait thirty years for a decent rave—and by then we'll be too old to enjoy it."

"Am I meant to understand what any of that means?" Maggie shook her head. She most likely had serious doubts about Atticus's time-travelling story, as anyone would, but the more she grilled Atticus, the less cynical her tone became, and the more inquiring. Well, except perhaps the part about raves. Apart from that, he felt he might be winning her over.

That was until her face changed once more. In an instant it transformed from good-humoured to deathly serious. Atticus instinctively leaned back, so drastic was the shift in her demeanour.

With tight lips, she avoided eye contact. "Did you have anything to do with Henry's... death?"

The abrupt change in conversation caught Atticus off guard. "No, of course not. That's absurd. Henry was a friend."

Clasping her hands together in front of her, Maggie seemed embarrassed to have suggested it. "You have to admit, your story is as flimsy as a King's Road suit on a Saturday, but I know you liked him. It seemed far too coincidental though—you turned up and everything went to hell in a handbasket."

It seemed to explain Maggie's sudden standoffishness. No wonder their little group of misfits had felt so fractured after Henry's passing. Atticus had to admit he would have thought the same if the situations were reversed. Though it didn't account for everything. Her disappearing when they were at Carnaby Street, for one. That was a subject for another day.

"I'm not disagreeing with you, it seems odd to me too. I can't think of anything I've done that would have caused this level of chaos. I can't be certain, but I'm pretty sure a murder of an MI6 staff member on our own premises would have still been remembered in my time."

Maggie shrugged. "Would it though? The government is in a right mess. They've only just swapped PMs, to a bleedin' Lord of all people. Philby, Profumo, JFK. Everything is on a knife edge. This could be buried so deep even our own organisation doesn't remember it."

"Maybe." Atticus wasn't convinced. "But that's part of what's driving me on. If I caused any of this, then I have to fix it. I can't have my presence here disrupt the timeline. I don't want to mess things up and have Russia win the Cold War or have England lose the World Cup."

Maggie tilted her head. "Does... does it happen? Do we win?"

"The World Cup?"

Maggie's face dropped, as if to say, *very droll*. "The Cold War, dummy. I think given our profession we'd be more interested in that than a bunch of idiots kicking a ball around a field."

"Speak for yourself." Oliver grinned.

With a smirk, Atticus addressed Maggie. "Remember what I told you about not wanting to screw up the time-line? Forget everything I just said."

Nodding with a smirk of her own, Maggie obviously had no intention of doing any such thing. Atticus found it difficult to retain a detached air around her. There was no denying his sense of relief that she was no longer angry with him. He tried his best not to dwell on what that meant.

"It's part of why we're here, in Berlin. I have to find out what's going on. If we can trace how Jayne leads to Henry, find the keystone, then we can see if I've caused any of this. I have to be sure."

Maggie's gaze went to the upper right; she was constructing thoughts. The faint clomp of footsteps could be heard from the hallway. Atticus assumed it was Kent or Brooker on patrol.

"If," Maggie raised a finger, "we assume Henry's passing is related, it happened after Jayne was captured. What would he know about who did it?"

"Less of who, more the why. Henry knew something, whether he was aware of it or not. Or he stumbled across something or someone he shouldn't have. Knowing how Jayne ties into all this will narrow down what that something could be. It gives us an avenue of investigation, rather than stumbling around in the dark."

"Then one may as well get on with it." They both turned to see Jayne in the half light of the hallway. His slicked-back hair wet from the shower. "Brooker brought me up to speed on you lot. Seems you've come an awfully long way to talk to me. I suppose it's the least I can do given the present circumstances. What?"

Atticus hadn't expected Jayne to speak with such a plum in his mouth. Stepping into the lounge, his full aristocratic profile became visible. His back rigid, Jayne's gaze swept the room casually, that was, until he saw Atticus. "Oh my. I wasn't aware we were now hiring—"

"I'd choose the next word very carefully if I were you."

"Irregular types." His eyes darted between the three. "You have to admit, you lot aren't standard-issue MI6, now are you?" Even with the highborn air about him, Jayne flashed a genuine smile, as if the fact amused him no end. "About time the stuffy old place had a jolly good airing, if you ask me."

All three "irregular types" stood and introduced themselves. Atticus motioned for Jayne to sit in the lone armchair, opposite he and Maggie on the couch. Oliver resumed his role as sentry by the window.

"We have some questions."

"No doubt." Jayne leaned forward. "Shall we begin?"

CHAPTER
SIXTEEN

B ut Jayne didn't begin his story, not immediately anyway.

Brooker's muffled voice interrupted Jayne before he'd even started. "Scout, eleven o'clock!"

By the window, Oliver checked his watch and looked back into the lounge, perplexed.

Atticus couldn't help but smile. Raising his voice, he turned in the general vicinity of the hallway. "Clock references only really work when we know which way you're facing, Brooker."

The blond agent stuck his head through the doorway and grinned sheepishly. He pointed in the direction of the window. "One bloke, slinking like he's in a pantomime."

Walking over, Atticus sat next to Oliver by the window. Oliver pushed his glasses further up his nose and leaned forward, his face almost against the glass. In retrospect, making someone who was optically challenged a sentry wasn't the wisest of choices.

"I can't..." Oliver squinted. "I can't see any... there." He sat up, animated. "By the big tree, see him?"

Atticus did. He observed what was happening. On the edge of the tree line a man moved slowly, comically. Hardly stealthy, the man was bouncing as he crept. It *was* like something out of a pantomime.

The strategy was reasonably smart, although mostly reckless. Even though his position was closest to the villa, it was too far for any human being who hadn't made the Olympic 100-metre finals to cross in daylight. Yet that's exactly what Mr Pantomime appeared to be readying himself for. Crouched, he had the stance of a man about to attempt to break a record of some kind.

"He knows he's visible, right?" Even Oliver, with his near-sightedness, could see exactly what the man was up to.

Atticus hefted up the old wooden window and locked it in place. He lifted Montgomery's pistol and took aim.

"You won't hit him from this distance." Oliver's gaze shuffled between Atticus and the man by the tree.

"I'm not aiming for him."

The shot shattered the late-afternoon stillness. Everyone but Atticus jumped.

Outside, Mr Pantomime was equally surprised. First by the shot, and secondly that he hadn't been hit. He even patted himself down to confirm the fact. His relief was short-lived.

A large branch, some ten metres above his head, cracked and plummeted to Earth. It just so happened Mr Pantomime was positioned between it and the ground. Landing with a sizable *thump*, the branch knocked him flat.

A pained but angry voice from the tree line cried out, "Scheiße!"

Behind him, Jayne let out a low whistle. "Look at Annie Oakley over here."

Atticus would have preferred Buffalo Bill, but he'd take it.

"How did you..." Oliver stared at him in awe. "That has to be two hundred feet."

Blowing imaginary smoke from the barrel of his gun, Atticus added a tug of an imaginary cowboy hat for effect. "I don't think they're going to be risking any more daylight raids."

"But they'll still come," Maggie's voice had a tenor of fear, "won't they?"

Atticus, Oliver and Jayne answered at the same time. "Yes."

In the far distance, Mr Pantomime limped away, not before yelling towards the house, "Dien Mutter geht der Stadt huren!"

Jayne chuckled. "I'm pretty sure he said your mother goes whoring in the city."

Atticus closed the window. "That should buy us some time."

"Why not just kill him?" Jayne's question wasn't accusatory, just curious.

"We kill their man, they get angry or worse, call for reinforcements. We don't want that. They think we got lucky that a missed shot hit a branch, they laugh it off and wait for nightfall."

"And then?"

"We use the terrain and elements to our advantage."

"But what does that mean?"

"Mr Jayne, we've come a long way to speak to you." Atticus did his best to keep the weight from his words.

Jayne straightened his back and nodded. "Right you are."

"About those questions..."

"Let's begin, shall we?"

~

JAYNE SPOKE in a slow unhurried tone, as if, contrary to all evidence otherwise, they had all the time in the world. He was a gifted raconteur and an engaging personality, ideally suited to ingratiating oneself to others. In other words, an ideal spy.

Atticus had the name of the operation confirmed: Operation Odysseus. For the first time, he learnt its aim. The mission was simple enough, at least on paper. Jayne had been sent to Berlin to become a double agent. His aim was to infiltrate the Soviet's weakest link, a subset of the Stasi called Hauptverwaltung Aufklärung, or the Main Directorate for Reconnaissance. They had suffered a recent set of humiliations at the hands of the Americans, and were desperate to claw back something, anything, to regain their prestige. Jayne was to give it to them—or at least, that's what they would be led to believe.

Jayne had been set up to appear to be an unreliable agent, supplied with one last mission to prove himself. He was to spend months discrediting himself. Appearing drunk in the streets, getting into fights, generally conducting himself as someone unfit to be a member of Her Majesty's Secret Service.

"The gambling debts." Maggie uttered the words more to herself. She glanced up, realising she'd spoken aloud. "The chequebook, the fake one I mean, full of the forged bookies slips and the like. It was planted to make it appear like you were living above your means, you needed the cash."

"I should be peeved you figured it out so soon, but it

would be rather boorish of me, would it not?" Jayne bared his crooked teeth in the fading light. "I see now why they put this team together. That shooting demonstration, the deductive reasoning." His eyes narrowed. "You're quite good, aren't you?" He pursed his lips, seemingly impressed. "The plan was for the Directorate to initiate the approach and one was, as the Americans are fond of saying, to go along for the ride. The debts were as fake as a thirteen-pound note, as you discovered. In reality, I'm as financially vigorous as J. Paul Getty himself, if you must know, but making oneself in arrears to unscrupulous bookmakers would provide an angle they could manipulate." He became more animated, enamoured with his own tale. "At first I was to deliver true information to earn their trust, including military exercises, treaty plans, troop movements and the like. All of it the Soviets would have known eventually, but hearing them from oneself ahead of time would cement one's devotion to the great and glorious revolution."

It made sense to Atticus. That kind of mission was common in the Cold War. Philby and the others had left MI6 flatfooted and embarrassed. They would have felt compelled to have one of their own infiltrate the other side of the Iron Curtain. They needed Jayne to act as a double agent, feeding them intelligence to manipulate the Soviets and ultimately embarrass them on the world stage. Bay of Pigs, the Cuban Missile Crisis, what would become known as the Cambridge Five; the UK was in an undeclared war where the right piece of information at the right time could alter the course of history. Tactically, Jayne's mission was serviceable on paper.

"But," Atticus spoke softly, "something went wrong."

"One could say that," Jayne rubbed his bruised jaw,

"indeed." His amiable expression hardened. "I'd only crossed the border a few hours before there was a knock at my door. At first I thought, what ho, it's going to be the new Station Chief with a bottle of sherry to welcome me on my first rainy day in Berlin, but alas it was not to be." He shifted in his seat. "It was a young fellow I'd never seen in my life, drenched like a drowned rat. As skittish as a blind cat in a rocking chair factory, he was. He turned up and asked if he could come in. The soaking man wouldn't give me his name, so I got to calling him Esther."

"Esther?"

"America's mermaid. Esther Williams. You know, the swimming movie star? He was wringing wet... look, I was a bit out of sorts and didn't have a lot of time to be frightfully witty."

"So what did this Esther want?"

"He was rather panicked, quite beside himself. He said he was being followed and had something urgent to tell me."

"What was it?"

"He explained that MI6 had a mole, quite high up. The Stasi knew I was coming, knew everything. The whole mission. My infiltration was going to be turned against us."

Atticus's mind raced. Whoever this Esther was, he knew everything they'd been trying to piece together since the beginning. He'd be a valuable asset to recruit.

Jayne went on. "Esther said on this side of the wall the mole went by the cryptonym Cardinal Wolsey."

Maggie scowled. "Why have I heard that name before?"

"You should read more history." Atticus sat back in his chair. "He was the Lord Chancellor to Henry VIII, practically ran the country. He was sometimes referred to as Alter Rex. The other king. Wolsey's sometimes used as shorthand to refer to the unseen person who wields the real power." Atticus scratched the back of his neck. "Which, when you think about it, does not bode well for us. If the mole has that code name, he must carry a lot of power, or at the very least be able to manipulate those in power at MI6."

Jayne nodded. "That was my assessment as well."

"What did Esther say next?"

Jayne folded his arms. "I'm not entirely sure. He started to tell me, then had trouble finding the right words."

"Why was that?"

"I can't say for certain, but I believe it had something to do with the knife through his back. Straight in the lungs. Certainly puts a crimp in one's day, or so I've been told. I pulled him inside and was about to call the office when the door was knocked down. There were four of the brutes. I gave them as good a thrashing I could, but I've never been much of a scrapper, especially not against four of the buggers. I was soon overpowered, and had a hood thrown over my head."

That explained one of the things that had always stumped Atticus about the whole situation. Sending a double agent into the field was always fraught with danger. Jayne being exposed so quickly never made any sense. Any half-decent spy agency would monitor a known double agent and manipulate the situation to their advantage; tease out morsels of information knowing full well they were dealing with an enemy agent. Or better yet, feed them manufactured intelligence which, if timed right, could change the course of the Cold War—which was exactly what Jayne had been tasked to do.

From the outset, Jayne's kidnapping had seemed so incompetent Atticus thought it may have been staged. Then again, it could have been deliberately executed to leave that impression.

If what Jayne was saying was true, this mystery man, Esther, may have been followed by the Stasi and led them to Jayne. He'd fallen into events already underway, ignorant of their history or ramifications. Then again, it could be completely fabricated—maybe Jayne was making the entire story up. Atticus was reminded once again that espionage was a hall of cracked mirrors where nothing was as it seemed.

"When you were captured, what did they want to know?" Atticus was aware he'd dropped into interrogation mode.

"They kept asking what I'd been told by the chap, which I could honestly say was nothing. It didn't seem to please them as much as one would have hoped." Jayne rubbed his chin. "Then there were the incessant questions about my connection with the man who turned up on my doorstep and why I'd been singled out. Again, my ignorance didn't seem to appease them. In fact, one could say they were downright incensed."

"We've seen the reports. They ransacked the place. Tore open books, cut into walls. They were searching for something."

Jayne shrugged. "There was nothing to find. I had nothing on me. I'd only recently arrived, hadn't even been given any assignments yet. I certainly wasn't carrying anything Top Secret."

Maggie tilted her head. "That you knew of."

With an impressed expression, Jayne unfolded his arms and leaned forward. "I hadn't even thought of that. You make a good point, young lady."

Atticus gave Maggie a *well done* wink. He turned back to Jayne. "You never learned who the man was, this Esther?"

"They gave me nothing. German, from the accent, certainly. He mumbled something about wanting to defect, but that he'd earn his place by what he had to tell me." He saddened. "He risked everything to see me and I didn't even get the poor blighter's name."

"Were you injured in your flat? Stab wound or shot?"

Jayne shook his head. "No, why?"

"Well, blood was found." Atticus flicked his index finger in Jayne's direction. "The same blood type as yours."

"My, that would have alarmed quite a few, I imagine."

Atticus dipped his head in agreement. "It did." Despite the encroaching attack, he was all business. If there was a chance any of them might survive, then he needed answers.

"I have to say, all this is terribly awful all round, but that's not the worst of it, I'm afraid."

"No?"

"No. The blighters mentioned my mission by name. They definitely referred to it as Operation Odysseus. Nobody but a very select few knew the name."

It was true. Atticus had to grill Rathdowne to give up the name, and he was the one charged with investigating Jayne's disappearance on the operation. He was never privy to the details of what the mission was about, and he was the one investigating the whole thing. This didn't seem like bureaucracy gone mad; it smacked of deliberate sabotage.

Jayne went on. "I'm reluctant to say, but I think Esther was telling the truth. There's a mole in MI6."

"I think you may be right." Atticus gave Maggie a sideways glance.

"Lads!" The shout came from the hall.

Oliver held up his hand to Atticus. *I'll handle it.* He left to see what Brooker wanted.

Atticus had more immediate concerns. "Who specifically knew of your mission at MI6?"

"No one. Only my direct superior, Flynn." Jayne gazed off into space. "That's it, I think. Not even the Head of the East German Bureau."

"Rathdowne?" Atticus had reason for asking.

Jayne scratched the back of his neck contemplatively. "No... no he wasn't in on it. Even the Big Man didn't know directly. The Chief knew there was an operation, of course, but according to Flynn, he only knew the scant details; no names, no timings and such. Flynn thought the less he knew the better. The lid was pretty tight on this one." Jayne scanned the room and sighed. "Or at least that's what I thought."

"I see." Trying for his best casual tone, but knowing he'd likely fail, Atticus pressed on as he checked the window. Night was falling, they didn't have much time. "How did you get out?"

"I would love to regale you with a heroic account of my brave and ingenious derring-do, but in the end it was just dumb luck. They held me in a wooden shack in some uninhabited housing estate outside of Ahrensfelde, quite isolated. There were four interrogators, you see. They took it in turns asking me the exact same questions over and over again, like some kind of violently incompetent round-robin. Needless to say, they didn't particularly like the answers. After a couple of days, beating me senseless must have become a bore and two of them went off discussing breakfast. One was asleep in the corner and the last one went out for a cigarette. I was strapped to a chair, but not terribly well. Whoever tied the knots was never a Boy

Scout, let me tell you. I managed to sneak up on the sleeping fellow and relieve him of his pistol. I left dear old Sleeping Beauty having a kip, and went out to relieve the chap outside of his filthy smoking habit, and his life. Sleeping Beauty ran out and suffered the same fate. I ran in the direction opposite the road in case Tweedledee and Tweedledum came back too soon. I eventually found my way back to Berlin on foot and left my message advising I needed immediate extraction."

The story was delivered without haste. The best Atticus could determine was it wasn't being made up then and there. Which either indicated it had been invented previously or it was indeed the truth. Atticus wasn't ready to make the call yet.

"When the three men were sent to extract you, what happened to—"

Footsteps came hurriedly from the hall. Oliver entered, face grave. "Sorry, I'm going to have to interrupt, folks." He was even more pallid than before. He inhaled unevenly. "They're coming."

SEVENTEEN

From the dim shadows of the woods, seven men stepped unhurriedly onto the grass, rifles at the ready. Dusk masked their features; from the back door they appeared like seven spectres slowly floating menacingly towards the villa. Their footsteps were unhurried, their few gestures precise but relaxed. The men displayed no urgency in their manner. There was no need; their prey were cornered, cut off and whatever they did would only stay the inevitable.

Rechecking his weapon, Atticus thought, *not if I have anything to do with it.*

Joining Atticus at the rear window, Brooker shook his head. "Jesus. They're armed like the damned 11th Cavalry."

Atticus thought this a misrepresentation, primarily due to the lack of tanks. Although he had no idea what else lay behind them in the woods, so anything was possible. Regardless, they were outnumbered and outgunned. They had to be smarter.

"When they get within thirty feet take a pot shot over their heads."

Brooker turned to him incredulously. "*Over* their heads? Doesn't that somewhat defeat the purpose?"

Amusement danced across Atticus's lips. "Over."

He explained his plan.

Brooker shook his head. "You're either a genius or the maddest bastard I've ever met."

"Can't I be both?"

Without waiting for a reply, Atticus crouched and made his way to Kent, who sat tensed on a rocking chair in the main bedroom, aiming the shotgun out the gap in the open window. Without preamble, Atticus outlined his hastily put together strategy. Kent's reaction was virtually an exact mirror of Brooker's.

"You're... you're not actually serious... are you?"

Giving him a wink, Atticus instructed him on how to get in position. With detectable reluctance, Kent did as requested.

Atticus strode to the lounge. Oliver was by the window, pistol in hand, Jayne beside him, unarmed. They observed the woods on the opposite side of the house from Brooker and Kent. Both men were vigilant, but visibly anxious.

Without turning, Oliver spoke. "Nothing yet. I'm keeping an eye on the driveway like you asked, but I'm not entirely sure why."

"It's logical to have someone guarding it if any of us make a run for it."

Oliver's voice was thin and frail. "Given the state of my legs right now, I don't believe running is a particularly practical option anyway."

Giving his friend a reassuring pat on the shoulder, Atticus chuckled, trying to make light of the grave situation. "You'll do fine. Keep your head low and your eyes open, and shoot at anyone you don't know."

Oliver blinked blankly, unconvinced. Jayne gave him a wary glance, as if he didn't know what to make of the newcomer. As far as Atticus was concerned, the feeling was mutual.

They went over the plan once more. Jayne's incredulity didn't change. One thing Atticus chose not to mention was that he had instructed Oliver not to issue Jayne a weapon. While his story seemed plausible enough, Atticus wasn't keen on getting shot in the back if he was wrong.

Making his way to the hallway, Atticus spied Maggie standing alone, glancing out the small window by the front door. She flinched at the sound of his footsteps, only easing her shoulders when she saw who it was. The woman was jumpy. In the space of a few hours she seemed to have aged five years.

Assessing him with dark eyes, Maggie scowled. "What else is going on, you seem worried."

"No, I don't. This is just my face now."

She eyed him sceptically, but at least there was a hint of humour in her expression now. It soon fell away. "Are we going to survive this?"

"Of course, we've got this completely under control."

"That right?" Issuing a dubious expression, she leaned forward. "If it's all under control then why does your face look like that?"

He shrugged. "I guess I was just born ruggedly handsome."

Maggie wrinkled her nose. "Are you trying to distract me by flirting?"

Atticus gave a not-too-subtle shrug. "Is it working?"

Leaning forward, she whispered, "A little." Her face became serious. Maggie straightened her back. "Before... all this happens, I should probably explain the other day when—"

She never finished her thought. From the back of the house a gunshot rang out, shattering the stillness. From the lounge room Atticus heard Oliver let out a startled yelp.

"Tell me later." Touching the side of Maggie's sheet-white face, Atticus slapped on the best brave smile he could muster. "For now, follow me."

Taking Maggie's hand, Atticus led her to a mahogany hall stand. It was a solid art deco number with multiple hooks for coats and a sizable seat where you could perch to put on your boots. Atticus lifted the hatch built into the seat. He'd cleared it of the clutter half an hour before. It was about the right size for a slim person. Maggie-sized, to be exact.

"If it all gets too much jump in here and wait it out, okay?"

Even with the fear enveloping her, Maggie planted her fists on her hips. "Like hell I will." There was a tenor of anger in her words. "I'm not some damsel in distress in some silent movie, Atticus Wolfe. Would you treat a woman from your time like that?"

Atticus realised he had to stop underestimating Maggie Dunbar. "Don't think this era is rubbing off on me. If the situation was reversed and Oliver was here, I'd tell him the same." He slapped the solid wood. "Use it for cover. This thing will stop a howitzer."

He lowered his head and raised his eyebrows to see if she agreed. In return she gave him a determined nod. *I got this.*

"If you see anyone you don't like the look of, shoot them in the chest." Atticus motioned to the gun. "It's the area with the greatest body mass and the best chance of taking them down. Make no mistake, they won't hesitate to do the same to you. Just make sure you get them first, okay?"

Seemingly unable to reply verbally, Maggie gave him a thumbs up and appeared to instantly regret the gesture, as if it were embarrassing. Knowing time was not their ally, Atticus gave her a wink and bolted for the lounge.

Hefting the trapdoor open by the fireplace, Atticus leapt into the dark and began crawling towards the back of the house. Once in position, he thumped the floor above his head. Receiving two knocks in reply, Atticus knew he was in the right spot.

"Glad you could join the fun." Kent's voice was muffled through the floorboards, but clear enough for Atticus to detect the tautness in his voice. "They're hunkered behind the mound of grass twenty feet from the back door."

Atticus noted he hadn't added, *just where you said they would.*

Kent went on. "Soon as Brooker took the pot shot over their noggins, they got their heads down faster than Oscar Wilde at Danny La Rue's."

Ignoring the gay slur, Atticus kept to business. "Brooker ready?"

"Affirmative."

"Give him the signal."

Barely able to detect the faint tap, there was no mistaking the next sound: the boom of a shotgun. Atticus had ordered Brooker into the roof, where he'd carved a hole in the thatch above the back door. From the high vantage point, the grass mound the attackers hid behind offered no cover. They were exposed and vulnerable. They just didn't know it yet. An old Gunnery Sergeant had once told Atticus that with the right planning, half a dozen soldiers could seem like hundreds. Atticus intended to pull off exactly that deception.

Brooker fired quick successive blasts from his shotgun. Cries of pain told them he'd hit his mark. As predicted, within seconds of the first shotgun round the men who weren't writhing on the ground scattered. With their only cover suddenly evaporated, they had no choice. They attacked, firing blindly while doing their best to escape the scything laceration of the shotgun. Two remained behind, one thrashing on the ground in agony, the other offering no movement whatsoever. It was Mr Pantomime, his slinking days now done.

Atticus and Kent opened fire simultaneously. The additional gunfire only panicked the attackers further. Their seemingly straightforward attack in disarray, they sprinted towards the back door—again, just as Atticus had calculated. Calling for his comrades to charge, the lead attacker's chest burst open in a bloody mess as Kent's bullets hit him dead centre.

Their assault having descended into chaos, the attacking group froze. From beneath the house, Atticus aimed his pistol at the stationary legs and fired in quick succession. Tibias and fibulas splintered; the cries of the attackers were drowned out by the incessant gunfire. They were being struck from above, below and dead on. They had no cover, nowhere to hide. Their choices were to continue their attack or retreat. Atticus had hoped they'd choose retreat; instead, they attacked.

The four remaining assailants focused their fire on the back door. No shots were returned. Atticus hoped that meant Kent had fallen back, not just fallen. The boom of the shotgun had gone silent, which either meant Brooker was out of shells, the attackers were below his line of sight or he'd met an unfortunate end. The attackers continued to come.

No longer able to see the assailants, Atticus scrambled across the dirt and made his way back to the trapdoor. His sudden appearance up through the floor of the lounge startled Oliver.

"Bloody hell!"

With no time to reassure his friend, Atticus hoisted himself up and raced to the door of the lounge. Charging forward, he had just enough time to see the pistol in Jayne's hand, unsure where it had come from.

Brooker was meant to have regrouped to the hallway, but it was empty. About to call out, Atticus heard the crack of the back door being kicked in. Taking a split second to poke his head around the corner, Atticus saw Kent prone on the ground next to the rocking chair, dead eyes staring at nothing.

Bursting through the back door, the three remaining men coordinated their efforts. One fired down the hallway, forcing Atticus to recoil while the other two peppered bullets into the ceiling: the exact position where Brooker had been positioned. A scream of pain confirmed their tactic had succeeded.

Brooker and Kent were gone.

Atticus reloaded his pistol and hoped wherever Maggie was, she was well hidden, or better yet, had managed to make a break for it and escape the carnage.

The strategy was a failure; the attackers had overrun the house. Atticus's slapdash plan was in disarray. He hadn't taken precautions this far ahead. Now was when the fighting became close quarters, bloody and desperate. Tactics no longer meant shit; this was when primal survival instincts kicked in. It was a fight for their very existence.

Sliding his pistol into the hall blindly, Atticus fired twice. He doubted the bullets would find a mark; he only wanted to slow down the assailants.

Turning to a terrified Oliver and Jayne, he pointed at the heavy green velvet couch in the centre of the room. "This is where we make our stand. We either kill every fucker coming through this door or die trying."

Atticus opened his mouth to warn Oliver to "protect the asset", but the words never formed in his mouth. Jayne was the reason they were here, the key to finding the mole and setting the timeline right again. Without him, their mission would be a failure and more importantly, there would be no way for them to avenge Henry's death. But there was no use asking Oliver to protect Jayne. Their fates were intertwined; they were destined to have the same end. Either they all lived or they all died. The next few seconds would determine which.

There was no discussion from the other two, they knew what was coming. The three men huddled behind the back of the couch, each aiming their weapon at the doorway. In turn, Atticus gave them a reassuring nod, as if saying, *we've got this*, which, of course, was a lie. He had no doubt they were going to die today. The only thing Atticus could control was when. Lining the pistol sights at head height, he intended to make them pay for every second.

After the frenzy of tumultuous gunfire and bloodshed, the sudden silence was jarring. Ears ringing, Atticus fought the tinnitus to listen for coming footsteps. And come they did.

A revolver was thrust into the doorway and fired randomly into the lounge. The shots were wild and indirect, but they forced the other two to duck. But not Atticus. He returned fire, forcing the hand to retreat. Atticus and Jayne swivelled their weapons skyward, readying for the next attack. Oliver fired for the first time, screaming as he did, splintering plaster and doorjamb.

Gently placing his hand on Oliver's shoulder, Atticus didn't take his eyes off the door. "Conserve your bullets. Wait for a target."

"Easy for you to say." The tenor in Oliver's voice made it clear he was petrified.

Oliver's tongue clicked on the roof of his mouth in a desperate attempt to bring forth any moisture. Atticus doubted he'd ever been in a firefight. His reaction was perfectly human. Even with training and experience, Atticus was scared. Anyone facing certain death would be.

Conscious of their depleted ammunition, Atticus exhaled slow and steady to calm himself. "Wait until you see body parts. Keep your eyes open and unleash."

From the corner of his eye he saw Oliver's shaking hands doing their best to keep hold of the heavy weapon. On the opposite side, Jayne held his pistol with two steady hands. The myth of a fearless field agent, able to withstand any emergency situation with unflinching fortitude and a square jaw was just that, a myth. The reality was they were just better at hiding it than most.

Urgent muffled German whispers could be heard from the other side of the doorway. Nothing happened for the eternity of a minute.

The first through the door was the first to die. Jayne's bullet flew true and decimated the man's skull in a sickeningly bloody explosion. His demise didn't slow his compatriot. Leaping through the breach, he fired two pistols as he dove. It was like something from a nineties action flick, thirty years too soon. Firing repeatedly, his bullets ricocheted off the solid couch, forcing all to duck from the onslaught.

Dropping to floor level, Atticus fired from under the couch as the man hit the floor. With nothing in the way of protection, the two shots found their target and exploded the man's neck and torso. The last two pulls of Atticus's trigger clicked.

He sat up with his back to the couch. His tone was hushed. "I'm out."

Oliver pulled the trigger of his weapon. "I was out about twenty seconds ago but kept firing anyway."

Jayne pressed the magazine release and held the empty vessel aloft.

With only one remaining attacker, they'd made it so close, only to be defeated within sight of the finishing line. They were out of bullets and out of chances.

"Does MI6 not conduct training on how to whisper?"

The accent was thick and German. There was no hiding his conceit. He knew he had them and was going to take his sweet time. The cacophony of the constant battle must have dulled their sense of volume. They'd spoken too loudly and given away their plight.

If Atticus had thought it through, pretending to be out of ammo would have been a great ploy to lure their enemy into a false sense of security. Unfortunately, there was no ploy, and the sense of security wasn't false, it was assured.

Stepping over the threshold, the man was older than Atticus anticipated. Grey temples and lines on his face displayed a narrative of hardship. The man had seen much.

"You hurensöhnes killed many of my comrades today." He raised his East German Makarov pistol, his movements unhurried. He didn't even glance at his fallen compatriots; he had other targets of his attention. "You will pay for that.

I am here to assure you that you will all die slowly and in complete agony."

"You first."

The shot rang out, shocking everyone in the room, but none more than the German holding the gun. Blood spread through the centre of his white shirt. He fell backwards, firing his pistol as if the action would forestall his inevitable passing.

When his lifeless form fell back through the doorway, Atticus could see the shadowy figure standing awkwardly in the hall holding a revolver. Face white as a sheet, Maggie's eyes were wide and locked on the body that lay sprawled at her feet.

Leaping up, Atticus bounded over the dead East German and raced to Maggie's side.

"Thank you."

Gazing at him, blank face devoid of all expression, she had to fight her dry mouth to speak. "That's twice I saved your pretty arse."

Rubbing her shoulder and relieving her of the revolver, Atticus tried to sound more casual than he felt. "When you hit three you get a badge."

With a great deal of effort, Maggie lifted her gaze and replied, "I'd prefer a sash."

"May I interrupt the flirting for a moment?"

They turned to Oliver, who was still positioned behind the couch. He was hunched next to Jayne. The latter had a blank expression on his face, primarily due to the bloody red hole in his forehead where his life used to be.

The East German's last dying reflex shot had been more accurate than those he took when he was alive. The gun dropped from Maggie's hand. Shock enveloped her entire being.

Oliver stared at the fresh body on the floor. "Criminy."

∽

THE LOCAL STATION CHIEF, head office and the Home Secretary were all of the same opinion: get the fuck out of Berlin.

Within two hours of contacting the Berlin Station, Atticus, Oliver and Maggie were wheels up in the belly of an RAF de Havilland Comet heading back to London. There was no cheer in their manner when they left East German airspace. Their mission had collapsed into chaos and death.

Yes, they'd found Jayne, but they'd failed to bring him in, failed to properly debrief him, failed to find any hard evidence and, in the end, failed to save his life. All they had was a litany of dead agents and more questions.

Who was the mysterious man nicknamed Esther who had tried to issue a warning only to be murdered on Jayne's doorstep? The mole now had a codename—Cardinal Wolsey—but they were no closer to finding his true identity. In fact, as Atticus watched the Netherlands give way to the North Sea, he felt further from the truth than ever before.

Of course, Maggie felt responsible for Jayne's death. No matter how many times and in how many ways Oliver and Atticus tried to convince her it was an unforeseeable accident, Maggie blamed herself.

The RAF doctor seeing to their welfare after take-off administered Maggie sedatives, which soon knocked her out. Despite the heavy medication, the smooth skin of her face contorted frequently, as if she was reliving the horrific events of the villa. It seemed likely she would be permanently scarred, and Atticus had to live with the fact that he had dragged her into this whole mess.

Oliver seemed to fare little better than Maggie. Once in the air, he'd done his best to hide his shaking hands. Now curled into a ball on the seat opposite, Oliver's resting face was as tortured as Maggie's. They weren't field officers. Neither had been trained for the brutality and bloodshed they'd endured. It was on Atticus's shoulders that their lives had been forever tarnished by the events he had actively embroiled them in. They would never be the same.

There was no way Atticus could sleep. Hopped up on adrenaline, he'd purloined a lined pad and a pen from a passing pilot officer who seemed barely out of school. Once he'd started scribbling down his wayward thoughts, he couldn't stop. Through his disordered notes he started to see some order, a report that tried to make sense of the madness.

He made sure he recommended Brooker and Kent to receive posthumous commendations for their selfless bravery. He even modified his language enough to make Montgomery sound less like the prat he was and more like the revered deceased.

No sudden revelations were made, there were too many unknowns for that, but at least writing the report helped Atticus compartmentalise what he knew, what he didn't and where the next steps in their investigation would take them.

If there were any next steps, that was.

Once Atticus arrived back at MI6 headquarters and submitted the report, there was the distinct possibility he would be fired. He hoped Oliver and Maggie did not suffer the same fate. MI6, the MI6 of this time, owed him no loyalty. He had never earned his stripes in 1963. If Rathdowne had indeed set him up for failure, then Atticus had certainly lived up to the promise.

Not that it would matter much.

Whether Atticus continued to be employed by his organisation was irrelevant. His task remained the same.

Even if it took his last dying breath, he would hunt down the man known as Cardinal Wolsey and make him pay for the blood on his hands.

Whatever it took, Atticus would make it right.

He had to.

EIGHTEEN

"Thirteen dead. Six of them bloody ours." Rathdowne paced before Atticus, his red face sweaty and furious. "The PM is screaming for blood. The Foreign Minister is calling this the biggest cock-up since the fall of Singapore." He used his hanky to wipe down his forehead. "You were tasked with interviewing one of ours, not starting a bloody war!"

For all the bluster Rathdowne threw around in the spittle-fuelled rage, for all the theatrics, the pauseless rants, Atticus knew one irrevocable truth: the man was right. They had screwed up. Good people had died. They had put the organisation in even more danger while trying to save it. Worse, they had nothing to show for it. If the situations were reversed, Atticus would be casting equally venomous vitriol.

"Five."

"Rathdowne's face was still red. "What?"

"Five dead on our side, not six."

"No." Rathdowne squared his jaw. "Six. Flynn, Jayne's superior, wrapped his car around a tree last night. Given what's been going on there's no bloody way in hell I'm chalking that one up to an accident."

There was no denying it now. Atticus's presence had altered the timeline. It was impossible that six MI6 deaths wouldn't be mentioned in hushed tones even in his day. Every move he'd made to try and correct the catastrophic impact of his presence only made it worse. Atticus had affected the past, and not for the better. Add to that the burden already on his shoulders with the passing of Henry. He slumped further into his chair, trying to stay focused on the moment. He had to set this right.

Even though he still had doubts as to Rathdowne's motives, the verve with which he dressed down Atticus made him question his own suspicions. Surely a mole would be overjoyed at their mission's failure. Rathdowne was anything but. There was nothing for Atticus to do than sit and take the reprimand, and throw in the occasional word of agreement when Rathdowne took a breath between castigations.

Thankfully Oliver and Maggie had given their statements before Rathdowne had arrived. The three had headed straight for MI6 headquarters from the airport in the eerie London pre-dawn. Both were visibly shaken, but had done their best not to appear so. Immediately after they had delivered their version of events, Atticus sent them home. This would be his burden to bear alone.

And bear it, he did. Rathdowne's tirade ran out of steam sometime around ten o'clock, when he called for tea. After the squat tea lady had delivered her tray and scuttled off, Atticus's manager passed him a cup and sat next to him, devoid of all the bluster that had been so rampant only moments before.

"So, this Esther chap Jayne mentioned, the fellow who

was stabbed on his doorstep. Is there a way to find out who he was?"

"My guess, and I have no proof of this, is that he was Main Directorate for Reconnaissance, got wind of a spy who was to be outed and tried to get ahead of the game by giving Jayne the heads up. Again, supposition, but he was probably looking to get himself a free ticket to the West. Jayne said he mentioned the bloke wanted to defect, so it fits the hypothesis."

"Only, he was followed."

Atticus nodded. "Pure guesswork on my behalf, but that's what I'm thinking."

"The kid not only tipped his hand and ruined the Stasis' sting, but got himself killed for his trouble. A fiasco for all concerned."

Taking a sip of the scalding hot and flavourless tea, Atticus's mind wandered. Rathdowne seemed far more reasonable now the ranting had ceased. It was as if he were obligated to issue a dressing down, and now that it was done the real spy work could proceed.

Atticus was only too happy to oblige. "The government organisation that pays GDR employees..."

"The Abteitsministerium?"

"Yes, that. I can never pronounce it." It was a lie, but Atticus thought it better than admitting he didn't know a key piece of information about East Germany, his apparent area of expertise. "Do we have an asset there?"

Rathdowne puckered his brow. "We do, as a matter of fact. A low-level secretary from memory. How is that going to help?"

The question was triggered by an incident in Atticus's recent history. In the 2010s, Chinese hackers breached the Office of Personnel Management, exposing the personal data of ten million employees. This would be of concern for most organisations, but when the data was for the US government's human resources unit, whose roster included the FBI, NSA and CIA it was a monumental espionage fiasco. Spies' criminal history, psychological records, information about past drug use and gambling habits were out in the open for exploitation. One of the simplest ways to target an ex-employee ripe for cultivation was to identify a list of those who had ceased to be an employee. Several were groomed and enticed to add to their retirement fund. Atticus was about to turn the idea on its head.

"Why don't we use the asset to find out who was recently terminated in the Stasi or Main Directorate for Reconnaissance."

"What use would that be?"

"Government bureaucracy may be notoriously inefficient, but they rarely make a habit of paying dead men. You find out who they stopped paying, you find out who Esther really was."

Slowly putting his teacup down, Rathdowne pursed his lips, impressed. "That's ... damn, why didn't our people come up with that?"

"I thought I was *our* people."

Rathdowne dropped his bottom lip, conceding the point. "I meant our old people, not *our* new people."

"Right."

Scribbling on his notepad, Rathdowne underlined the idea, hopefully signifying the urgency the task would be given. A silence descended on them once more.

Glad of the stillness, Atticus began formulating his own interrogation of Rathdowne, ideally without the man even knowing. According to Jayne, only Flynn had been aware of his mission, and not the man sitting beside him. Determined to uncover the truth, Atticus had to take a meandering route to get to his destination.

"The mole, this Cardinal Wolsey—"

"Mightily odd reference, if you ask me." Rathdowne took a bite of his digestive biscuit.

"Jayne virtually confirmed there is a mole, if we are to take him at his word."

"And why on earth wouldn't we? The man died in a shootout with the enemy, it hardly seems likely he'd be making things up for a lark."

"In espionage no one should be taken at their word."

Rathdowne gave Atticus a curious glance. Nodding, he prompted him to continue.

"Therefore, the leak came from this office. No one else had the information, not the Foreign Office, not the Americans. This was a closed-door operation. If Flynn was killed because of what he knew of the operation, and there's no way in hell I'm betting against that, then there's nowhere else for the information to have come from."

"Perhaps Flynn was the mole?"

"Then why kill him?"

Rathdowne threw up a conciliatory hand, accepting the point. "Logical. Therefore?"

"Given no one has left the organisation, and this mission took place after Philby escaped into the night, they have to be right under our noses." Atticus watched Rathdowne's face for the slightest of movements.

"Could Henry have been the mole?" Rathdowne must have caught the distaste on Atticus's face. "Terribly sorry to speak ill of the dead, but we can't be sure why he was here at such a ridiculous hour, or with whom. You just said yourself no one in espionage should be taken at their word, did you not? Who knows, he could have come in with an enemy agent, had a disagreement, got cold feet or what have you and then come to a sticky end."

Granted, it was an angle Atticus hadn't considered. It seemed farfetched, but not something to be dismissed entirely. He frowned. "A possibility."

"But you don't buy it?"

Atticus shook his head. "Again, why kill him?" He blew air out his nose. "How well did you know Flynn?"

Rathdowne twisted his face. "I don't wish to denigrate the departed."

Atticus snorted. "But you will."

He tilted his head in agreement. "He was the usual insufferable MI6 toff. Country estates, driving his MG, wearing a beak cap above his unpleasant chinless face. Why?"

"You didn't meet with him or Jayne about the mission?"

"No, of course not, we've been through this. They were the only ones who knew about the mission."

"You're sure?"

"Yes." Rathdowne's tone indicated the question *and?*

"Until we have any evidence to the contrary, I'd say Flynn's still the prime suspect."

Rathdowne scoffed, then upon seeing Atticus's face became sombre. "His family name is revered; his grandfather was bloody Speaker of the House of Commons, for Christ's sake. The man was beyond reproach even before he was the honoured dead. It's all in the breeding, you see."

"Are we spies or corgis?"

That seemed to amuse Rathdowne. "There was an internal investigation. He was cleared."

"An internal..." Atticus straightened his back. "I thought *I* was the internal investigation?"

"You were, er, are," Rathdowne shifted uneasily in his

seat, "well, one of the investigations. It was... the Heads Of deemed it inappropriate that an underling question a superior."

"Inappropriate? Jesus. Is this the fucking dark ages?" Incensed, Atticus did his best to head off a tirade of his own. "So, I really was set up for failure, then?"

"What's that?"

"I'm an outsider, for multiple reasons. I don't know your people, I don't know their capabilities, their strengths and particularly their weaknesses. I'm practically the worst person to investigate a mole in an organisation I don't know."

"I thought an impartial eye—"

"So you've said, but I don't buy it." Atticus put the vile tea down; it wasn't worth the effort. "The reputation of the entire organisation is on the line, the stability of the nation, and you hand the investigation to someone you only met a couple of hours before."

"I'm a fast judge of character."

"But you don't like me."

"That's not true, and besides, I don't need to like someone if they get the job done."

"Ah, but I haven't."

"Well, not yet. There's still time, although not much. We are on the clock here. What is this about? You yourself boasted you have the best people on it."

"Not as far as the organisation is concerned." Atticus threw in what he hoped was a wry smile to soften his words. "We're the outcasts, the refuse of MI6."

"I won't deny there's a few around here who had, let's say, inappropriate names for you all."

"I'd like to hear them."

"I'm sure you wouldn't."

Atticus crossed his arms and glared. In response Rathdowne lurched backwards, giving his head the slightest of shakes. Atticus continued to glare.

"Fine, but don't hold me accountable for the distaste of others. You lot have been referred to as the spook, the shirt-lifter and the walking pair of tits. Now, I obviously don't—"

Lifting his hand, Atticus silenced the man. He'd expected as much. This wasn't exactly an enlightened time. He'd experienced the sneers hidden behand hands, the reluctance to move aside in the hallways. His complexion was considered more suited to punching tickets than walking these hallowed halls. Atticus had a well-honed thick skin against the bigotry of others. But that wasn't what bothered him. It was the insinuation that Oliver and Maggie were deemed far from equal. While it was suspected, it still stung.

Atticus spoke carefully, watching for a reaction. "All the more intrigued as to why you let us be your point team. Hardly what the leadership of this organisation would traditionally call the elite team, wouldn't you say?"

Rathdowne eyed Atticus suspiciously. "I can't help but think I'm the one being questioned here."

"I have no idea why you'd think that." Atticus tried the tea again in the hope that after cooling from its molten heat level it might now offer some flavour. It didn't.

Rathdowne's eyes narrowed. "What was it you did at the Navy again?"

"Oh, all manner of espionage business. Classified, clandestine, covert. Lots of lurking in shadows, that sort of thing."

"How very... cryptic." He lit a cigarette and contemplated the glowing tip for a moment. "I still can't quite reconcile a naval tactician being able to single-handedly take down a heavily armed Stasi assault team. It strikes me as a might peculiar."

Determined not to be distracted from his aim, Atticus ignored the bait. He was doing the interrogating.

There was the faintest hint of humour in Rathdowne's features, as if he knew Atticus hadn't been thrown off topic. Atticus knew the man could be a prime suspect, but he just couldn't see it. He had always had Rathdowne down as the possible mole. The man did have a working-class contempt of his elitist superiors. In this time, working class did lend itself to socialist leanings, which could slide towards communism given the right nudge. However, the man seemed genuinely dedicated to the same organisation Atticus was. There was nothing in his facial tics or mannerisms to indicate deception or deceit. As far as Atticus's well-honed skills could tell, they were on the same side.

That simple fact only made the situation more disheartening. The list of suspects was slim, and no doubt heads would start to roll following the Berlin disaster. If Rathdowne or Flynn wasn't his man, Atticus was more out to sea than ever before.

Deprived of Jayne and his inside knowledge and unable to provide even an arbitrary physical description of Esther, they had little to go on. Even the fragments of what they'd uncovered failed to reveal why Henry would have been lured to MI6 headquarters in the middle of the night and murdered. The fact weighed him down.

"I'd like to see the report on the other investigation where Flynn was apparently cleared."

"Of course, of course." Rathdowne sipped his tea and stared off into the middle distance.

Atticus glared in return. "Now is a good time."

"Oh, *oh*. Right, I didn't think you meant..." Rathdowne

went to his disorganised desk, picked up the heavy black handset and mumbled a set of instructions.

Within a few minutes a pimply kid slunk into the office with a sweaty forehead and even sweatier hands. Rathdowne dismissed him with a wave and handed the damp manila folder to Atticus.

"I can't believe you didn't even mention another investigation." Atticus shook his head and examined the report.

"Like I said, beyond—"

"Reproach, yes I heard the first time." Struggling to contain his exasperation, Atticus went on. "When I first arrived weren't you the one banging on about the ongoing battle against privilege? And yet here you are automatically exonerating your superior because of his breeding. Sounds awfully elitist to me."

Rathdowne's jaw clenched. "Do you ever *not* say what's on your mind?"

Not taking his eyes off his boss, Atticus replied, "Constantly."

Turning his attention to the brief four-page report, Atticus allowed the world to fall away. The typewritten report, the only copy in existence, detailed information that would have made Atticus's own investigation infinitely easier. It contained the details of every meeting Flynn could recall where he'd planned Operation Odysseus. It contained not only the details of what was discussed, but also the initials of who attended.

When he'd finished, Atticus turned it over and started again. After his fourth reading he lifted the typewritten document close to his eyes and examined the third page closely. Screwing his face up, Atticus placed the report on his lap, sighed and rubbed his eyes.

"You see?" Rathdowne waved in the general direction of

the report. "There's nothing there, all above board. He was an aristocratic twat, incompetent at times even, but he wasn't a traitor. At best he was—"

Rathdowne stopped as Atticus stood. Marching to the door, the newest member of MI6 didn't look back.

"What... what is it, Wolfe?"

Finally turning to his superior, Atticus found it impossible to rein in his fury. "I've just found your fucking mole."

Atticus marched out and slammed the door.

"I... I DON'T BELIEVE IT." Maggie's response mirrored Oliver's reaction not twenty minutes before.

The two of them sat across from Atticus in their tiny office, trying to come to terms with what he had told them. An uncomfortable stillness filled the room.

It had taken far longer to get them into MI6 than he was used to. What once would have required five seconds to send a group message or text message took comparatively forever. First, he'd had to obtain their home phone numbers, then actually call them—a novelty in itself—then wait for an answer and explain himself. Twice. It was laborious and mundane. Everything took far longer in the past.

Pushing the four-page report away with her finger, Maggie then wiped her digit on her skirt, as if afraid she'd catch mole. "Now that we have this information, what do we do?"

Unsurprisingly, Atticus had a plan for that. In fact, he had a plan behind the plan. And a spare plan if needed. He loved a plan.

Oliver picked up the report and shook his head as if he didn't believe it either. He wasn't the only one. The report seemed innocuous enough. It detailed the times and dates when, to the best of his recollection, Flynn had anything to do with Operation Odysseus, including the discussions with Jayne himself. It was all rather dull—that is, until the third page, when it became incendiary.

It was the minutest detail, easily missed. In shorthand notes it outlined the content of half a dozen meetings discussing everything ranging from whether MI6 should conduct the operation, a short list of names, and when it should run. It was the notes on one meeting in particular that brought down the entire house of cards. The minutes themselves were mundane, almost non-existent. When it came down to it, the mole had been uncovered with just two letters.

That was enough.

Atticus checked his no-longer-smart watch. "It's time."

Maggie and Oliver wore the exact same expression: foreboding apprehension. Unfortunately, Atticus had no time to soothe their anxiety. They had somewhere to be.

The three of them made their way up to the sixth floor. Their mission was brought closer to home as they stood in the space once occupied by their lovable team-mate. Atticus felt Henry's absence every time he stepped into the elevator. As the doors shuddered open, they stepped out onto the path to bring his murderer to justice.

The men stood in a clump. Some were bemused; more, perhaps the majority, radiated an expression akin to gleeful self-satisfaction. They were all there. Henderson, Pillar, Hildebrand-Burke, Vincent, the whole chinless gaggle. There were two more members of the mob who had been specially invited. Without a word, Atticus stormed past them all and strode towards Rathdowne's office. The horde joined Oliver and Maggie in Atticus's slipstream and followed him as he burst into the office.

Startled, Rathdowne dropped the heavy black phone handset. Fumbling to pick it up again, he mumbled that he'd call the other party back, then hung up without waiting for a response. On seeing the mass of bodies streaming into the office, he stood, horror blanching his features.

"What the hell is this all about?"

With hands on hips, Atticus's jaw clenched. "I've successfully completed my assignment."

Face crinkled in confusion, Rathdowne stared. "You, you found the mole? Well don't leave it hanging, man." He eyed the crowd in his office and gulped. "Who the bloody hell is it?"

Atticus just glared.

"I knew it!" Hildebrand-Burke slapped his hands together and turned to his compatriots. "I told you, didn't I? I damn well told you. The little weasel was more red than pink. I *knew* it." He glared at Rathdowne gleefully.

Rathdowne's mouth dropped open. "What... what?"

Oliver held up the report. "The super-secret second report. You really should have read what Flynn reported more thoroughly. One part in particular, a meeting he had with a certain party with the initials O and R. There's only one O.R. at MI6, and that's Oscar Rathdowne, is it not?"

"A meeting? What meeting? I never... What are you insinuating?"

"I knew it." Pillar shook his head. "I damn well knew it. Class will out, you lecherous little toad."

It was then Rathdowne noticed the final members of the mob: two Metropolitan Police officers. Neither MI6 nor MI5 had the ability to arrest anyone. That's where the two stern men came in. There was no hiding the delight on the faces of the elite in the room. The upper-class toffs watched on with rapt delight, thrilled that one of their inferiors had lived up to their expectations.

Rathdowne skittered backwards, aghast at what was unfolding. "This is ludicrous! What the hell are you up to, Wolfe?"

"You're the mole, Rathdowne." Atticus crossed his arms. "We figured it out ourselves. The spook, the shirt-lifter and the walking pair of tits."

NINETEEN

The consequence of the earth-shattering revelation was as swift as it was devastating. The news spread like wildfire. The drama of Rathdowne being manhandled, shackled and, screaming bloody murder, walked out of the MI6 building shook the entire organisation to its core. Even those who didn't witness the theatrics of the expulsion were visibly stunned at the revelation that one of their own—*another* one of their own—had betrayed them so thoroughly.

In the aftermath of the drama, Oliver, Maggie and Atticus stood in Rathdowne's office, which was eerily silent given the events of only minutes before.

"Two little letters?" Oliver shook his head in disbelief. "Well, I'll be."

Tapping the table a few times with the tips of fingers, Atticus spoke. "That and setting us up for failure, sending us to Berlin unprepared and letting the East Germans know where to find us. I knew Rathdowne had a thing against the upper-crust types in this organisation, but not enough for him to be the actual mole. But you said it yourself, Oliver, he was deliberately setting me, us, up for failure."

Maggie shook her head. "I honestly thought he was innocent."

"I can't deal with this right now." Atticus heaved a sigh and surveyed the office. "Oliver, can you secure Rathdowne's effects? Maggie, I need you to work on the report for The Met. We gave them a summary for the arrest, but they'll need more detail for the arraignment."

Both agreed absentmindedly, stunned by the pace of events. Atticus had to guide Maggie out of the room as she seemed to be finding it difficult to put one foot in front of the other. He really felt for her. He unfortunately knew that, for Maggie, far worse was yet to come.

They made their way past the scuffed and mismatched desks. Past the smoke-stained walls. Past the hordes of gobsmacked staff in their ill-fitting woollen suits. It still seemed odd for Atticus to think of these strangers in their old attire as his colleagues. But that's exactly what they were, his colleagues at MI6. He felt their anguish, their despair. He felt saddened that they had to face yet another scandal, another blow to send the entire organisation reeling.

In the coming days the people they passed in these halls would need Atticus, just as, in return, he needed them. His presence in this timeline had changed history, and affected each and every one of the dazed faces he passed. His loyalty to his MI6 was unwavering and absolute; his loyalty to this MI6 was becoming just as all-encompassing. For a second, he thought perhaps that was the most surprising aspect of the day. A moment later he recanted the notion. There were more revelations to come.

Maggie walked into their tiny little office in a daze.

Without a word to prompt her, she shook her head and went about her task with forced vigour. She had a job to do and she was doing it to the best of her ability. Back slumped, she placed a piece of paper in the typewriter and pecked away.

She sniffed. "After all this at least we caught our mole." She shook her head, exhaustion slowing her movements.

With sympathy in his voice, Atticus spoke quietly. "I'm sorry to say we haven't." He met Maggie's in her startled eyes. "Rathdowne isn't a traitor."

Suddenly animated, Maggie sat bolt upright. "Um, did you miss the part where he was arrested and all that? Seems a lot of hassle for someone who's not guilty, wouldn't you say?"

"Not when you're setting up the capture of the real mole."

Maggie shook her head in confusion. "The real...so Rathdowne wasn't—"

"The mole? No, he wasn't. Never was."

"But...but..." It was clear Maggie was having trouble keeping up. It was to be expected, she didn't have all the facts.

"Rathdowne was in on it." Atticus caught his smile before it developed. "Well, the theory of it, not the bit where he'd be paraded out by police. That part I improvised as a surprise to illicit the right reaction. Seems to have done the job." He could see Maggie had no idea what he was on about. Best to start at the beginning. "When Rathdowne finally gave me the report on Flynn the last piece fell into place." Atticus gaze went up the wall on the left. "Well, eventually. At first, I naturally assumed he was the mole as the report he gave me had him attending a meeting with Flynn. The initials O.R. It couldn't be anyone other than

Oscar Rathdowne, right? As the other person attending the meeting was Flynn no one is left alive who could tell us otherwise."

Maggie screwed her face up. "But you asked Jayne if Rathdowne knew about the mission, he replied he didn't."

"Correct." Atticus waggled a finger. "But I left it out of the report. It usually doesn't ingratiate oneself with one's superiors when you ask incriminating questions about them specifically." He grinned. "Rathdowne wouldn't be stupid enough to give me a report that implicated himself. It was the reason for the meeting with O.R. which put me on the right track. It said O.R sat in on a meeting with Flynn about travel documents."

Maggie shrugged. "I'm not following any of this. Maybe I'm too dumb."

"That's a ridiculous thing to say, especially since you were the one who solved it."

"Of course, I did." Maggie's voice dripped with sarcasm.

"No, I'm serious. The first time I met you, you told me the story when you identified the Minsk letters as being fake, remember? You said you solved it because they were written by two separate typewriters, that all typewriter slugs had unique characteristics." He poked two thumbs at his chest. "Sometimes the men of this organisation listen to your cleverness. That's how I knew someone had doctored the report. Look."

Opening the Flynn report to the third page, Atticus pointed to the meeting headed "Documentation prep.". Without his usual tools of computer imaging he forced to go old-school. Holding a magnifying glass to the page he enlarged a particular R in the third paragraph. Enlarged it was apparent it was slightly different when compared to the other Rs on the page. The P had been made into a R. Atticus nodded when Maggie saw it too.

"The forger's quality was good. Too good, in fact. The shape of the line forming the R for Rathdowne was perfectly formed. The thing is, the rest of the report, the R isn't as perfect. There's an imperfection in the slug which forms the capital Rs, see? The malformed extra part to the bottom left of the letter. He was too clever for his own good."

Maggie stared at him blankly. Atticus was unsure if she hadn't twigged yet or simply refused to believe it. He thought it best to lay it out plainly.

"It wasn't O.R. The person attending the meeting was not Oscar Rathdowne. It was O.P." He hated the sound of his own voice. "The person who attended the meeting was Oliver Preston."

Twisting her mouth to the side Maggie seemed unconvinced. It was only natural. Oliver was one of her best friends, her only ally in a hostile work environment. Her loyalty to the man was understandable, as was her scepticism.

Atticus went on, conscious he'd have to stop should the office door open at any minute. "Oliver wasn't in the room when Jayne told us Rathdowne hadn't been in on any of the meetings. He didn't know we even asked the question in Berlin. It was before all hell broke loose, it's no wonder we never went back and discussed it. As far as he knew Jayne never mentioned Rathdowne at all. There's also the fact we were attacked at the safe house in Berlin. Ever think that was coincidental? Oliver was one of the very few who knew where Jayne was holed up. Rathdowne certainly didn't. I think we all know how that turned out. Add to that Oliver was the only one of us who didn't shoot at anyone, only a blank wall."

Maggie nodded her head slowly but seemed far from convinced. "I see what you're getting at, but—"

"You need more, of course." Atticus went on. "Flynn's report says he met with, what we now assume to be O.P, for travel documents. Oliver Preston is the only O.P. we have and coincidently the resident forger, so it makes sense. It's logical to assume a discussion around travel documents included a passport, yes?"

"With Jayne's photo on it?"

"Now you're getting it."

There was no way they could verify Oliver was in the meeting or created travel documents himself. With Flynn dead in suspiciously mysterious circumstances Oliver would deny he was there, of course, like any good traitor would. Just like Rathdowne had pretended to.

"No. Oliver's my friend. He's not a traitor. I teach him Mod, he came to my house and made soup when I was sick. He pushed me to get promoted into Signals." Maggie shook her head. "This is ridiculous."

"I owe Oliver so much as well. I'm able to live in this time period because of him. He set me up with a job, a place to live. I wish it wasn't true either." Atticus placed his hand on hers. "You're right to question it all. A spy should never take anything on face value. Go through what I've said. Pick it apart. Point out the flaws in logic. I've never wished I was wrong more in my life."

It took Maggie a few minutes, but she came up short. The logic was sound, or at least seemed like it. "But he's *Oliver*. We can't mess this up. How can we know for sure?"

Atticus conceded it was all a bit too circumstantial. Did

it fit? Yes. Was it enough for a court of law? Not yet. They did indeed need more.

Atticus explained the next part of the plan. He'd left Oliver alone in Rathdowne's office for a reason with tantalising bait. The thought still made him sick. *Please be wrong about this, please.*

"You left bait, didn't you?"

He bobbed his head in agreement.

"What if he doesn't take it?"

Atticus frowned. "Then I'm wrong."

Maggie's face danced with a thousand emotions. At first, she seemed pleased, either from the fact that Oliver would have an opportunity to prove his innocence or Atticus was reasonable enough to give him a chance. Her face soon darkened, likely realising what would happen should her worst fears be realised.

Letting her ruminate on the thought for a while, Atticus remained mute. A lot had been thrown at her in the space of a few minutes. She needed to catch up.

"Uh, if he was in on it..." Maggie scratched the back of her head. "Rathdowne was a good sport to be paraded around like that. He was very convincing."

"Ah, well," Atticus tugged at his collar, "he knew he was going to be fingered as the mole. He just didn't know it was to be so public and...well, I didn't tell him about the police either."

Like she was some Warner Bros cartoon heroine, Maggie's jaw dropped open. For the briefest of moments despair gave way to mirth. "You...hauled your own boss *publicly* out the door, pretty dramatically I have to say, yeah? And he didn't know it was coming?" She whistled. "Old Rathdowne's going to give you a right bollocking next time he sees you. He's not going to be happy about that."

Despite the professional dressing down there was an awestruck admiration in Maggie's voice. The sheer audacity of Atticus' handling of Rathdowne seemed to have momentarily distracted her from thoughts of her best friend's deception.

Atticus couldn't help but match Maggie's smile. "My thinking was the more it was uncomfortable for Rathdowne the more believable it was for everyone else." He pursed his lips. "I think I may have gone overboard a tad. They would have taken him to the local station, had a laugh at how convincing it all was and should be having tea and biscuits right about now. At least, I hope he and the police are whooping it up."

He very much doubted it. In fact, he envisaged Rathdowne sitting in a room somewhere making a voodoo doll of his most recent employee. Atticus couldn't really blame him.

After he'd detected the forged letter, he'd stormed out of Rathdowne's office in a rage. It wasn't directed at his superior. It wasn't even directed at Oliver, though he'd be lying if some weren't some percentage aimed in that direction. No, the main focus of his fury Atticus held for himself. How could he have been so blind?

He'd worked so closely with the mole yet hadn't suspected him. For all the hunting his team had done they'd failed to uncover the most basic of mistakes. The error wasn't sloppiness, no, Oliver had been far too clever for that. *Clever.* Being clever is what had ultimately done him in. He'd been *too* good at his craft, *too* clever.

Once Atticus had calmed down, he'd returned to a bemused Rathdowne, explained his discovery and formed a plan. Well, less of a plan. More of a trap. Rathdowne hadn't particularly liked the idea of setting himself up for public ridicule but eventually went along with it. In part because what Atticus had explained made sense, but there seemed to be more to it. Rathdowne appeared to genuinely want Atticus to succeed, to earn the trust of the organisation by bringing down the man who was ripping them apart. If he had to suffer the humiliation of false accusations, then so be it. The sacrifice only elevated Atticus' opinion of the man. There wouldn't be many in the building willing to endure the ignominy of such dishonour.

Atticus was left to wonder what would have happened if he hadn't stumbled into this timeframe. As far as he knew, no spy by the name of Oliver Preston had ever been discovered at MI6. It likely meant he'd gone his entire career undiscovered. What secrets had he told, what destruction had he wrought?

That was, if Atticus' assumptions were correct.

As the two of them sat alone with their thoughts the truth would be making itself known several floors above. There were two reasons Oliver had been left alone in Rathdowne's office. It gave him ample time to place more fake evidence. This time they were ready. Photographs had been taken of all surfaces to know what had been moved, they'd know if Oliver had planted anything further. In Atticus' time there would have been pinhole cameras with multi-spectral lenses, DNA sensors, chemical markers, anything else the tech boffins could throw at it. Instead, they took fifty still photos with a manual-winding black and white camera. Hardly bleeding edge.

The real reason for leaving Oliver alone was to ensnare him even further. They'd planted a report any self-respecting double agent couldn't ignore. Laid out in plain sight was a NATO communique marked in highly visible Top Secret red, detailing a sudden change in foreign policy.

It seemed the Prime Minister was about to accuse the Soviet Union of having a direct hand in the assassination of JFK. This revelation would have a devastating impact on already heightened international tensions across the entire globe. If the USSR had advanced warning of this diplomatic attack, they could prepare a defence or even a counter strike. It was to occur tomorrow. For a mole, the time constraint necessitated immediate action.

It was a test Atticus hoped Oliver would fail.

There was a rap on the door. Pillar's face was ashen. "He...he's gone."

"Gone?"

Pillar nodded ashen faced. The first time Atticus had seen the man unpretentious.

"And the report?" Atticus didn't want to know the answer.

"Gone." Pillar gulped. "He made some excuse about feeling ill and left in a rush."

Maggie and Atticus exchanged glances. Without a word spoken they stood and grabbed their coats. This was no longer time to dwell in self-doubt and supposition.

They had a mole to catch.

TWENTY

The elevator trip down was the longest Atticus could remember. It was made more painful as they shared it with the ghost of Henry Morton. The moaning gears of the ancient mechanism echoed with painful memories of laughter.

Atticus clenched and unclenched his fists.

He and Maggie stood in silence. What was there to say? Their colleague, their confidant, their friend was a double agent. A traitor. A mole. Silence was the only choice.

The doors juddered open and they raced out. Mrs Abernathy called to Atticus and without breaking stride she tossed him another Browning Hi-Power. It seemed she didn't hold a grudge he'd lost the last one she'd issued. There wasn't a word about halting to fill in a form on her precious clipboard. It seemed Rathdowne had briefed the formidable Mrs Abernathy well.

She said only one word. "East."

Outside the cold was bitter. *How fitting.* He and Maggie folded their overcoats around them and trudged against the London drizzle. The spectre of Westminster loomed closer with every step. Atticus donned a trilby he'd purloined from an intern earlier in the day. His bald dark head would surely catch Oliver's eye if he turned their way.

Not that they intended to get too close. The Met had surveillance on Oliver as soon as he'd left 52 Broadway. Their three teams of two had been deployed to catch him in the act. Even without all the technological gadgets unavailable in this time, mobile surveillance was still a formidable practice. Luddite tools like reversable jackets, interchangeable hats, switchable team members could successfully allude even the most proficient anti-surveillance practitioner. If the Met were as good as they claimed, they'd have Oliver in their sites until he performed a dead drop or as the police hoped, a face to face meeting.

There was still an element of doubt in Atticus' mind Oliver was their man. Or was it an unrealistic hope? Every-thing still pointed to him as the mole, the mysterious Cardinal Woolsey. Short of a miracle, there seemed little doubt Oliver would soon be exposed for the world to see.

Without warning, Maggie extended her hand, her deli-cate fingers interlaced with Atticus'. She didn't turn to face him, focus on the target before her. Did she believe a couple would be less conspicuous? Was it something else? Her determined silence had no story to tell.

After several blocks, she finally spoke. "Given that by your time we've been to the moon, I suppose you track people in hovercars and jet packs?"

Atticus stuck out his tongue sarcastically. "Not quite. We use computer software, a lot of technology, but in the end, we still need actual people. They're still the best at reading human expression, gestures, anticipating what the target's going to do next. A computer can't match that intuition. We haven't replaced human spies just yet, though many have tried."

In the far distance, Oliver braced himself against the cold. Examining the body language and trajectory of the individuals between Oliver and himself, Atticus took an educated guess as to who the surveillance team was, though it was just that, a guess. He hoped The Met had good people on the surveillance team. They only had one shot at this.

Ahead, Oliver crossed the road and occasionally stepped aside to let people pass, creating opportunities to scan the street using his peripheral vision. He used little fakes to see if he could detect shadow indicators. It was simple and subtle. He was using all the right counter-surveillance techniques, far more proficiently than one would expect a desk-bound Business Support Officer to be capable of.

Atticus remembered the last time he'd followed a Tango. Pursuing Omar Ganim had led him to this place and time. It seemed a lifetime ago. It *was* a lifetime away.

Recently, Atticus had been so obsessed with the hunt for a traitor, he'd given less attention on his own fate. As he thought about it, he realised he was getting used to this era. It had taken far less time than he'd thought to grow accustomed to the idea that this was where he lived now.

Everything had happened at breakneck speed. His arrival, joining MI6, being assigned to the mole hunt, everything. He hadn't had proper time to meditate on any of it. Hell, he hadn't even meditated. It used to be a daily practice to still his thoughts, fight stress and sharpen his mind. He needed to get back to that. He needed to get back to a lot of things.

Was this his life now? Did he even want to get home? He

looked down at his hand intertwined with Maggie's. He honestly didn't know.

~

It was near St George's Circus that it all fell apart. Even from a hundred feet away, Atticus saw the deliberate head check. Using the reflection in a storefront window, Oliver lingered a fraction of a second longer than was natural. For a moment it was written all over his face.

Atticus squeezed Maggie's hand. "The police have been made."

"How... how do you know?"

Before he could answer, Oliver broke into a sprint.

"Just a hunch."

The two let go of each other's hands and ran. Several others joined them; members of the surveillance team Atticus hadn't spotted. They all had one goal now: catch Oliver. The gloves were off.

As he ran, a new thought occurred to Atticus. There was the realistic concern that exposing Oliver would mean that he would in turn expose Atticus. Even if MI6 dismissed the far-fetched story of a time-travelling spy, any cursory investigation would uncover the lies his life was built on. He had no past here, no history with the Navy, hell, no history of ever being born. The story of his existence was a house of cards, liable to collapse in the slightest breeze.

It mattered little to Atticus. Oliver had to pay for the death of Henry and every other person who had been slaughtered due to his actions. His supposed friend had betrayed his country and murdered someone dear to Atticus. The kid was innocent, and should have had a long life ahead of him. Oliver had denied him that, and so many others. No, Atticus's destiny was unimportant compared to bringing Oliver down. That was all that mattered now. Atticus ran on.

Once again, he was reminded of the total absence of CCTV cameras. What Atticus wouldn't give to be able to call in Tactical Operations Centre, tap into the city's closed-circuit network and activate facial recognition tracking. In his time London was called the CCTV capital of the world for good reason. The design of a city dictated much about the nature of the crimes that take place in it, rather than the other way around. A city like Los Angeles encourages a different type of criminal; the wide, high-speed (at least, in theory) highways crisscrossing its surface were what made it the bank heist and drive-by shooting capital. Such crimes are impractical in other cities. London, with its narrow, chaotically planned streets necessitates CCTV cameras, as it is all too easy for an offender to disappear into the labyrinthine streets and lanes.

It was a fact Oliver would understand all too well. He knew the city, he knew the streets. The man was cunning. He wouldn't have run if he hadn't had a destination in mind. *But where?*

When Atticus and Maggie rounded a corner they stumbled, almost literally, into two men doubled over and wheezing.

"We... lost 'em guv."

The young officer addressed the one member of the surveillance team Atticus had met, a lean string bean of a man with a humourless face and yellowing teeth. All four of them gaped at the five streets branching off the intersection.

"He could be anywhere."

There was despair in Maggie's tone. They'd come far, but had failed at the most critical of moments.

Anger infused Atticus's joints and he circled the group in frustration. What had tipped him off? How had he detected their presence? Of course, these questions were irrelevant. It didn't matter. Oliver had seen he was being followed and taken the only course available to him: bolt.

The two police were soon joined by two more, and together they started to devise a new plan to create a grid to search for any sign of their prey. Maggie observed Atticus's pacing and jerked her head, as if to say, *we should join in.*

Atticus shook his head and continued to pace, thinking. He *knew* Oliver. Or at least, he thought he did. Did that help them or hinder them? Where would Oliver go when in trouble? Where would he hide?

Atticus stopped pacing. He regarded the streets anew, getting his bearings, and realised where he was. Not only did he know this part of London from his own time—streets don't change—he'd been in the area recently, in this time. *Yes, that's it.*

"I know where he's going."

In the midst of issuing orders, the string bean officer, whose name Atticus had already forgotten, turned to Atticus, irritated. "I beg your pardon, Sambo, we're running an operation here. Not you."

Clenching his fist, Atticus strode forward to deck the police officer. Maggie stepped between them, her face determined.

"Where is he headed, Atticus?"

The sound of his name from her lips calmed him, focused his attention.

He uttered only one word in reply. "Underground."

Well below London's streets, Maggie and Atticus trod carefully through the dark maze below the city; the hidden world known only to those who needed it. It was a world Atticus had visited once before.

The damp underground tunnel was roughly bricked and crisscrossed with pipes, conduits. All manner of detritus lay across their path, abandoned long ago. The local constabulary elected to stay topside, guarding the possible exits, but they'd said it with such little enthusiasm Atticus worried they'd head for the pub instead. They'd at least issued the two of them torches, but offered the bare minimum in the way of encouragement. As they walked away he'd heard one say under his breath that Atticus and Maggie were off for a subterranean frolic. The cobwebs and damp didn't exactly stir Atticus's romantic loins.

He was doing this from memory, and a hazy one at that. When Oliver had led Atticus down this path it had been late at night and they'd both been drunk. In the past ten minutes they'd already turned down a few dead ends and his confidence was beginning to wane.

"Are young people happy in the future?"

Atticus turned to shine a light on Maggie. "What on earth made you ask that?"

She shrugged. "The silence was freaking me out."

Bowing his head in acknowledgement, he walked on. "Kind of. It's a sad generation who take happy pictures of themselves."

"I... I don't know what that means."

"To be honest, neither do I, but it sounded wise."

Behind him, Maggie made a grunt of agreement.

"What's the greatest song ever recorded from where you are?"

"'Far from Over' by Frank Stallone."

"Wow, you answered that really quickly." She chortled. "Is it really?"

"For all you know, sure."

The cryptic answer seemed to sate her far a minute or so, and they trudged on.

"Are you sure about this?" Maggie's voice was at once determined and full of doubt. "Finding Oliver, I mean."

It seemed her distracting questions hadn't served their purpose, and she'd been forced to confront what was truly on her mind.

Atticus could sympathise; her thoughts echoed his own. "As with anything to do with espionage, one can never be absolutely sure."

"You do that a lot," Maggie ducked under a steaming pipe, "trying to give me spy wisdom."

Amongst all the gloom, Atticus chuckled. "Would you prefer I give you some typing to do?"

"Cheeky. It's just... uncommon, that's all."

"I've been called worse things." The beam from his torch which startled a rat, who scurried away. "I hope I don't come off as some know-it-all mansplaining douchebag."

"A man-whating, what, what?"

"Mansplaining is a word we use for an explanation of something by a man to a woman, in a manner regarded as condescending or patronising."

"Oh, you mean my everyday life?" She brushed away a cobweb as she followed. "I once had a bloke explain how a coded signal worked. Took every ounce of willpower not to whack his wedding tackle in the typewriter, let me tell you."

Atticus chuckled. The story wasn't amusing, and certainly not confined to this era, but Maggie's delivery, her approach to life always filled him with joy. They walked on for a time in silence.

It was several minutes before Maggie spoke again. "I just realised, by your time, your native time, I'll be eighty something. Hopefully I'm a hip old granny type with long hair and eccentric outfits who continually embarrasses my family."

"Sounds about right."

"Did you ever have an oddball but fashionable old lady smash you over the head with an umbrella for no reason?"

Atticus grinned. "Not that I recall."

"I'll have to remember to do that now."

The mental gymnastics required to think that one through hurt Atticus's brain. Was his reality still there? Could an old Maggie meet him in the future? What if she did and told him what was to happen? Would it alter the future and negate him ever coming here? He stopped walking and rubbed his temples. His brain felt like it was boiling in his skull. He needed to focus.

It had been at least five minutes since Atticus had seen anything familiar in the subterranean world. A growing sense of panic overcame him. Were they wasting their time? Sure, police were watching Oliver's flat, but there was no way he would be crazy enough to return there. No matter how many times Atticus ran through scenarios, this was the only one he kept coming back to. It was a hunch, but it was the one place that made sense. It was an environment where Oliver had said he felt safe. The place had multiple points of entry and escape. In other words, it was the perfect place for a double agent on the run. As hunches went, it was the best they had.

Maggie interrupted his wayward thoughts. Her voice was full of sadness. "Do we have to catch him?"

"That's what we do." Atticus had expected the question earlier.

"Yes, but, if he's innocent."

"Then we'll both be pleased. If he can explain the forgery, how they found us in Berlin, stealing the document from Rathdowne's office and running when he saw the police, all of it, then I'll be honestly quite happy." Atticus stopped walking and turned to Maggie. "But you need to accept the very real possibility that he won't have an explanation, and this is exactly as it appears."

"And then?"

"Then we hand him over to the awful racists on the street and let justice be served. Especially in the name of Henry."

Maggie had opened her mouth at the mention of Henry's name. "Did you have to say his name?"

"If it put your head in the game, yes."

With her mouth twisted to one side, Maggie mulled it over. It was plain to see there was an inner conflict still raging within her. It was a battle that had to play out. Atticus hoped there would be a decisive victor by the time they faced Oliver. *If* they faced him, he corrected himself. He could be in a thousand different locations by now.

If he was the mole, a Soviet spy, he'd want to escape the country as soon as humanly possible. Given the nature of the man, he'd surely have multiple fake passports, travel documents and all the necessary paperwork ready to go. They had to find him fast or he'd become a ghost. The window was closing.

A bend in the tunnel ahead seemed familiar. Atticus recalled the change in brickwork from higgledy-piggledy red bricks to the smooth curved brown bricks of an old railway shaft. Oliver's underground club was nearby.

Glancing in his direction, Maggie's face turned serious, reflecting Atticus's expression back at him. Without an exchange of words, they knew it was time. Game on.

Handing the torch to Maggie, Atticus extracted the Browning. Their steps were more deliberate, careful. The air seemed cooler, laced with tension. As the two followed the smooth railway tunnel, the darkness at the end seemed even bleaker than the rest of the underground world. They'd arrived.

Doing his best not to breathe, Atticus stepped into the dark underground bar. It was still silent and bereft of any sign of life. The mismatched Persian rugs, velvet couches and art deco mahogany bar were the same as he recalled. There was no one single point of entry or exit, with multiple doorways and tunnels snaking off in all directions. The absence of people only added to the ghostly atmosphere. The silence was all encompassing.

Momentarily perplexed by the myriad of choices, Atticus took in the room. The amazement on Maggie's face told him she was doing the same.

Flicking her thumb to the left, Maggie directed him where to start. He was thankful for the guidance. The two explored the expansive space, each footfall sounding like the beat of a bass drum.

Targeting the archway behind the bar, he went to peel back the green velvet curtain. It was heavy and he tucked the gun down the back of his pants to properly move the hefty drape. Atticus stared into the darkness.

The darkness stared back.

Two faint flickers of light blinked in the blackness. Amongst the darkness the reflection from glasses flickered. Stepping into the half-light, the slight man gave Atticus an equally half smile.

The figure shrugged as he aimed the pistol at Atticus's chest.

"Hello, Atticus." Oliver's voice was low and menacing. "I suppose some sort of explanation is in order."

TWENTY-ONE

"You two are about as stealthy as Napoleon's cavalry charging over a tin bridge." Oliver shook his head. He flicked the pistol towards Atticus, motioning for him to re-enter the cavernous bar.

When the two stepped into the room Maggie gasped. Oliver reached behind Atticus's jacket and removed his pistol. With a gun in each hand, he directed the pair to the centre of the room, indicating that they should sit on a cracked brown leather couch. They had no other option than to comply.

"The thing about the underground is that sound really travels." Oliver shook his head and waved his gun hand around his ear. "You two have been chatting away like lovers for half an hour."

Atticus hefted an eyebrow. "Is that jealousy I hear?"

"Oliver isn't interested in me, Atticus." Maggie waved a hand, dismissing the notion.

"I didn't say he was." Atticus hefted an eyebrow.

Head tilted, Maggie attempted to process the statement. In response, Atticus scoffed.

"Surely you know?"

Maggie half shook her head. "Know what?"

"That subject isn't exactly what we're here to discuss." He turned to Oliver. "If you're innocent, we can get this sorted. I still have a flicker of hope I've got this all balls-up somehow. Tell me that's the case, please. Tell me I've got this wrong, Oliver."

Oliver's shoulders sagged. Leaning heavily against the bar, he let the guns dangle, but it would only take a flick of his wrist for them to become lethal. He groaned heavily and wiped his nose. "The JFK communique was bogus, wasn't it?" Without waiting for a response, he went on. "I realised it about Parliament Square. It was all too perfect. I should have listened when my mother warned me about something being too good to be true." He shook his head. "I have to hand it to you, Atticus—I assume it was you, of course, no one else there would have the brains for it—it was a masterstroke. You don't mind me complimenting you, do you? No, I didn't think so. You do so like being the smartest man in the room. It's most infuriating that you often are." A sinister sneer crossed his lips. "When I'm not there, of course."

"So," Atticus didn't take his eyes off the gun, "it's all true, then?"

"What is truth?"

"If we're going to debate Aristotle's nature of truth I'm going to need to raid the bar behind you."

The statement was a test. If Oliver's mind was distracted, even in a small way, the mention of the bar should have drawn his eyes involuntarily. His gaze didn't even flicker. As tests went, Oliver passed. Atticus wished he hadn't.

"Why?" Maggie held back tears, her jaw clenched. "Why did you kill him?"

"Oh, my dear child. As with everything in life, the answer is complex and fraught with misconception, deception and shades of reality, whatever that may be."

"Cut the bullshit charm. It doesn't fucking work anymore." Her voice was barely below a shout. "Why did you kill Henry?"

Genuine pain darkened Oliver's features. "I... I... it was an accident."

It was the first time Oliver had openly admitted he was behind it all. Atticus studied every gesture Oliver made, reading, anticipating, searching for an opportunity to pounce. Right now, the man held all the cards. Surely his luck couldn't hold. *Surely?*

Face dripping with remorse, Oliver dipped his head, though his eyes didn't stray from the two on the couch. "He... shouldn't have been there. It started out perfectly. I'd set up the alibi, everything."

"You mean me?"

Dinner with Atticus had been Oliver's alibi. They'd gone out drinking until late, and they'd both gone home at an hour at which any reasonable person, or jury, would assume it would be humanly impossible to call into the MI6 office. Perhaps Oliver had consumed far less alcohol than Atticus had thought. Oliver having to bail him out was an added bonus; it had rounded out the story perfectly when they'd both arrived at MI6 the next morning.

Oliver sighed. "I only needed a small window. Minutes at most to forge a report implicating Flynn. I needed him out of the way, obviously. What I hadn't anticipated was being discovered. He shouldn't have been there. There was no reason for him to be there."

"But he was." Maggie's words were as hard as marble.

"But he was." His nod was sad. "He came in with some revelation that wouldn't allow him to sleep. It was about the second investigation. Something he'd part heard in the elevator. His assiduousness cost him dearly, unfortunately. He stumbled in, spotting me at my desk laden with forgery equipment. I asked him, begged him to keep it to himself..." Oliver shook his head morosely. "He...he could have just agreed, I probably would have believed him, let it go, but... but he insisted on telling the truth. It was loyalty that made him unable to promise fidelity, loyalty to *you*." Oliver spat the last word with venom directly at Atticus, "A man he barely knew. A man who shouldn't even be here."

"A man you brought into the organisation."

"And don't I regret it?" Oliver let loose a humourless chuckle. "I had a nice little operation going until you bumbled into it."

In a calmer voice, Maggie asked, "Why are you telling us this?"

"My last confession? Guilt? Remorse? I honestly don't know." He rubbed a gun barrel on the side of his head. "No. That's not true. It's important to me for the two of you know his death was an unfortunate accident. There was no backing out of it, no fooling Henry into believing I'd been caught doing anything other than treason. It shouldn't have happened, but there you are. Henry was my friend. Henry was quite dear to me."

"But you killed him."

The guilt in Oliver's eyes screamed far louder than mere words could convey. For Oliver, Henry's death was self-preservation. For Atticus it was a brutal and soulless murder.

And that murderer had to pay.

The gap between Oliver and Atticus was too great for him to make the distance without being cut down. Even if Oliver was an average shot, he'd have multiple chances to land the right one to take Atticus down. No, a direct assault would be suicide. He needed a distraction.

The fact Oliver was talking to them was interesting. He had brutally killed Henry on being discovered, yet here he was confessing his sins in no apparent hurry. *Why?* Atticus may as well keep him talking until there was an opening he could exploit.

"You explained Henry, but you haven't explained why you became a traitor, betraying the very thing you confessed to love?"

"Oh please." Oliver rolled his eyes. "That's overly flowery patriotism, even for you, Atticus. They give you that speech when they issue you with the stupid little MI6 identity card? You tell me, why does someone betray their country?"

"There are four main reasons." Atticus counted off his fingers. "Greed; they need money for a divorce, gambling debts, you name it. Then there's ideology where you simply sympathise with other side. Compromise where they've been pictured in a shameful position to exploit. Finally, there's ego, a powerful motivator, mostly men, because of male pride and ego where they perceive they've been passed over for a promotion, that kind of thing."

Oliver frowned in approval. "All quite neat and compartmentalised. I'm curious, which one am I?"

"Like you said, it's quite compartmentalised. It's rarely all in one category. Unless it's you, of course."

Suddenly rigid, Oliver stood up, taking a step forward. *Closer, you little fucker.*

"Explain that." Oliver's calm façade was melting. He thrust a gun toward Atticus. "Explain what you mean."

"No."

"No?"

Atticus folded his arms. "You heard me."

Closer.

Frustrated, Oliver's pasty complexion took on a rosy hue. His hand shook in anger. "Tell me!"

Atticus shrugged and inspected his nails.

"Tell me or..."

He swivelled the gun to aim at Maggie. She gasped and writhed backwards, burrowing into the leather of the couch.

"Oliver!"

"Maybe you'll choose to tell me if I threaten something you care for, hmmm?"

"You won't shoot her, Oliver, and we both know it."

Maggie's head swivelled to him, mouth agape. "You realise you're playing poker with my life here?"

Atticus squinted at Oliver. "No, I'm not."

To show so much remorse for the loss of Henry, Oliver was never going to shoot the only friend he had. It had drawn him closer, but not close enough.

Oliver had to be stalling. If he was, it meant time was not on their side. He had to get Oliver nearer for Atticus to strike. But how?

Assuming he was prolonging the moment, why engage them in conversation? Why not gag them and be done with it? It had to be Maggie. She was the only reason he was explaining himself. He had to alleviate his guilt. It was important to him. *She* was important to him. He'd never intentionally harm her.

"Ego." The word startled both Oliver and Maggie. "Ego

is why you're a double agent, Oliver." Atticus went on. "You feel you haven't been given your due. You said it yourself, you're the smartest man in the room. Pure ego if ever I've heard it. You're a shimmering beacon of intellectual superiority in a building rife with dullards, aren't you? They belittle you, not see you, treat you like an intellectual midget when you're actually a giant, right? They refused to accept you for the magnificently luminous brilliance. That's what drove you to betray all you're meant to hold dear, isn't it? Because some mean boys wouldn't acknowledge you're smarter than they are? Well boo fucking hoo, Oliver."

"Steady on. He's still got the guns, remember?"

"Am I getting warm, Oliver?"

Oliver's eyes were wide, manic. "Shut up."

"Sounds like I am." Atticus leaned forward. "People have died because of your pathetically fragile little ego, Oliver."

"Shut up!" Oliver stepped forward. "You don't know anything! You fucking shut up!"

Oliver thrust the Browning in Atticus' face. Like lightning, Atticus acted. Using the base of his palm he shoved the pistol skyward. At the same moment his left hand darted to the gun in Oliver's other hand. It wasn't a clean grab, unable to slide his fingers between Oliver's palm and the grip panel his grasp faltered. Atticus frantically clutched at the weapon trying desperately to get any hold.

Hoisting his body upward Atticus shouldered Oliver in the chest pushing both his feet off the ground. Using the momentum of the two intertwined bodies, Atticus ran full pelt at the solid mahogany bar with a rugby tackle. Oliver's back hit the bar in a teeth rattling crash. One of the guns clattered on the floor. It wasn't enough.

Atticus' two hands fumbled for the other pistol, Oliver

fighting his every move. They grunted as their sweaty hands grappled for any leverage, desperation in their hitched breaths.

The shot shattered the silence in the underground cavern.

The two staggered from one another, shock etched on both their clammy faces. The two men stared at one another, stunned.

Stiffening his back, Atticus clenched his teeth but it was a useless gesture. He collapsed, clutching the bullet wound on his lower thigh. It had missed bone, but it hurt like a son-of-a-bitch. He let out a cry. It was a mixture of pain and anger.

He'd taken his one shot.

And lost.

"This is what you do, Atticus." Stepping back, Oliver inhaled deeply. "Do you see now? You bring chaos to everything. You mess it all up, everything." His face dripped of with sweat. "You should never have come here, to this time. You bring disorder and death everywhere you go." The man was unhinged. He leant down to pick up the dropped pistol and shook his head. "You are the bringer of disorder, not me!"

Barely able to focus on anything beyond pain, Atticus writhed on the ground, blood oozing through his fingers. Maggie leapt to his side, removing his tie and creating a tourniquet high on his leg.

"Oh, how quickly the princess dashes to her knight's side. I'd be impressed if it weren't so nauseating."

After several frenetic moments, Maggie had the impromptu bandage in place; the bleeding had been arrested temporarily. Her hands were slick with blood. The loss had been significant; Atticus was having trouble staying conscious. He needed medical attention, urgently.

"Why don't you piss off, Oliver?" There was anger in her voice now. "You've stopped him, I won't follow you."

"You mean you won't leave his side?"

"Is there a difference?"

"Oh dear child, there is a chasm between those two things, I assure you." He checked his watch. "I do believe it's time to go now."

Closing his eyes, Atticus tried to filter out the pain; a futile act. "It's all pointless, Oliver. You know it. Whatever you do is absolutely meaningless. We've already discussed how the Cold War ends; your efforts will be for nothing. You picked the losing side."

"Ah," Oliver waved his finger, "but what if, just *what if* someone in the glorious Socialist Republic had foreknowledge of what was to happen?" A sadistic grin crossed his lips. "Imagine what that would mean? Can you envisage how much better the world would be? Communism triumphs— the right kind of communism, the kind that cares for its people, not a backwater tinpot regime that represses them. How glorious would it be, don't you think Atticus?"

His eyes were crazed, tinged with menace. He leaned down to Atticus, out of striking distance. "Remember what Jayne said? The right piece of information at the right time could change the course of history."

With a Cheshire cat smile, Oliver reached into his jacket. He pulled out Atticus's phone and gleefully waggled the black rectangular device.

"I do recall how you mentioned you had history books in here." He shrugged. "How the Cold War was won—or in my case, lost?" His baleful expression grew more fevered.

"Imagine, just imagine, if someone had that information ahead of time. The next hundred years are about to get very interesting, Atticus. All thanks to you."

"Good luck finding a charger cable in the next fifty years."

Oliver chuckled humourlessly as he stood. "I'm sure our scientists will come up with something. Soviet scientists are the smartest in the world, after all."

"Not smart enough to get to the moon first."

"That's your history, not mine, Mr Wolfe." He gazed at the phone reverently. "I have a feeling history is not going to be what it used to be."

"You're a monster, Oliver."

He sighed, regarding Maggie with a softer expression. "You could always come with me. Women are treated far better on the other side of the curtain. You'd have all the opportunities for advancement denied you here. You could be happy there, Maggie."

Her bitter laugh echoed around the yawning space. "You don't know me at all, do you?"

"A little, I think." Oliver pouted. "I knew you wouldn't accept, but I had to ask anyway."

Maggie shook her head. "You hate the cold, Oliver."

"No, I don't."

She placed her hands on her hips and raised an eyebrow.

"Okay, fine. I'm sure they'll give me one of those big fur hats. I'll be just fine." He gave her a genuine smile. "You've always been kind to me, Maggie, when others weren't." He leaned over the bar and lifted up a tattered grey folder. "Which is why I have something for you." He placed it on the top of the bar and gave it a gentle tap with his hand. "A parting gift, if you will."

"I don't want anything from a traitor."

He bobbed his head in response, as if expecting the reply. "Wednesday seventh of June 1944."

"What?"

Oliver looked up. "The day your mother died, Maggie."

Her mouth dropped open.

"It's all here." He ran a finger over the file. "Top Secret, of course. That's why you could never find it. Took me some digging, let me tell you. This is your mother's file. The missions she was on, where she was deployed, all the information you've been seeking your entire life. Of course, it also reveals how she died. If it's any consolation, it was a heroic death. She stayed behind in Caen, against orders, to aid Operation Overlord. Unfortunately, she was discovered two days before the Allied landing. She was executed by firing squad four days later. Worse ways to go, I suppose. She wouldn't have suffered. I thought it was important for you to know."

Tears in her eyes, all Maggie could do was nod. Oliver returned the gesture.

"Now if you two don't mind, I must be off. I have history to change." He doffed an imaginary cap. "I bid you both good day."

"I'll hunt you down, Oliver. You know that, don't you?"

"Oh, I know you'll try, Atticus Wolfe, I know you'll try."

Oliver gave Maggie an elegant bow and pivoted on his heels. As he strode confidently through one of the myriad tunnels leading away from the bar, Atticus's vision grew murky. Before everything went black, he saw Oliver turn and give him a friendly wave.

"See you around, Milli Vanilli."

CHAPTER

TWENTY-TWO

" I say, there are worse places to be shot."

"He's just lucky someone got there before I did."

"What ho, he's coming to."

Atticus's eyes flitted open to see half of MI6 crowded around his hospital bed. The whole crowd. Pillar, Hildebrand-Burke, Henderson, Bridgeman and, of course, Rathdowne. The latter wasn't quite as pleased as the others to see Atticus regain consciousness. He made to sit up.

Hildebrand-Burke, who had a cigarette dangling from his lips, gently pushed Atticus's shoulders back on the bed. "Steady on, old boy, you've lost a lot of blood." He gave a nod to the room. "Half the rutting office rolled up their sleeves to donate."

Feeling lightheaded, Atticus accepted the suggestion, sinking back into the bed. There was an IV in his arm and lots of archaic-looking machines making pinging noises.

Pillar slapped him on the shoulder. "He'll be up and about in no time, won't you Wolfe, er, Atticus?"

It was clearly a strain, but the man seemed to be

attempting to build bridges. Atticus was too weak to fight it. He simply nodded.

"See? Good man!"

It seemed all a black man had to do to earn respect in the organisation was to get shot and almost die. If he'd known that earlier it could have saved a whole lot of angst.

Atticus turned to Rathdowne. "Sorry to have you paraded out like that. You can't say it didn't garner a genuine reaction."

Rathdowne's mouth twisted. There was no denying an underlying anger, but he eyed the others gathered around the bed and then, seemingly against his better judgement, he grinned what was almost a genuine smile. "It was all sorted rather quickly. No hard feelings." Atticus didn't believe that for a second. "You smoked out the right man in the end. Good job."

"Good?" Hildebrand-Burke scoffed. "The man's taken a bullet for Queen and Country, exposed the mole and saved us all. I don't believe *good* quite cuts it, old chap."

It seemed Atticus had suddenly acquired some new allies. Rathdowne tilted his head, conceding the point, but Atticus suspected there was going to be a long period of building bridges with his superior officer to get over that one.

There was a commotion behind the group in the private hospital room, the sound of raised voices overlapping one another. Only certain words were distinguishable from the babble. The main word that garnered Atticus's attention was Maggie saying his name.

"Let her in!"

The sheer force of his words parted the men like the Red Sea. In the doorway, two nurses in their ancient Flying Nun outfits were blocking Maggie from coming in. They turned to Atticus.

The elder nurse tugged at her starched uniform. "This is highly irregular."

"So am I." Atticus smiled to soften the words. "She's with us."

The confused nurse viewed the rest of the group, seeking confirmation. Eventually, they all nodded and her shoulders slumped in defeat. Maggie ran to Atticus's side and held his hand, concern etched on her beautiful features.

She seemed distressed, but was doing her best to hide it. "I'm sorry it took so long to get help, Atticus. I got lost a few times." She rubbed the back of her neck. "I used lipstick to mark my way back."

"Lipstick? Ha, just like a woman." Bridgeman shook his head in amusement.

"A good field officer uses all available resources to his," Pillar turned to Maggie, "or her advantage. I think that was ruddy crafty of you, Dunbar. And if you don't mind me saying, rather ballsy too."

Maggie gave a faint nod by way of thanks, then turned to Atticus. "I took so long. I'm sorry."

Atticus took her hand and squeezed. "You did great. I'm here, aren't I?"

She shrugged, then, seemingly realising she was holding his hand, relinquished her grip and stepped back. For once the men of MI6 seemed to notice Maggie.

"You're well, Miss Dunbar?"

"Quite well, thank you, Henderson. It's Mr Wolfe here who deserves all the attention. He was willing to put his life on the line for all of us."

"Quite right."

All heads turned as Dick White, the Chief of MI6 strode into the hospital room, his silver hair shimmering in the afternoon sun. He made a beeline for Atticus and stood beside the bed, rigidly straight.

"On behalf of Her Majesty's Government, let me thank you for your noble efforts yesterday, Mr Wolfe."

Yesterday? How long was he out?

White went on. "I've read the reports, and also heard an account firsthand from Miss Dunbar here, and I believe your efforts beyond reproach. You've gone to exceptional lengths to perform your duty. I've spoken to the hospital administrator and ensured you'll be given the finest of care." He rocked on his heels, seeming pleased with himself. "Obviously we'll bury all this. State security, of course. There was no mole. It will all be swept under the carpet, for the good of the country. I'm sure I have your word on that, of course?"

Atticus inspected his expression as well as the man himself. Beneath the veneer of surface cheer and glad-handing was a wary man. Almost scared. *Wasn't that curious?*

"Thank you, sir." Rathdowne bended, a few inches short of a bow. "He agrees, of course. The last thing we want is to rock the boat. Isn't that right, Atticus?"

It seemed the Chief of MI6 made the trip to see his own man for fear Atticus may not be as loyal to the organisation as he needed him to be. As far as White knew, Atticus had just joined MI6 and been shot on his first assignment. The Chief had no knowledge of Atticus's real history, of the years of blood, sweat and sacrifice. The man was wrong to ever question his loyalty. His own organisation would never slight his name in such a way.

Slowly, Atticus exhaled. "You do." The words were thick and heavy.

Suddenly elated, White threw his hands in the air and slapped them together. He went around the bed shaking hands with every man there.

He didn't shake Maggie's hand. And there was someone else he didn't offer his hand to. Atticus looked down at his dark-skinned hand, then back at White as he exited the room with a cheery wave.

"Alright, you lot!" Rathdowne raised his voice. "You've seen he's alright, there's plenty of work to be had and it's not going to do itself, now is it? Off you pop."

Grudgingly, the men moaned as they were manhandled out of the room. Within a minute there were only three people left. Maggie sat halfway down Atticus's bed, while Rathdowne sat in the visitor's chair.

"You didn't catch him?"

Rathdowne grimaced painfully. "We threw up a net around the city. He either slipped through or is up for the next Olympic hide-and-seek gold medal. We're not giving up hope, but..."

"He's gone."

Rathdowne tilted his head, as if to say *probably*. There was sadness in his features. If he knew the truth as to what Oliver possessed, he'd be more than merely sad.

"Look, I'm sorry about the whole," Atticus rolled his hand, "dragging you through the office in chains... thing."

"It wasn't exactly what we agreed to, now was it?" The edges of Rathdowne's mouth turned downward.

"You can't say it didn't get a natural reaction."

"No, you can certainly say that."

Atticus grimaced exaggeratedly. "Sorry."

"Hmmm. We'll deal with that another time."

The three sat quietly for a moment.

"The Cockneys."

Both men turned to Maggie.

"The what?"

Maggie sat upright. "Who were the Cockneys? In Jayne's flat. That bit doesn't make any sense to me. They weren't Russian, so who the bloody hell were they?"

"Language, Miss Dunbar."

"Right you fucking are, boss. So, who were they?"

For the first time, Rathdowne seemed sheepish. "They, ah, were apparently working for MI6."

"You could have fooled me."

"Yes, well, they did take to their roles a little too vigorously, I will admit." Rathdowne rubbed his chin. "They were rather convincing, I have to say. Those two you chased across half of Soho were there to convince the Russians Jayne had severed ties completely with the UK, that he'd run up debts with loan sharks. Quite ingenious of Flynn to come up with it, I must say. Trouble is, they turned up at the office demanding hazard pay after, in their words, some lunatic started shooting at them and, I quote, a crazy lady broke one of their arms with a Union Jack cricket bat, I believe it was?" He eyed Maggie amusedly. "They couldn't get hold of Flynn, for obvious reasons, so turned up on our doorstep. They incurred Mrs Abernathy's wrath before we figured out where they fit into the whole scheme of things. But I get what Flynn was trying to do. Hiring men with no affiliation to us, who we had no knowledge of, to gallivant around telling the world Jayne owed them money. Tantamount to Cortez burning his ships and all that."

"Hang on," Atticus was still lightheaded, he was having trouble keeping up. "That was after Jayne had been made, after he'd been captured. Why keep up the act?"

"We *assumed* he'd been made. We weren't completely sure then. No body, remember? He might have needed the charade more than ever. They could have been interrogating him and needed verification of his story. There was still a chance our man could have pulled off the mission, so I assume Flynn thought he'd better keep up the pretence, you see?"

"I would have preferred if they'd kept up the pretence without shooting at me." Atticus tilted his head.

"As I mentioned, perhaps they took to their part a little too vigorously."

"They did at that." Atticus remembered the incident all too well.

"Wait a minute. How did they find my flat?"

"I'm sorry?"

"The bloke outside my flat late at night. I tried to have him arrested but got thrown in the clink myself."

Rathdowne shook his head, not understanding. "Wouldn't have been them. They swore off the job as soon as people starting wielding cricket bats."

Atticus scratched his head. "So, it may have just been a random guy in a car?"

Shrugging, Rathdowne said, "I suppose so?"

That one, Atticus would have to mull over. "What about the Esther guy? The one the Stasi murdered on Jayne's doorstep?"

"Ah, right, that one we do know. Your suggestion worked wonders. Our person in the Abteitsministerium found out they'd stopped paying wages to a certain Albrecht Schmidt. He was working as a bookkeeper in their anti-spy wing. Quite young, only twenty. It seems the East Germans didn't take kindly to an accountant taking it upon himself to chat to Western spies."

It struck Atticus as odd that the actions of one lowly public servant had set so many events in motion. If the young man hadn't tried to defect to the West, hadn't confronted a spy so brazenly, Jayne wouldn't have gone missing, the mole wouldn't have been identified, Oliver would never have been exposed, wouldn't have stolen his mobile phone and wouldn't have the potential to erase history as Atticus knew it.

That thought would keep him awake at night, he had no doubt. He tried to convince himself it would be impossible for the Soviets to leverage the technology. Even if they somehow managed to power it, his phone was locked with a passcode. The best hackers in his time wouldn't be able to unlock its secrets. The history books Oliver had bragged about reading would be safe from prying eyes. *Hopefully.*

Then there was the phone itself. The leap was too far for the other side to make any sense of at all. It was too advanced, too sophisticated to pose any real threat. It's not like they could leap from transistors to quantum computing overnight. If they pulled the phone apart it would be a cacophony of incomprehensible circuits and chips. The Soviets would have no technology capable of deciphering its secrets.

Or at least, that's what Atticus kept telling himself.

"You're off with the fairies." Rathdowne waved his hand in front of Atticus's face. "You need some rest. I'll send someone over later to take your statement. Come into the office when the doctors give you the all clear." He turned to Maggie. "Miss Dunbar?"

"I'll be a few minutes. You go, sir."

Rathdowne paused for a moment to take both of them in, then nodded but said nothing, his calm exterior giving nothing away. He bid them both farewell and exited the room with the faintest smirk on his face.

Maggie playfully poked Atticus on the thigh and he squealed.

"Oh, I'm so sorry, I was being all cute and all and ended up stabbing your wound, I'm so sorry."

Floating down from the ceiling, Atticus chuckled. "It's fine, really."

Maggie seemed less convinced. She tucked a stray hair behind her ear. "I'm glad you're okay."

"Me too."

"Is it alright if I stay?"

"Always."

Her normal sunny disposition returned, and she beamed.

As candour was flying thick and fast, Atticus thought he'd chime in too. In a short amount of time, he confessed to Maggie that he'd seen her in Brixton with her friends late at night. Repeating several times that he wasn't a stalker, he explained how he'd been trying to walk off the booze, with limited success. He hadn't meant to come across her and her boyfriend.

"Oh, he's not my boyfriend." Maggie couldn't meet his gaze. "Well, not anymore."

"You two seemed pretty chummy."

"We were... once."

"That right?"

Maggie nodded firmly. "And then we weren't. I took my friend Mary along because I needed her to keep me on track. He, uh, didn't take it so well. I mean, who would? No one wants to hear their girl is falling for another man."

"Wait. What was that last part?"

She rolled her eyes. "Remember when I left suddenly on

Carnaby Street? I knew all the way back then. But it never seemed to be the right time to say anything."

"And now?"

"Too much talk." Maggie leaned forward and kissed him.

EPILOGUE

I t was three days before Atticus could leave the hospital. MI6 wanted to ensure their new star had properly recovered. His wound was apparently healing well, although the doctor was reluctant to advise when he could do yoga again, primarily because he didn't know what yoga was.

Rathdowne had visited several more times, each successive call slightly more friendly than the last. Atticus was to return to MI6 on Monday, and would be given his own office. He was to be assigned to the Eastern Europe bureau.

Maggie visited several times a day, often having to be kicked out by hospital staff. They spoke of all manner of subjects; the future was a regular topic. Not only did they discuss what was in order for the world, but also for the two of them. They had a date planned for after work Monday, and they'd see what that particular future held.

The taxi stopped outside number seventy-two. Everything on the busy street was as Atticus recalled; that is, as he was now used to. The sixties fashion intermingled with the old, staid London, the clash of cultures writ large.

History was being made before his eyes and he was seeing it firsthand.

Paying the driver, Atticus gingerly exited the taxi. Extracting his cane, he let out a quiet moan at the Herculean task before him.

Sticking his head out the driver's window, the cabbie called out, "You alright there, mate?"

"Yes, thank you."

Waving off the call for assistance, Atticus hobbled across the pavement. He unlocked the weathered door and gazed up heavily at the tall, narrow flight of stairs. This was going to be tough. Atticus groaned.

Trudging his way up, he was quite pleased with himself. He'd only sworn eleven times, way down on his initial estimate. Unlocking the door, Atticus entered his light-filled flat. Instinctively he knew something was wrong.

Scanning the flat, everything seemed in order. No upturned furniture, nothing ransacked. But the uneasy feeling remained. Then he heard the creak of a floorboard.

In the small kitchenette an elderly man stood casually stirring a cup of tea. He seemed unperturbed at being discovered in another man's flat. His hair was a wiry grey, his face creased with wrinkles from a hard life. If Atticus were to hazard a guess, he'd estimate the man was in his seventies. There was something oddly familiar about him.

He smiled amiably. "Your landlady, Mrs Astor, was kind enough to let me in."

"Who are you?" Realising he was still standing at the threshold, Atticus limped into the flat and shut the door. He hefted up his cane in case he needed to brandish a weapon.

Placing the spoon on the bench, the old man chuckled. "That is a far more complicated question than you'd think."

He shuffled across the floor and sat in one of the green cocktail armchairs. He motioned for Atticus to do the same —in his own flat. Without any logical reason not to, he complied, and sat across from the intruder.

His craggy, weathered face seemed amused at Atticus's confusion. "You really don't know who I am, do you?"

Atticus squinted. There weren't many people he *did* know in this time period.

This time period.

Realisation washed over him and he recoiled. He reassessed the man from the ground up. The eyes were far less fiery than he remembered, but there was no mistaking the proud Romanesque nose. But this man was old, far older than Atticus had seen him just days before.

"And there's the recognition." The wide grin only crinkled his face further. "Welcome back, Mr Wolfe."

"Omar Ganim." Atticus shook his head. "You're a murderer, a terrorist. I should arrest you on the spot."

"For what?" Amused, he theatrically threw his hands in the air. "I haven't committed any crimes in this time. Well, not that you're aware of."

Squinting, Atticus asked, "How long have you been here?"

Regarding Atticus from stem to stern, he said, "A lot longer than you, obviously." He sighed. "I've been paying someone in the tenancy office a quid a week for forty years to tell me if anyone rented or bought a property in your name. Guess what finally happened?"

"Forty years?"

"I came around the other night to talk. You must have been out and about living it up, no doubt."

"That was you on the street in the Vauxhall?"

The other man nodded quizzically, as if wondering how

Atticus knew that. He sipped his tea. "We have much to talk about."

"I don't think I have anything to discuss with a terrorist."

The old man frowned as he nodded. "I suppose that's fair. Unless…"

"Fine," Atticus rolled his eyes, "I'll bite. Unless what?"

He may have aged decades in the days since Atticus had last seen him, but Omar Ganim's eyes now shone with the same intensity Atticus remembered.

From his pocket he extracted the keypad that had been found next to Atticus's unconscious form when he first arrived in this era. The one he'd thought was well hidden in the flat, with the big red button at its base. Tentatively, Ganim placed it on the armrest of the chair and glanced up. "Unless, of course, you want to get back home, Atticus Wolfe?"

The End

To be the first to find out when new novels arrive and to win prizes and get free stuff (who doesn't like free stuff?), sign up for my VIP Book Club at:
https://davesinclair.com.au/newsletter/

ACKNOWLEDGMENTS

This book almost killed me.

It took at least three times longer to write than my other novels. It wasn't that Atticus was a tough character to write, just the opposite in fact, but external factors kind of put writing on the back burner for a bit. First Covid hit, and here in Melbourne, Australia we were the world's most locked down city. Fun times. Then we had to cancel our wedding and honeymoon to the Maldives. But fear not – my lovely now wife and I had a sneaky Vegas style wedding. And it was awesome. Then, my amazing wife was diagnosed with breast cancer. Month after month of chemo, recovery, surgeries and everything else meant writing wasn't exactly my number one priority. But all throughout, even on her lowest days, Kristi encouraged me to get some words down. And I did. So even though the first Atticus Wolfe novel took a long time to fully form, he was always in the background, patiently waiting for his story to unfold.

Since then, Kristi is doing amazingly well. She's one hell of a strong woman and of course the person this book is dedicated to. She's everything.

And ladies, check your boobs!

Now for the acknowledgements.

What more can I say about my beautiful wife? Monkey heart unicorn.

To my remarkable girls, Quinn and Esther, a BIG thank you for supporting my writing and still getting excited when they see a new cover or when I show them a good day on the book rankings. I love that they both write their own books and adore reading as much as I do.

As always, thanks to the G-Mob, my writing tribe. The G-Mob are amazing writers and even better friends. Craig, Justin, Luke, Nathan, Steve, Kat, Amanda and Amanda, thank you for your support, encouragement and laughs.

A big thank you to my editor Vanessa Lanaway for her talented and speedy work. She really does make me sound like I know what I'm doing.

Thanks to Phil Poole who did an incredible job on the covers for the Atticus Wolfe series. He not only nailed the brief I gave but knocked it out of the park!

There's a sneaky reference in the novel of Susan Palinosky. She won a competition in my VIP Book Club to be murdered horribly. Congrats (?!) again Susan!

And to my fabulous Book Ninjas who receive an advance copy of my novels – thank you for the amazing feedback! You guys are brilliant.

Don't be afraid to reach out on Facebook, Twitter, Instagram. It's always great to hear from readers. You can stalk me at all these semi-reputable places:

www.davesinclair.com.au

https://facebook.com/DaveSinclairAuthor/

https://www.instagram.com/davesinclairauthor/

https://twitter.com/thedavesinclair

https://www.goodreads.com/author/show/ 22167525.Dave_Sinclair

https://www.bookbub.com/authors/dave-sinclair

If you can, please drop a review, it is greatly appreciated. It helps new people discover my work.

Thank you and here's to many more adventures!